# What Happened to the Boy?

## by

## June Summers

Cover Art by *Teddi Black*

The Wild Rose Press, Inc.
PO Box 708
Adams Basin, NY 14410-0708
Visit us at www.thewildrosepress.com

Publishing History
First Edition, 2024
Trade Paperback ISBN 978-1-5092-5913-7
Digital ISBN 978-1-5092-5914-4


Published in the United States of America

## Dedication

To Emily and Steve

To Wendy, my brightest star in the sky

Prologue

*Friday, shortly after 9:00 p.m.*
"9-1-1, what is your emergency?"
The muffled voice of the female caller sounded weak and labored. *"Ple-ease h-help m-me. H-house on fire. I've b-been sh-shot!"*
Quickly, the dispatcher responded, "Ma'am, what is your address?"
*"T-two… t-two… f-f-fi… uh, f-f-fiv… ohh! F-fifth A-ave… Ohh!"*
Silence.
"Ma'am, are you there?"
*"I-I'm sh-h-ot, f-fire, hus-s-b-band d-dead. S-s-sam-my-y-y-y!"*
Silence again.
"Ma'am?"
A pause.
"Ma'am?"
Then the dispatcher heard only a soft hissing noise, then a series of pops which she attributed to the sound of an intensifying fire. She immediately had the police, paramedics, and fire department dispatched to Fifth Avenue, hoping they could quickly determine the exact location. The caller had used a cellphone, and when she spoke, her address was incoherent, but the operator did determine it was probably somewhere in the twenty-two hundred block of Fifth Avenue on the north side of

Youngstown, Ohio.

The police and the fire department had no difficulty finding the exact location, for as they approached, the house at 2255 Fifth Avenue was ablaze with flames shooting out of almost every window of the capacious dwelling. The firefighters began the challenging task of drenching the violent blaze with endless gallons of pressurized water from the thick fire hoses they laboriously carried and stretched across the immaculately landscaped yard. Others crashed through the main entrance, breaking down the scorched door and entering into a grand foyer. These officers dispersed into various sections of the house, searching for any victims, alive or dead. Making their way through the dense smoke and the angry blaze, two firefighters promptly entered the living room off to the left of the foyer. Amid flames and charred, falling debris, they discovered two bodies lying prone and motionless on the living room carpet.

They called for assistance and rapidly removed a man and a woman from the burning house. When they were safely away from any danger, they determined that the male victim was not breathing. Even though the paramedics attempted to revive him, their efforts were futile. He was pronounced dead. The female, though still alive, had a very weak pulse. Both were rushed into two waiting ambulances. The paramedics in the female's ambulance directly started working to keep her breathing. As they administered to her injuries, over and over, she whimpered the name, "Sammy."

Despite all measures, she weakened and was pronounced dead at 2145 hours just before arrival at Saint Elizabeth Hospital on Belmont Avenue.

Back at the location of the ongoing fire, rescuers

continued to thoroughly search the entire house for survivors or fatalities, each floor, every single room, but no other bodies were found. Even after the flames were completely extinguished, no evidence was discovered to indicate any other living being had survived or perished in that fire.

Chapter One

*Friday, around 9:00 p.m.*

The main branch of the public library system was located on Wick Avenue just above the hill from downtown. The facility had closed for the day about a half hour earlier. The woman who went by the name Thin Lizzy was secretly hiding in the women's bathroom on the first floor, but she knew she couldn't stay in that location for much longer. From her precarious perch on top the toilet in the stall furthest from the bathroom door, she heard that lady with the very black hair who wore a blue outfit come into the restroom. She always had on that stark blue outfit. Thin Lizzy knew that lady was coming in the bathroom to clean all the toilets, including the one on which she was squatting, for she had been in this predicament several times before.

Just as Thin Lizzy was about to jump off the seat, dash out of the stall, and rush out the bathroom door, hoping the blue outfit lady wouldn't chase after her, an upbeat melody loudly pervaded the room from the cleaning lady's cellphone. The woman retrieved it from the right pocket of her pants and answered it, talking on it for less than a minute.

To Thin Lizzy, her response sounded like, "Jibber, jibber, jibber." She had no idea what the blue outfit lady had said. Through the crack where the stall door met the partition wall, Thin Lizzy saw the lady stop talking on her phone, shove it back into the pocket of her pants, and rush out of the bathroom. Thin Lizzy didn't know where the lady went, but she knew she would be back very soon. She always cleaned the bathrooms in the library every night.

This was her chance to escape and find a new place to hide. She had to get out as quickly as possible before the cleaning lady returned. She cautiously crept off the toilet seat and slowly opened the stall door. Sneaking over to the heavy bathroom door, she pulled it open just enough to peek into the hallway. Casting her eyes around the surrounding area, she verified the hallway was empty and the cleaning lady was nowhere in sight. This was now her opportunity. She darted out of the door, up the wide staircase, and found a new hiding place on the second floor among the shelves with the large volume books. She planned to stay in the library all night, just as she had done for the last few weeks. However, everything she owned was not currently in her possession.

The large, black plastic trash bag that contained all her belongings was shoved under a parked car a block away on Rayen Avenue. That abandoned car with only three tires left, rested on its axle and had been at that location for a couple of days. She hoped the car would still be there when she went to retrieve her things later that night. She knew she'd soon have to find a new hiding place for her bag.

Thin Lizzy was very hungry. The only food she had eaten that day was a partial candy bar she had found earlier when she was walking downtown on Federal Street. She had picked it off the sidewalk near a trash can in front of one of the restaurants, then pulled the sticky piece of candy from its ripped paper wrapper and devoured it. It still lay heavy on her empty stomach.

That afternoon, she had also gone to the university campus up the street from the library to search for food, but it was the start of a weekend, so not too many students were around to throw away containers of unfinished food. Besides, it was best to find food at night—really late, when the restaurants downtown threw away most of their leftovers and the scraps their customers hadn't eaten off their fancy plates. Especially, the big hotel on Federal Plaza. Sometimes lots of food was in the dumpsters, particularly, if the hotel had held some type of party or event where many people attended. Maybe a wedding reception, a Bar Mitzvah, a charity event, or some big-wheel business convention.

Oh, she was very happy then. She would find fancy chicken dishes, savory beef cooked in exotic sauces, vegetables smothered in flavorful seasoning. Sometimes she even found sweet and tasty cake or other scrumptious goodies. She was so hungry she could probably eat anything. Anything at all. Actually, one time her hunger was so demanding she ate a handful of grass. It tasted nasty, actually horrific, and her stomach remained queasy for the rest of that day. But when she was desperate, she had no choice. She'd try anything to keep from starving to death.

On this particular Friday night, she hid in the corner by the shelves of books until all the lights were turned off and the library was silent and still. That meant the cleaning crew had finally finished their work for the evening, had left the building, and wouldn't return until tomorrow after closing. Only then did she decide it was safe to go fetch her bag of belongings and bring it back to the library before she would hunt for food downtown. It was plenty dark enough outside to make her escape.

The first time she had stayed overnight in the library, she was lucky enough to find a small flashlight in one of the unlocked drawers behind the counter at the main entrance. Then in the early morning when she left the building before any personnel arrived for work, she would routinely replace it exactly where she had found it. The library opened at nine, and some of the staff came in as early as seven o'clock. She was always gone from the premises by then. She knew she had to be very careful to be out of there before anyone caught her inside. Otherwise, she would be in serious trouble.

Along with the use of the flashlight, the streetlights and headlights from the traffic outside would also channel through the windows to help her find her way around the dark and desolate library late at night.

A single door at the back of the library was marked "private" and was used only by certain staff members. However, those employees who used that door were either unaware or didn't care that its alarm was broken and didn't buzz if someone opened the door. But Thin Lizzy knew about it, and she kept a rock about the size of a large fist underneath the shrubbery on the side of the building. Near closing time each night before she entered the library, she would retrieve the rock and hide it under her clothes, bringing it into the building with her and placing it behind a shelf of old books that nobody seemed to care about reading anymore. Then she would take it with her after hours to keep the door from closing and locking while she left the building to forage for food. She would open the door and place the rock inside on the floor next to the bottom of the door. The rock was just heavy enough to hold the door slightly ajar—just enough so the security guards checking the perimeter of the building at night on their drives around it couldn't tell the door was barely open. And just enough so she could reach her boney fingers in the opening and grasp it when she wanted to get back inside the building after her search for food.

One time on her trek back to the library, she caught sight of a hefty, bushy-haired, scraggly bearded man with dirty, bare feet lurking near the door. She stopped suddenly and hid in the shadows a short distance away so he wouldn't see her. She became aware that he had noticed her rock holding the door slightly open. She stood silently, observing him as he struggled to firmly grasp the door. After opening it wide enough to enter, he glanced around the outside darkness before slinking into the doorway and picking up her rock. As he entered, he raised his arm and heaved the rock far away, narrowly missing Thin Lizzy in her hiding place.

Lucky for her, she later overheard two of the librarians whispering about that bushy-haired guy. Apparently, he had fallen asleep somewhere on the second floor, and a staff member called the police when she found him in the morning loudly snoring and spread out comfortably on a couple of wide, upholstered chairs he had pulled together. The police escorted him out of the building. She didn't know what happened to him or where they took him, but thankfully, he hadn't returned since that incident. As far as she knew, she was now the only street person who used that door. That time when he took her rock away and went inside for the night, she had to find a new place to stay and ended up in one of the back alleys downtown. She didn't like to sleep there because too many others hung around in those dim, murky alleys. Darkman and Mojo, two really evil men, were always there. It seemed they were just about everywhere she went. She had to hold onto her personal stuff, or they would steal it. No place was safe from them, and she didn't get much sleep that night, being too busy guarding her meager possessions.

Lately, Thin Lizzy routinely slept in the library at night and roamed around various areas of town during the daytime, always being observant of her surroundings and anyone who might present a threat to her. Sometimes, when she walked around the university campus, she'd find a bench to sit and watch the students as they rushed from class to class, carrying heavy backpacks. When they threw bits of food or even leftover coffee in the trash barrels, continually mindful that no one saw her, she would scavenge through the containers, retrieving anything edible or drinkable. One or two swallows of coffee helped rejuvenate her a little. Other times, she ventured a few blocks away to Wick Park, where she'd remove her tattered shoes and walk on the soft, pliant grass, feeling its moisture and texture beneath her tired toes. Or she might stretch out on one of the picnic tables to take a nap in the shade of the tall oak and maple trees located throughout the park.

Other times, she might walk down the hill on Wick Avenue and wander the streets downtown—Federal Street, Front Street, Commerce, Phelps, Andrews. All of them. Once in a while, she'd stand on a corner and beg for food or money. But while doing this, she had to be very watchful for the police. They were always out looking for people like her. Occasionally, they arrested them, or maybe they just gave them a warning and made them move on. The best way to protect herself was to be vigilant, keep walking, and mind her own business.

So far, she had never been arrested, but once, she had come very close to being caught. She and Aggie Bee, her friend, had been panhandling on the plaza about ten o'clock at night. Some event was happening downtown, and the streets were crowded with pedestrians. Neither of them was paying attention to what type of cars were going by their location on the corner.

Suddenly, Aggie Bee shouted to her, "Run, Thin Lizzy, run!" And she did. She ran to the nearby hotel, where several cars at the entrance were unloading their occupants who were about to enter the hotel lobby. She ran among them, dodging through the incoming guests to get away but also to use them as a concealment from the eyes of the police in the patrol car. She heard some of the offensive remarks coming from these hotel guests as she passed by them.

"Oh, how disgusting!"

"Oh, my Gawd! It isn't safe around here."

"Can't they do something about these trashy vagrants?"

"What a disgrace!"

But Thin Lizzy managed to get away unseen by the police. The snide critiques from the guests didn't bother her. Not anymore. She was used to their abrasive remarks and disparaging looks.

That night, Aggie Bee hadn't been so fortunate. The cops caught up with her as she ran down East Federal Street. But lucky for her, they just gave her a warning and told her they didn't want to ever catch her panhandling anywhere in the city again. Of course, she didn't obey their coercive suggestion. She was simply more careful after that close encounter.

Thin Lizzy tried not to take her bag of belongings with her when she walked around town, the university campus, or even the park. It was too heavy to lug around, especially if she wanted to look for food. Besides, if she carried it downtown, Darkman or Mojo would surely try to steal it from her. Then she'd have nothing. They were rough, mean, and vulgar, usually high on drugs or drunk on something. If she saw those men or the police, she ducked behind a parked car or a trash receptacle. She always remained cautious and keenly aware of her surroundings in order to stay safe and survive this cruel life.

Of course, her real name wasn't Thin Lizzy. No one seemed to use their real names in this community of the homeless. For sure, Darkman and Mojo didn't. She didn't know anybody's real name, and she didn't want to know them. Not even Aggie Bee. Yes, she was her best friend around town, but Thin Lizzy wasn't sure if she could trust even her. Nothing about living on the streets was safe or trustworthy. Or easy.

Thin Lizzy's first destination that Friday evening was to retrieve her trash bag full of her belongings from under the parked, abandoned car on Rayen Avenue. Even though she knew the library was empty, she was still guarded as she crept out of her hiding place. She had become so familiar with the layout that she could find her way in the dark and didn't always have to use the flashlight, but she grabbed it anyhow—just in case. Since she never knew where she might end up at night, she felt more at ease having it with her as she roamed the streets around town.

When she reached the back door of the library, she

opened it cautiously, making sure no one was lurking anywhere in the darkness. After scanning the area with her eyes, her night vision, still good from being inside the shadowy building, she saw no one. When that bushy-haired man had thrown away her original rock, she had found another suitable for her purpose. She opened the door wide enough to exit and placed her rock on the floor, so the door wouldn't slide closed completely.

It was a cool, September night. Her meager sweatshirt was threadbare with holes in the elbows and the seams. Many months ago, she had found it in a trash bin on the university campus near one of the dorms. There was a time when the sweatshirt was a light, fluffy pink with deep pockets. Not anymore. The pink, now faded and dirty; the pockets, riddled with holes. Thankfully, at least the holes weren't so big that the flashlight would fall through them. Underneath the sweatshirt, she wore a long-sleeved T-shirt. That is, it originally possessed long sleeves. Those sleeves were also tattered and torn. The cartoon penguin embellishing the front of it was covered in so much dirt, grime, and whatever else that it was difficult to determine what kind of animal it actually represented. It too was found in the trash on campus.

Her jeans were two sizes too large for her meager body frame. She had lost so much weight since she had been on the streets. She used a rope she had found tied to a fence to weave through the belt loops and fastened it at her slim waist, holding up the threadbare jeans. Her once white sneakers she had confiscated long ago from the trash bin behind the second-hand store were now ripped on the seams. She had placed pieces of cardboard inside them to cover the holes worn on the soles and heels.

She'd have to find some new pieces of cardboard soon, knowing she'd probably never again be lucky enough to find a pair of shoes that somewhat fit her small feet.

After leaving the library, she began walking down the sidewalk on Rayen Avenue to get her bag from under the abandoned car. When she neared its location, she stopped suddenly, noticing two slovenly dressed men wandering near the car and inspecting inside its windows. She immediately hid on the side of a nearby building, watching them intently to see what they planned to do. No way was it safe to approach the car with them milling around it. She waited anxiously, snuggled flat against the building. As she observed them, the men tried unsuccessfully to open the car doors, but each one was securely locked. Thin Lizzy heard them mumbling to one another, but she couldn't make out what they said. One of the men began looking around on the ground near the car, probably to find something with which to break a window. He was getting close to where she was hiding. She cautiously backed up a little.

Just as he was about to come closer to where she stood, the other guy near the abandoned car called out loudly enough for her to hear, "Forget it, Torro. We'll try somewhere else."

She breathed a sigh of relief as the guy called Torro turned around to follow the other man away from the car. Then she waited for a couple more minutes to be sure they had disappeared from the area. When she finally came out from the side of the building, she hurried to the car and crouched down to recover her bag from underneath it. She knew she'd have to find a new hiding place because either the police would soon come and tow that car away, or some of the street people would be back and eventually break into it. She was surprised that something hadn't happened to that car already.

After stooping to the ground and tugging out the bag from under the car, she trudged back to the library to wait until it was late enough to walk downtown, anxious to find some food. She removed her rock from the private door and lugged the bag up the stairs to her current hiding place. Breathing a sigh, she dropped the bag and rock in her corner and sat on the floor with her back against the wall and legs spread out in front of her. With her head down, she dozed while she waited until it was late enough for the hotel to have thrown out their garbage, dreaming of finding juicy morsels of fabulous food and devouring them slowly, enjoying every bite.

It was sometime after midnight when she awakened, rubbed the sleep from her eyes, and picked up her rock to go to the hotel on the plaza. Food! She had to get some food soon. She left the library, once more placing the stone to hold open the door, and walked through the parking lot to Rayen Avenue, then turning right toward Wick Avenue. Her hunger was giving her nausea and cramps as she turned left and began hiking down the sidewalk of the hill toward downtown. The thought of finding food at the hotel dumpster made her mouth water, and her mind was singularly focused on what possibilities she would find waiting for her in that huge garbage bin. Her focus was solely on her extreme hunger and the pain in her stomach because of it.

As she moved forward and approached Wood Street, she happened to look up in the direction of the roadway. And she couldn't believe what she saw. Were her eyes playing tricks on her? All alone in the middle of the quiet street, stood a small child. A boy, standing perfectly still. "What da hell is *he* doin' dere?"

She was totally confused. All thought of food and hunger instantly escaped her mind and body. She noted the boy was dressed in dirty, red pajamas with nothing on his tiny feet. He simply stood there, stiff as a statue, arms straight down to his sides, staring at the street. She yelled out, "Hey, you! Kid! Whatchu doin' dere? You better get outta da street."

The boy didn't respond. Had he even heard her? Did he even know he was in the middle of the street? He continued to stand rigidly in place and stare straight ahead.

Thin Lizzy's eyes were riveted on the boy, wondering what he planned to do. Since it was so late at night, traffic was extremely light, but that was no reason for a small child to stand there all alone in the middle of an empty street.

But the street failed to remain deserted. Suddenly, she heard the roaring sound of a vehicle approaching from the top of the hill, coming south on Wick Avenue. She turned to look and saw a huge black SUV barreling toward the boy at a high rate of speed. The kid just stood motionless, limp arms still dangling at his sides, unaware of the impending danger.

What was she supposed to do? He just stood there, and that car was swiftly getting closer and closer to the boy. It was definitely going to run him over if he didn't move immediately. Coming down the street at that rate of speed, the result would be bad, real bad.

She stopped thinking about the possible crisis and took action. Bolting into the street, she scooped up the boy in her scrawny arms and, stumbling slightly, raced back toward the sidewalk. The SUV's horn blasted as it whizzed by her and the boy, mere inches from her backside. She felt the hot, swift air of its rapid motion smack her left side before she careened over the curb.

When she reached the sidewalk, she staggered upright and placed the small child down onto the pavement. Unsteady on her feet and clasping his shoulders, she stared at him. "What's wrong which you, kid? Why you standin' in da middle of da street like dat? You could a been killed. You know dat?"

The boy stared up at her with huge sad, crystal blue eyes but didn't respond in any way—no trembling, no crying, no fear, no words.

She gently nudged him away from her to get a better look at him. Most of his face was covered in a cloudy gray residue, but she thought he must have been crying because light pink, wiggly stripes funneled down his round cheeks. His soiled pajamas smelled like smoke and urine.

She tried to talk to him once more, "What's da matter which you, kid? Where you come from? What you doin' in da middle of da street with no shoes on yer feet?"

But he didn't answer her; his somber, blue eyes simply stared into her panic-stricken face.

Chapter Two

*Friday night, before the fire.*
Since no one planned to get up early the next morning, being it was the start of a weekend, Sammy was allowed to stay up a little later to spend some quality time with his mom and especially, his dad, who was a very busy man and not often available to hang out with the family. Sometimes they played games together. Sometimes they watched a movie of Sammy's choice on the large screen in their media room. Sometimes they went to the playground and out for ice cream afterwards. This Friday night, Alyssa and Samuel Nagy, dressed in matching, buffalo plaid loungewear, were in the living room playing Sammy's new card game with him, also in his favorite Titaniuman pajamas, red with bright yellow sun rays emanating from a depiction of the planet earth and super-imposed with the image of the superhero. Sammy's favorite dinner of hot dogs and macaroni and cheese had recently been devoured, and the kitchen was cleaned up and back in order. Sammy and his mom had previously played a few games of checkers with Sammy winning four out of the five games. He was also winning the current card game, and his dad was losing badly, mainly because he wasn't paying much attention to the card game. A local high school football game broadcasting on the gigantic television screen on the opposite side of the luxurious room had captured his

attention, and his father's eyes tended to drift more toward that football game than to the all-important card game with his son. As always, Sammy's mother was trying to lose the game. She believed in building her child's confidence in any way possible. In her eyes, even winning a simple game of cards or checkers was a successful step in the right direction to develop a strong, self-confident adult.

Attempting to distract him from the football game, Sammy tapped his father on the shoulder and coaxed, "Daddy, it's your turn to pick a card," His dad did not respond immediately. "Daddy?"

Abstractedly, his father finally took his eyes off the television and glanced at his son. "Uh, okay… My turn." He still remained engrossed with the game on the television screen. Then momentarily, his father focused back on the trivial card game, looking down at the scattered deck in the center of the coffee table.

Just as he finally reached over to select his next card from the messy pile, his eyes still darting back and forth between the top of the coffee table and the television, an ear-splitting noise came from the foyer. Each of the Nagys immediately sat upright and looked toward the sound, eyes wide, bodies rigid, mouths gaping open. A second later, two unmasked, muscular men dressed all in black and carrying semi-automatic weapons entered the living room.

The gut reaction of the adult Nagys was to stand upright and face the intruders. Their cards and drinks tumbled to the floor, producing wide spots of deep red splashing the cards scattered over the somber gray carpet.

Alyssa's motherly instincts kicked in. Sensing grave

danger, she pushed Sammy toward the attached dining room behind them. "Go! Run and hide. I'll come get you later."

Both terrified and confused, Sammy stood frozen, staring at the two men. But his mother pushed him harder. "Go!"

Frightened, he instantly jerked his head, first at his mother. She really looked scared, and her voice was high and squeaky. He had never seen her look or sound like that before. Then he gawked at the intruders with the guns one final time before dashing into the dining room. At the entrance to the hallway, he stopped for a second, darting his head left and right, wondering where to go next. The stairs were nearby. He rushed up them as fast as his short legs could carry him.

At the top of the stairs, he stopped again. What now? Where should he go? Tears fueled by fear rolled down his cheeks. He was so scared, but he couldn't let those bad men find him. He had to hide. But where?

Across the hall was the big bathroom. He shoved the door open and looked around for a hiding place. He tore open the door of the sink cabinet. Too much stuff was in there. He wouldn't fit. The door to the supply closet was a teeny bit open. Sometimes when he and Mommy played Hide and Seek, that's where Sammy would hide. He staggered to the door, opened it, and snuggled underneath a comforter way in the back of the bottom shelf, covering himself completely after closing the door behind him. Through the louver doors of the closet, he heard shouts and screams routing up the staircase. Then the sound of gunshots caused his heart to skip a beat. Bang! Bang! Every part of his body shook with fright. Confused and petrified, he didn't even realize that he had urinated in his Titaniuman pajamas. His teeth couldn't stop chattering, and his body wouldn't stop trembling.

A few minutes passed, and everything grew eerily quiet. Then he heard heavy footsteps mounting the stairs and clomping into the hallway. Hoping and assuming, it was his mother coming for him, he started to push away the comforter to exit the closet. But suddenly, the sound of the clatter of doors slamming open and furniture roughly being shoved around stopped his progress. His mommy wouldn't be doing that kind of stuff. She would probably be calling, "Sammy, where are you? You can come out now." She wouldn't make all kinds of noise looking for him. He immediately hustled back into his position in the closet and burrowed under the comforter again.

The very second he was settled and quiet, the brilliant light in the bathroom lit up the entire room, casting narrow, horizontal panels of brightness into the supply closet through the slats of the louver door. Sammy heard the daunting footsteps on the tile floor just inches away from the closet. Unexpectedly, the door sprung open. Sammy held his breath and willed his quivering body to stop trembling. He waited as the shadow rummaged through the shelves, knocking over bottles and jars, throwing towels out of the closet and onto the floor. The shadow started tugging and pulling to remove the comforter covering Sammy when a loud voice shouted from the hallway, "Let's go!"

The hand roughly released the comforter as it dangled partially to the floor, and the man withdrew from the entrance to the closet, leaving the door open. He disappeared from Sammy's limited view and left the glaring light still lit as he went out of the bathroom.

Sammy remained trembling, his body still partially beneath the comforter while the sound of the footsteps in the hall grew fainter. He closed his eyes while he waited for the noise to stop and his mother to come and get him.

And he waited. Where was she? She said she would come and find him.

While he hunkered in that small space, Sammy began to notice a funny smell in the air. After another minute or so, he found he was having trouble breathing. At first, he didn't know what the smell was. Then he realized it reminded him of when he and his daddy went camping. When it got dark, his daddy would always start a fire to cook hotdogs and roast marshmallows. If he stood too close to the fire, sometimes that smoke came in his face, and he had a hard time breathing. Did he smell smoke like that now? He began to cough and gulp for air. He had to get out of the closet. Since his mommy didn't come to get him, maybe he should find her. Maybe she smelled the smoke too.

That's what he would do. He'd get out of the closet and look for his mommy. He wasn't sure where the bad men were, but he didn't hear them anymore. And he didn't hear any more gunshots.

He tossed off the comforter and climbed down from the shelf.

Once in the open bathroom, he still had trouble breathing, and he felt so hot. Whew! He wiped his hand across his forehead. What was he going to do? He could hardly breathe, and he began to cough and choke for air. Maybe if he got out of the bathroom…

He stumbled into the hallway, jerking his head in both directions. Where was his mommy? Maybe she ran away from those bad men like he did. Maybe she ran into the dining room too. Maybe she was waiting for him somewhere downstairs. He looked toward the main staircase, the one he had previously mounted, but it was hidden in smoke. Hesitating again, he snapped his head toward the back set of stairs that led down to the kitchen, and then he lurched toward them.

Never had Sammy been this terrified as he tripped down that back staircase. But his mommy would surely be there waiting for him, and she would know what to do. Yet, when he reached the end of the stairs and entered the kitchen, there was even more smoke. And his mother was nowhere in sight.

"Mommy! Mommy! Where are you?" He choked as he stood in the middle of the expansive room filled with acrid heat and even more noxious smoke. He could barely see in front of him. But his mother didn't answer his screams.

Struggling to breathe, he had to get fresh air. The room was getting hotter and the smoke was becoming denser as each second ticked away. He saw flames coming from the dining room. He had to get out of the house. He staggered to the French doors on the opposite side of the kitchen and grasped the door handle. "Ouch!" he yelled. The hot metal had burned his tender hand. But he had no choice; he had to get outside.

Pushing the door open, he rapidly took in the fresher air as he escaped from the blistering heat. Upon his exit, he bolted off the patio onto the backyard grass below, coughing, choking, gagging, and spitting out gray globs of phlegm while gulping in the cleaner air. When he was finally able to breathe more easily, he was completely terrified and bewildered. He stood motionless, staring at his home being inundated with garish flames, tears streaming down his cheeks.

What was he to do? Where was his mother? She promised she would come for him. Should he wait for her to come out of the house? But it was almost completely engulfed with the fire, and even while he stood in the yard, the heat was so fierce on his body that he needed to back further away.

Maybe she was in the front yard of the house. He promptly circled the entire house, screaming as loud as he could, "Mommy! Mommy! Where are you?" Like a frightened rabbit, he crazily ran helter-skelter, back and forth, finding no one, only more fire immerging from the windows and the heat getting even stronger.

Then he heard the shrieking sound of sirens growing louder and appearing to come closer. What should he do? Where should he go? So agitated, so petrified, so confused, and so overcome with mounting shock, he didn't realize what he was doing. He began to haphazardly drift away from the blazing structure. He couldn't free his mind of the vision of those awful men and the guns they carried. He had seen the way they looked at his daddy and mommy when they had burst into the living room. He might be only five years old, but he knew they were bad men and wanted to hurt him and his family. But why didn't his mother come and get him before the fire started? She said she would. She had always found him when he hid in the closet when they played Hide and Seek. Why couldn't she find him this time? And who were those men? Why did they want to hurt his family? That's why she told him to run and hide. But then he heard the gunshots while hiding in the closet. What did that mean?

He began to wander through the lawns of the houses

along Fifth Avenue, rambling far south from his own blazing home. If he heard a car coming, he hid behind a tree or a bush. It might be those bad men trying to find him. His feet were bare, having removed his slippers while playing the card game and not having the time to put them back on when his mother ordered him to run and hide. As he walked, he stepped on stones and small branches, which poked and bored into the skin. His feet began to throb with pain, and his right hand felt like it was also on fire like his house. But he couldn't stop moving forward. He had to escape the unspeakable scene he had left behind. He had to get as far away as possible from the sound of the gunshots, the volatility of the fire, and the oppressiveness of the smoke. If his mommy were okay, she would find him. If she wasn't? His mind refused to think of that alien alternative. He had nothing else to do but to trudge forward, dazed and totally alone.

He constantly blew on his singed hand to try to ease the blistering pain, but that didn't help much. His short, little legs and his injured feet sent sharp jolts throughout his body with every step he took. He felt like he had walked a hundred miles.

When he had gone camping with his daddy, they would go for hikes together on the narrow paths through the shaded woods, admiring the wild plants and vibrant flowers that were so pretty. They searched for the small animals who burrowed, roamed, and inhabited the woods. His dad would tell him the names of each one they would see. Sometimes they knelt down on the damp, musty moss and dirt to watch the tiny insects go about their diminutive lives. If they were walking and Sammy got tired, he would tell his daddy to slow down or ask to take a rest or go back to camp. Sometimes, his dad would even heave him onto his shoulders to carry him back to their car. He loved to perch there, reaching high in the air and picking leaves off the branches of the trees nipping at his head and shoulders.

But his daddy wasn't with him as he silently plodded through the dark night on unfamiliar terrain, not knowing where he was going or how far he had walked. He was all alone. He didn't know how much further he could go. He kept blindly looking straight ahead as he stumbled on and on, passing house after house, street after street.

Finally, after walking for what seemed like an eternity, he stopped to take a breath. He slowly turned his head from side to side, looking at his unfamiliar surroundings. To his right were buildings and houses, and to his left were trees and grass. No buildings or houses. He saw a large sign at the edge of the grassy area. He had just started kindergarten a couple of weeks before, but his mommy had already taught him how to read. He could say his A-B-C's faster than anyone else in his kindergarten class, and he was the only one in the class who could actually say them backwards. He was having so much fun learning everything. Since he wanted to be an astronaut when he grew up, his mommy told him he had to be good at reading and writing and stuff like that. He could already add and subtract numbers as long as they weren't real big like a million or billion.

Thus, when he looked carefully at the letters on the sign above him, aloud, he spelled them out. W.I.C.K P.A.R.K. Okay. He knew how to do this. "Wwwkk Ppprk. Wik Prk. I-I think that's it."

He remembered Crandall Park, where his mother sometimes took him to the playground. He thought he passed that park a while back on the other side of the street. Could this be another park? It kind of looked like a park. Wick Park. If it was a park, maybe he could find a bench where he could sit and rest for a little bit. At least they had benches at Crandall Park.

Tired, weak, and in pain, he turned and staggered onto the lush surface of the park's ground. The soft, cool grass felt soothing on his bare, injured feet. As he walked a little further, sure enough, he found a bench. No matter what, he had to rest for a while before walking another step. He wasn't sure where he would go next or what he would do, but he had to take a break. He was so tired, more tired than scared, and he hoped he was far enough away from those bad men so they would never, ever find him. He climbed onto the bench, lay down, and put his left hand under his face for a pillow.

Soon he drifted off to a restless sleep, and before long he was lost in a dream. A happy dream. He and Corbin and Jace, his two best friends, were playing tag in his backyard. Jace was "it" and was running after him. When Jace caught up to him, he tagged him on the shoulder. But he kept tagging Sammy over and over again. Sammy was getting irritated with Jace. He tried swatting him away. Then suddenly, he realized that it wasn't Jace but someone else touching his body. His eyes popped open wide, and he jerked upright on the bench, instantly frightened and alert. Standing over him was a scary looking man with red eyes, a crumpled face, and wearing ripped, grubby clothes. The smell from his body took Sammy's breath away. He scrambled to the end of the bench, so the man couldn't touch him again.

"Leave me alone!" he shouted as he tightly gripped the metal arm of the bench. "Leave me alone!"

The man stared at the child. "Whatchu doin' here, kid? Why ain't chu home? You could get hurt around here. Git outta here! This ain't no place for no kid."

Sammy repeated once more, "Leave me alone!"

The man stared at Sammy for a few more seconds, then shook his head and simply moseyed deeper into the park, mumbling to himself as he walked away.

Sammy's heart thumped against his chest. He didn't know whether he should continue trying to sleep again or move on to somewhere else. His nerves were all frazzled, but he was still just so weak and tired. Instead of lying back down, he leaned against the back of the bench, bowed his head, and closed his eyes. Soon his nerves settled, his body slumped over, and he dozed off again.

About fifteen or twenty minutes later, he was awakened by a sudden noise and a weird odor, unlike that from his burning house. This time when he opened his eyes, his neck was stiff and achy. He reached up to rub at it with his right hand, but that made the skin burn like fire. He looked around to check out his surroundings. Where was he? Had anybody heard him?

A group of older boys sat on top of a picnic table several yards away. They talked in loud voices, smoked funny smelling cigarettes, and were drinking out of beer cans. Sammy didn't want them to see him, and they were making so much noise on their own that they hadn't heard his shriek when he reinjured his burnt hand. He'd better get out of there. No more sleeping. He scrambled off the bench and crept through the park in the opposite direction of the boys—and Fifth Avenue.

After reaching the other side of the park, he came out at the corner of two streets. Looking up at the street signs, the one going along the edge of the park read, E.L.M. S.T.R.E.E.T. The other sign going in the opposite direction read, I.L.L.I.N.O.I.S. A.V.E. Which way should he go? He started to walk east on Illinois Avenue. He walked for several blocks on that street when he came to a sign that read, W.I.C.K. A.V.E. That was the same name as the park, so he turned right onto Wick Avenue.

He walked and walked for at least another hundred miles—what it felt like to him. Every inch of his body ached. His legs were so tired and numb it felt like he was dragging his daddy's big car instead of just his legs. His feet were so sore that every single step shot jabbing pains up to his groin. At one point he stopped under a streetlight to look at them. They were bloody and swollen. He wasn't sure how much longer he would be able to walk.

But he walked on, so exhausted and aching all over that he was to the point of being completely unaware of what he was doing. Step with the right leg; step with the left leg; step with the right leg; step with the left leg; on and on. Like a robot walking on Jupiter or Mars. That would be fun. He tried to pretend he was walking with his dad on a camping trip as they meandered on the trails through the woods. He tried to keep his mind in that place—away from the fire, away from the big men dressed in black, away from the gunshots. Maybe his mother would find him in this new place. Maybe his father would carry him because he was too tired to walk any longer on his own.

When he was so exhausted that his legs just wouldn't move him even one more step, he suddenly stopped. He closed his eyes and stood motionless with his arms dangling at his sides. And when he finally opened his eyes, he realized he wasn't with his mother and father at all. He had somehow gotten himself at the top of a hill in the middle of the street, looking down at a bunch of tall buildings. And from the sidewalk, a skinny lady was screaming at him.

**Chapter** Three

*Saturday, past midnight, after the fire.*

The struggling firefighters spent hours at the house on Fifth Avenue containing the horrific blaze. It was too soon to predict much about the cause or circumstances of the fire. The first thing they determined was that only two bodies were found in the living room—a man and a woman. No other human or animal remains were discovered in the rubble anywhere else in the house.

The authorities acknowledged that the fire presumably started in the front foyer and spread rapidly throughout the structure. It was also soon learned that the man and woman taken from the house had both been shot before the fire enveloped the living room. It wasn't official yet, but those at the scene were fairly certain the fire was deliberately set. The accelerant was believed to be plain, old gasoline—one reason why the fire advanced so rapidly.

"Well, what do you think?" Detective Willard Hamilton addressed his question to his partner, Detective Stacey Atkinson.

They were the officers who Marlon Rutherford, Youngstown's Chief of Police, immediately assigned to the murder case after he had received word of the death by gunshots to two individuals at the scene of the fire. The male victim had been shot in the middle of his forehead and had died instantly. The female victim wasn't so lucky. She was shot in the stomach with the bullet fragments damaging several of her internal organs. She had lived for only a short while in the ambulance on the way to the hospital.

The two detectives were outside what was left of the destroyed house. They had been questioning the firefighters and the inspector. For their own safety, they were prohibited from getting near the burned-out shell of the house. They were then informed the residence had been comprised of six bedrooms, five baths, an expansive attic, and a finished basement. The fire inspector would present his full report to the chief within a few weeks.

One firefighter had told them that the female was still alive when she was placed in the ambulance, but he didn't know anything else about her condition. The detectives had previously been informed that the 9-1-1 call for help had originally been made presumably by the woman inside the house.

Detective Atkinson said, "I think we need to talk to the 9-1-1 dispatcher who took the call and find out if the woman was alert at all and able to speak to her. And if she was, what she actually said. We also need to verify that the couple found in the living room are truly Samuel and Alyssa Nagy, the owners of this house. It's probably them, but we'd better make sure. You never know about these things. Could be relatives or friends. Maybe house-sitters, something like that."

Detective Hamilton nodded. "Yep, I think our next stop is the hospital where they took the couple and see what we can learn there."

Hamilton was a tall, portly man, pushing retirement age. What little hair he had left was a golden white, almost iridescent. His gray suit was clean, but somewhat rumpled, as if he had been in it all day, which was actually the case. His shift on duty had ended at six o'clock, but the chief had contacted him just as he and his wife Marion were in their living room relaxing on the couch and enjoying a glass of smooth, red wine after finishing up his delicious roast beef dinner. When he received the chief's phone call, Hamilton had immediately contacted Atkinson, informed her of their new assignment, and told her to pick him up in a half hour.

Detective Atkinson, a tiny woman in her mid-thirties, barely came up to Hamilton's shoulders. They were an odd combination, but they worked well together. Atkinson wasn't looking forward to Hamilton's retirement. He had taught her so much over their partnership of almost four-and-a-half years, and she wasn't ready to get accustomed to a new partner. Of course, she knew the choice wasn't hers to make. She would deal with it.

After they had finished examining the scene on Fifth Avenue as much as they could at that particular time and talking to the professionals on the scene, Atkinson drove them to Saint Elizabeth Hospital. When they arrived, they asked to speak to the doctors who had attended to the couple from the Fifth Avenue fire. Both doctors affirmed that the two individuals were DOA at the hospital. The coroner had been notified and the bodies would soon be taken to the Cuyahoga County's Medical Examiners facility for the autopsies to determine the official causes of death.

"But I can tell you this," Doctor McKay said. "The female victim was still alive when they put her in the ambulance at the scene of the fire. However, she succumbed before reaching the hospital. In addition, both victims died of gunshot wounds. Their bodies may have been compromised by the fire, but the gunshots were what killed them."

Hamilton and Atkinson both paused. Gunshot wounds? Detective Hamilton asked, "Do you know if they were able to speak before they passed?"

The doctor responded, "No, I don't know. You'll have to check with the paramedics who brought them here in regard to that."

Hamilton then asked, "How about the bodies? Were they officially identified?"

"Yes, they were. We notified the next of kin to both victims. Samuel R. Nagy was identified by his brother, Adam Nagy. Alyssa Dawn Karis Nagy was identified by her mother Mrs. Patricia Karis and her sister Madelyn Winthrop."

"Thank you, Doctor. We'll get in touch with the Medical Examiner for more details on the conditions of the bodies and the causes of their deaths," offered Hamilton.

The detectives planned to eventually seek out the relatives of the deceased to ask them if they had any theories on who could have shot their family member. First, though, the relatives needed a chance to grasp the consequences of this terrible family tragedy.

The two detectives then left the hospital and rode to the 9-1-1 call center to talk to the operator who had taken the emergency call. Cynthia Dornan was still on duty when the detectives arrived at the center. She joined them in the break room. Detective Atkinson started the interview. "Ms. Dornan, what time was the call and what did the caller say?"

Dornan consulted her records. "The call came in at 2113 hours last evening. Truthfully, it was difficult to understand her. Her voice was very hoarse and low in volume. I understood from what she said that there was a fire. That part I got. Then I believe she said she was shot, and her husband was dead. Like I said, it was really difficult to make out what she was saying."

Hamilton inquired, "Was that all she said, then?"

"Yes, I think so. Actually, I can play the call back for you if you like."

"That would be great," agreed Hamilton.

The trio went into another room, and the dispatcher adjusted a recording machine to the time the message came in from supposedly Alyssa Nagy.

Caller: *"Ple-ease h-help m-me. H-ouse on fire. I've b-been sh-shot!"*

Dispatcher: *"Ma'am, what is your address?"*

Caller: *"T-two… t-two… f-f-fi… uh f-f-fiv… ohh! F-fifth A-ave… Ohh!"*

There was a pause.

Dispatcher: *"Ma'am, are you there?"*

Caller: *I-I'm sh-h-ot-t, f-fire, hus-s-b-band d-dead. S-s-sam-my-y-y-y!"*

The recording ended.

"That was it," said Cynthia.

The two detectives looked at each other. Atkinson spoke, "Could we get a copy of that recording?"

"Oh, of course." Immediately, Cynthia began to make the copy. "I sure hope it helps you. What a shame."

Taking the recording with them, when they got to their vehicle, Hamilton said, "I think we're missing something, here, Stace."

Atkinson had started the vehicle and was pulling away from the call center. "What do you think we missed? And why?"

"I… I don't know." He paused. "I think I want to talk to the paramedics who transported Mrs. Nagy to the hospital. If she actually died in the ambulance, did she say anything there, or was she too far gone by that time?"

"You've got a point there. Let's check that out."

Detective Atkinson drove to the main fire station on Martin Luther King Boulevard. She pulled into the guest parking lot, and the two detectives entered the administrative area of the building. Inside the station, the detectives walked up to the uniformed firefighter at a desk. Showing his badge, Hamilton said, "I'm Detective Will Hamilton with the Youngstown Police Department. This is my partner, Detective Stacey Atkinson. We'd like to talk to one of your paramedics who was on duty around 2115 hours last night."

The firefighter responded, "Sure thing. Can you give me a little more detail so I know who you're talking about?"

"Yes, I can," said Hamilton. "He or she would have responded to a fire on Fifth Avenue. Two ambulances were dispatched, one picking up a deceased male and the other, a female who passed away on route to the hospital. We need to speak to the paramedics who handled the female victim."

The fireman checked a clipboard on the desk, flipped a page, then another. "Okay… That would be EMTs Craig Hodgins and Maura O'Donnell. They're out on a call right now, but they should be returning momentarily. Would you like to wait? Can I offer you a cup of coffee?"

Hamilton and Atkinson looked at each other. Atkinson said, "It's kinda late for coffee. What do you think?"

Hamilton sighed, "Hell, we're gonna be up all night anyhow. Might as well have a cup." He turned to the firefighter. "I'll take mine black. She'll take hers with one cream."

After a few minutes, the firefighter brought out their coffees in Styrofoam cups, and the detectives sat on two comfortable padded chairs in the small waiting area. Hamilton groaned as he lowered his body to the chair. "Been a long night, hasn't it?"

Atkinson agreed, "You got that right. This isn't exactly what I had expected to be doing right now. Friday night, you know."

Hamilton looked over at her and grinned. "I suppose you were planning a hot date with that new guy you've been seeing. What did you say, he's a guitar player or something?"

She scowled at him. "You talk as if he's some fly-by-night, has-been musician. Dude, he's a very successful guitarist for a pretty well-known band. They even go abroad for some of their gigs—England, France, Sweden." She paused. "So there!"

Hamilton shook his head and smirked, then took a sip of his hot coffee. "Whatever."

They waited for about fifteen minutes before the EMTs to whom they needed to speak finally returned to the fire house. Both Hodgins and O'Donnell came out to greet them. Hodgins spoke, "You detectives wanted to talk to us? Come on back."

Hodgins opened the door and led the detectives back to a small room with a table and a half dozen chairs.

"Take a seat," he said, pointing to the metal chairs around the table. "What can we do for you, detectives?"

Atkinson started the conversation. "I understand the two of you were the EMTs who responded last evening to the fire on Fifth Avenue and tended to the dying woman at that location?

"That's right," answered Hodgins. "What do you want to know?"

Atkinson asked, "Did she say anything before she died? Anything at all?"

Hodgins glanced over at O'Donnell. "Maura, you were closer to the upper part of the victim's body. Did she say anything?"

Maura O'Donnell looked up and tapped her forefinger on her closed lips. "Uh, you know, she tried to say something ..."

"What was it? Do you remember?" asked Atkinson.

O'Donnell struggled to recall the words uttered by the dying woman. "To me it sounded like she said, uh, the name 'Sammy.' Come to think of it, she actually said it a couple of times before she passed."

"Nothing else?" asked Hamilton.

O'Donnell slowly shook her head, her mind still going back to that ambulance ride. "No... No. That was all. Just 'Sammy.' Her voice was very weak."

"Is there anything else we can help you with?" asked Hodgins.

Hamilton replied as if his mind was somewhere else, "No, that's all we came for. Thanks for your time."

Everyone arose from their seats. As they exited the room, Hamilton and Atkinson turned toward the front of the building, Hodgins and O'Donnell, toward the back. Hodgins called out to them, "If there's anything else we can help you with, just let us know."

Atkinson and Hamilton responded at the same time, "Thanks."

Back in their vehicle, Atkinson turned on the ignition but didn't shift into reverse. "Where to now, boss?"

Hamilton didn't answer. Instead, he asked another question that was bothering him. "So the man's name was Samuel, right?"

Still waiting for instructions on where to go, she said, "Right."

Then Hamilton queried, "And the nickname for an adult male named Samuel would normally be Sam, right?"

She looked over at him, wondering where he was going with this. "Right. Probably. Why?"

Instead of answering, Hamilton continued to speculate, "On the 9-1-1 recording, it sounded like the woman said 'Sammy,' and the EMT also agreed that the woman said 'Sammy' in the ambulance, not 'Sam.'"

"Okay?" Atkinson wasn't catching on to what he was thinking.

"So why do you think she said 'Sammy' instead of 'Sam'? Do you think she called her husband 'Sammy'?"

She looked over toward him. "I don't know. What's your idea here?"

He was silent for several seconds. "I'm thinking she may be talking about a kid. A boy and not her husband. Did the Nagys have any children?"

Atkinson stiffened. Eyes wide, she quickly turned toward Hamilton. "You think that a kid—"

Shaking his head, he revealed, "Yep. I think maybe they have a son. But where is he?"

"Shit!" she cried as she tore out of the fire station parking lot.

*Chapter* Four

*Early Saturday morning, after the fire.*

The unlikely pair stood on the sidewalk at the top of the Wick Avenue hill. Both the boy and the thin woman shivered, not so much from cold but from the emotional overload controlling their minds and bodies. Thin Lizzy had just saved this little boy's life. At the speed it was going, that SUV would never have been able to avoid hitting him as it swept down Wick Avenue.

And the boy? How much could a child take? No doubt, his body was in an extreme stage of shock. The fire, the gunshots, the never-ending walk. The pain in his legs, feet, and hand. This weird lady who smelled really bad unexpectedly grabbing him. It was such an emotional and physical trauma for a young boy of five.

Thin Lizzy stooped down to be closer to the boy's height. Still breathing heavily, she tried once more to get the grimy child to talk. "What's yer name, li'l kid?"

Sammy had lost all sense of time and reality. Maybe he was having one of his nightmares. Will his mother magically appear to comfort him and take him back to where he belonged? He looked at the scrawny lady kneeling in front of him on this strange sidewalk far away from where he lived. This was definitely not a nightmare, and that lady was absolutely not his mother. He began to cry, not just sobs as he had been doing ever since he escaped from his burning house, but a full blast bawling episode. Tears flowed non-stop fluidly down his dusty cheeks, creating blotches and smudges as he rubbed his face with the back of his hand. And he wailed.

Astonished, Thin Lizzy opened her mouth. It had been a long time since she had dealt with a crying child. She looked around the area to see if anyone noticed the two of them standing there with the boy bellowing so loudly. But they were alone amidst the buildings and the quiet, early morning darkness. However, the kid's voice was so deafening she knew she had to do something to calm him. No telling what would happen if somebody like Darkman or Mojo would notice them standing there. She had to shut him up.

"No, no," she warned the boy as she hastily lifted him into her spindly arms, turned around, and briskly strode back in the direction of the library.

Sammy was so startled by her sudden actions that he abruptly stopped crying while he was held tightly against this woman's bosom and jostled up and down with her rapid movements. While she carried him, Sammy had no choice but to focus on her. Who was this person? Why did she smell like a garbage can? Where was she taking him?

But the strangeness of his situation stopped his crying as the woman joggled and bounced him while she swiftly walked to wherever she was taking him. For some reason, despite the turmoil and insanity of his situation, he didn't know why, but he felt calmer than he had since leaving his living room and hiding in the closet.

She turned off the sidewalk and wandered to the back of a big building. Sammy knew that building. His mother had taken him there lots of times. It was the library. But it was dark. None of the windows showed any light shining out of them. Why was this lady taking him to the library when it was dark outside? He didn't want any new books. He was too upset and worried about his mom, dad, and the fire to think about getting anything to read.

When Thin Lizzy reached the back door of the library, she promptly plopped the boy down next to her. "Now you stay right dere. I'm gonna open da door, and we gonna go inside."

Wide eyed and confused, he did exactly what she told him. He saw her remove a big stone that had propped the door open a tiny bit. He stood there as she grasped the heavy door and pulled it open. She held her back against the inside of the door and spoke to him, "Now you go inside, and you just stand dere until I gets da door closed."

Sammy obeyed. What else could he do? He was so tired, and in a way, he was thankful someone else was making decisions for him. He walked inside the very dark library, and stood perfectly still, just as the lady had said. It was even darker than outside. He was afraid to move. Breathing heavily, he stood stiffly while the woman closed the door behind her.

When she entered the library, Thin Lizzy reached in her pocket and pulled out the flashlight she had been carrying. She turned it on and held the big stone out to the boy. "Here. You carry dis and follow me."

Bewildered with what was happening, Sammy had never experienced anything like this before. However, even though everything seemed so strange and unusual to him, he felt less alone and lost. This weird lady seemed to be helping him. At least he hoped so. He took the stone from her and held it with both of his hands even though the pressure on his right hand was very uncomfortable.

The skinny lady walked in front of him, beaming the flashlight so they both could see where they were trudging through the dark building. He heard her say, "I don't really need dis light, but I know yer probably havin' a hard time seein'. I don't wanchu knockin' into anything."

Sammy kept following her as they started up a wide staircase. After all the walking he had recently done, he had a difficult time climbing the stairs. He had to rest a couple of times, grabbing onto the railing with his left hand as he caught his breath and slowed his racing heart. Each time he stopped, the lady looked back at him and also stopped and patiently waited for him to catch up to her. She didn't say anything. She just waited.

When they reached the top of the staircase, she led him into a large room with lots of huge books on big bookshelves. She walked over to a corner on the opposite side from the wide windows. She knelt down on the carpet and pointed the flashlight up like a lamp so Sammy could see her and the area they were in a little better. "How 'bout sittin' here wit me for a li'l bit, okay?" She twisted her body and sat down against the wall.

Sammy stared at her for a few seconds, still holding the stone. Then he also sat on the carpet and leaned against the wall. It felt so good to finally get off his worn-out legs and injured feet. He crossed his legs in front of him and placed the stone beside him, releasing an enormous sigh as he dropped his shoulders and sat.

After she saw that he had finally settled down, Thin

Lizzy asked, "So can ya tell me who ya are and why yer all by yerself when it's so dark outside?"

Sammy stared at the stone he had placed beside him.

"So what's yer name, li'l kid?"

Sammy had calmed down enough that he thought he might be able to talk to the lady. She didn't seem to want to hurt him. He wasn't so afraid of her like he was when he had seen those two men holding guns barge into his living room. Or even when he had been in the park when that man had touched him or when he saw those big boys nearby smoking and drinking. He also was worried about his mother and how he could get back home to her. Maybe the firemen had already put out the fire. Maybe this lady knew how to get him back to his mom and dad.

He folded his hands, brought them close to his face, and said, "Sammy." He paused. "That's my name."

For some reason, Thin Lizzy hadn't expected him to speak. Therefore, she was startled when he did say his name. Pleased with the progress they were making, she responded, "Sammy, huh? So dat's yer name? Well, my name's Thin Lizzy."

Normally, Sammy, a very outgoing, bubbly child was not shy around strangers. His mother always said he was perceptive and precocious and could hold his own in a conversation with most adults. But the situation he was currently in, and the condition of his battered body made him wary and cautious. However, he was beginning to feel a little more comfortable around this odd lady. He gave her a strange look before he responded to her. "That's a funny name."

Thin Lizzy smiled. "Yeah, I guess it is. Well, it ain't my real name, anyhow. Nobody goes by der real name 'round here."

44

Despite his new predicament, since Sammy was an inquisitive little guy, he asked, "How come you don't use your real name?"

Surprised, Thin Lizzy opened her eyes wide and frowned slightly. "Well, I don't think I know why. I guess 'cause nobody wants nobody else ta rat on dem to da cops."

Sammy had never heard that phrase before. He was confused as to what it meant. "What do you mean about rats and cops?"

Thin Lizzy didn't know how to explain it to a small child. "Oh, heck! I don't know. Can we just furget about it, and ya just call me Lizzy?"

"Okay... Lizzy."

Sammy really didn't feel like talking anymore. His head hurt; his legs were so tired; his feet felt like all the bees in the world had stung him a thousand times; and his hand burned so much that he wanted to cry. He was just so tired he didn't know what the lady would say if he simply lay down on the carpet and went to sleep. "Lady, uh Lizzy, I'm really, really tired. Can I just answer your questions after I sleep a little bit?"

Thin Lizzy saw his eyes kept closing on him as he sat propped against the wall. She certainly wanted to know what had happened to him, but he looked so overwhelmed by fatigue she knew he would have a difficult time answering any of her questions. Nevertheless, she had a dilemma. She was still very hungry. Finding the boy on the street had thwarted her plan to find food. Maybe the kid was hungry too. If she passed out before she was able to get some food, she wouldn't be any good to either of them.

While the lady stared at him, Sammy couldn't stay

seated any longer. His body gently sloped down the wall until his head touched the floor.

Thin Lizzy lightly shook his tiny shoulder so he could be awake long enough to tell him she had to leave. Sammy opened his eyes slowly, looking at her in a sleepy daze.

"Okay, uh, Sammy. I got to go out for a li'l bit. But I'm gonna leave ya here so you can rest. I won't be gone too long, but don't move from dis spot. So you go ta sleep and stay right here. Okay? Don't move, okay?"

Sammy nodded before he curled himself into a ball. Whether or not he actually heard what Thin Lizzy had said was debatable, and despite his harrowing ordeal, his body gave out on him. He immediately fell into a deep sleep.

Thin Lizzy hated to leave the boy, but she had no choice. She would hurry through her task, and hopefully, he would stay asleep until she returned. She grabbed the flashlight, picked up the stone, and left the boy lying asleep on the dark, deserted library floor.

After fixing the stone to hold open the back door, she hastened her walk to the Wick Avenue hill, then rapidly walked downtown. When she reached the plaza, she saw no one on the quiet streets. Marching with a purpose, she scurried to the dumpsters behind the large hotel. Thankfully, the hotel had hosted some type of event the night before, and plenty of food had been tossed away. No one else had foraged through the food yet. Lucky for her. The aroma of the food made her think of the zesty chicken, savory roast beef, and spicy pasta and sauce she might find. She could tell from the scent of the food it was still warm and fresh. She was also lucky that she had arrived before the rats.

Heaving open the lid of the dumpster, she confiscated one of the garbage bags full of food and trash. Routing through it, she discarded what wasn't food, taking bites of a chicken leg as she worked to satisfy her immediate keen hunger. She went through three bags and ended up with enough food to feed her and the kid for a while. She knew she could never take all the food. Some of it would spoil before she'd be able to eat it. She also didn't want to be selfish. This way whoever hunted through the dumpster after she was gone would still find some decent food for themselves.

When she had scavenged enough food, she picked up her bag, scanned the area to be sure no one was nearby, slung the bag over her shoulder, and promptly took off toward the hill and back up to the library.

After retrieving her stone at the doorway and tightly shutting the door, she dragged her bag of food and the stone up the stairs to where, thankfully, the boy was still sleeping. She placed stone and bag gently on the floor in her corner and took a couple of breaths, short-winded after the hike up the stairs with her heavy load. The boy was still in the same fetal position as he had been when she left him. She searched in her food bag for something more to eat. Even though she wanted to gorge herself with food, she knew better. Too many times in the past she had done just that and paid the price afterwards. When she had eaten an ample amount to satisfy her hunger, she closed up her bags and lay down beside the child.

She had hoped she would fall asleep immediately, like the boy had done, but her head was too full of the current events. What was she going to do with this kid? Who did he belong to? How could she get him home?

She surely couldn't take care of him for very long. The streets were no place for children. Things were dangerous around here. Sure, she saw teenagers roaming around town sometimes, but this kid was not a teenager by any means. She had to find out why he was standing in the middle of the street so late at night. Maybe then, she could determine what she should do with him. After tossing and turning for another hour, she finally fell asleep.

***Chapter*** Five

*Monday, 8:45 a.m., eighteen days before the fire.*
"Mr. Banetti, your niece is here to see you."

Louise Tellesco, a woman in her late sixties with straight, coal-black hair cut just below her ears, had been Rocco Banetti's secretary since he started his professional career years ago and moved his office to the third floor of the REB Enterprises building on Market Street in Boardman. Since then, his enclave had expanded and made him a very wealthy man. And Louise, a friend of the Banetti family, had known Rocco since he was in diapers. He trusted her explicitly. In his type of business, he had to have a loyal, reliable, and confidential staff that he could count on to be discreet at all times.

"Send her in, Louise."

Banetti pushed aside the documents he'd been analyzing before his secretary informed him of the visitor. It was always a pleasant surprise to see his niece, the daughter of his dear, deceased sister, Angela. And recently he was even more pleased to see her and to hear what she had to relay to him.

The graceful and attractive young lady entered Banetti's plush, enormous office, tossing her shining, sable hair over one shoulder. She immediately went behind the sleek, metal desk to his side and kissed him on the cheek. "How is my favorite uncle today?" Then she walked around the front of the desk and agilely sat into one of the tasteful chairs facing him, sitting up straight and crossing her slender legs.

As Banetti watched her get seated, he reminisced how she looked so much like his sister Angie at that age. Natural tawny complexion; wide chestnut brown eyes; thick, ebullient hair, and a delicate nose—not like many of the Italian women with their copious, bulbous features and manly faces.

"I'm doin' great today, love, especially since you stopped in to visit me. Do you have anything special to tell me this morning?"

She leaned forward and placed her narrow elbows on his polished metal desk. "Well, I think I'm getting close."

Banetti clapped his hands together. "Damn! It's about time!"

She leaned back on her chair. "Gimme a break, Uncle Rocky. This thing takes time. You should know that better than anyone."

He got out of his chair, came around his desk, and reached down to hug her. "I know. I know. But you can't blame me for being impatient. You know how important this is to me. He straightened back up and sat on the matching chair next to her.

She placed her hand on his forearm laying on the arm of his chair, and momentarily, rested her head on his shoulder. "I do know how important it is." Then she scooted her body to face him. "That's why I'm working so hard on it. But I have to be very careful. You know how it is."

He clutched her delicate hand in his beefy one. "Yes, sweetheart, I know. I'm just a busy, impatient man, and it's hard to trust anybody these days. That's all." He hesitated. "Do you love me anyhow, sweetheart?"

She reached down and kissed his hand that was holding hers. "Of course, I do, Uncle Rocky, you know that."

He turned to face her more directly. "So tell me what has happened, what you've learned."

She took a deep breath. "Well, not much—not yet. But what I can tell you is that he's getting ready to talk." She shook her head. "He's so full of himself, thinking he's such a big shot. I'm sure he's going to open up soon."

"Well, what has he said so far?"

She paused before tilting her head to her left and nodding. "He just said he was working on a client that was really into some corrupt activities."

Banetti jumped out of his chair, dropping his niece's hand. "That snake! That weasel! Those men know better than to mention anything about me, anything at all to anyone." He paced around the office, breathing heavily, visibly upset. Then he sat back on the chair next to his niece. He took a deep breath, and while staring at the map of Italy behind his desk, asked, "What else did he say?"

She looked him directly in the eyes. "For sure, he didn't mention your name, but one other time he told me he worked on one client, one that had many different entities and businesses. Although back then, he hadn't mentioned anything about corruption."

Banetti stared at her, not really seeing her, his thoughts going elsewhere. Then he once more got out of that chair and walked back to his own chair behind the desk. He sat down and placed both his elbows on the desk, folded his hands together and bounced them back and forth against his mouth. He said nothing for several seconds, maybe an entire minute.

His niece also remained quiet, watching and waiting for his next remark or directive, her legs crossed and one leg swinging up and down.

Finally, he dropped his hands to the desk and sat upright. "I'll have to think about this for a while."

"Do you want me to continue to keep picking his brain to get more information from him?"

"Oh, yes, yes, of course, but be discreet. You don't want to spook the guy."

She chuckled. "I don't think that's possible. He loves me too much for that."

There was silence for a bit.

"Uncle Rocky?"

Deep in thought, Banetti looked up. "Yes, sweetheart?"

"You know I love you."

"I know you do, honey."

There was another moment of silence before she said, "Please don't hurt him, okay? He's not really such a bad guy, and I really like him.

When Banetti didn't respond, his niece got out of her chair, went around the desk again, kissed him on the cheek. Then she walked to the door and turned one last time to look at him. Without saying another word, she opened the door and was gone.

Banetti silently sat in his chair, staring at the office door through which his niece had exited. Five minutes later, he picked up his intercom. "Louise, get me Benny on the phone. Right now."

It took several minutes before Louise buzzed Banetti. "*I have Benny on the phone now, Mr. Banetti.*"

"Thanks, Louise," he said and waited to hear Benny's voice.

*"Mr. Banetti, you wanted to talk to me?"*

"Yeah, Benny, I have a job for you and your boys?"

*"What is it, sir?"*

"I want you to harass a certain attorney."

## *Chapter* Six

*Monday, 2:00 p.m., twelve days before the fire.*

Samuel R. Nagy, the owner of the house on Fifth Avenue, was a prominent attorney with prestigious offices in downtown Youngstown. On a part-time basis, his wife Alyssa worked at the firm doing clerical and administrative duties. Sam's partner in the law practice was Carl N. Padgett. Padgett & Nagy, LLP had formed after Sam received his law degree from Michael E. Moritz College of Law at Ohio State University. Carl Padgett had also attended that college but had graduated three years before Sam. They had been fraternity brothers and had become good buddies during their coinciding years at Moritz and had planned to start a firm together after Sam's graduation.

Prior to the start-up of the partnership, Padgett had started his private law practice and had permanently taken on a few very lucrative clients. Carl was lucky his father, a high-powered state senator, had many friends and acquaintances in the Youngstown area to whom he had recommended his son's firm. Therefore, by the time Sam came aboard, the law firm was already well established. His addition and the resulting partnership just made it more profitable and productive.

Although they had many clients and several employees, including attorneys, paralegals, investigators, and administrative staff, the most important and successful client who engaged their firm was Rocco Ettore Banetti, a very ingenious and resourceful man who had his hands in an abundance of legitimate operations and businesses throughout northeast Ohio and western Pennsylvania. As well, he was a very wealthy and influential man in the community. However, perhaps some of those associations and companies might not have been as completely bona fide or honest when scrutinized more closely. Some, in fact, were outright unscrupulous and unlawful. Racketeering, sex trafficking, illegal gambling, drugs.

In other words, what this meant for Padgett & Nagy, LLP was that even though Banetti was a very profitable and successful client for them, he was also a very dangerous and risky client to represent.

The firm had to be extra vigilant in their attentiveness when dealing with Banetti's legal issues. Their policy was strict: only selective staff members worked on any of Banetti's business or personal matters. Because Alyssa was the wife of a partner and therefore, could be trusted explicitly, she was the only administrative personnel permitted to handle any of Banetti's affairs.

Besides Carl and Sam, the lone professional who worked on Banetti's accounts was Attorney Ryan Nesbitt. Only those four members of the firm had the combination to Banetti's keypad locked filing cabinet containing all of his files and records. This was the way Banetti required his accounts to be handled, and this was the way the law firm acknowledged his demands.

Ryan Nesbitt was young, only two years out of Cleveland State's Marshall School of Law, when he was hired by Padgett & Nagy, LLP. His drive and ambition was a big reason why he was hired. Before he was offered a position with them, he was thoroughly interviewed and vetted by both Sam and Carl. The partners believed Ryan would be the perfect addition to the law firm and specifically, for the work they did for Rocco Banetti. Nesbitt was well aware that his position with the firm depended on his ability to keep everything and anything about Banetti's accounts strictly confidential. If the partners found that he broke that edict, he would be fired immediately. Both Carl and Sam warned him that Banetti might offer Nesbitt his own form of punishment if he didn't keep all knowledge on Banetti's businesses in strictest secrecy. Nesbitt had been with the firm for three and a half years, and no issues regarding this matter had ever become a problem.

Twelve days before the fire that destroyed the Nagy home on Fifth Avenue. Ryan Nesbitt asked Sam Nagy for a private meeting in his office. At two o'clock that afternoon, he approached the partially opened door to Sam's office. He knocked and peeked through the opening. "Are you ready for me, Sam?"

Sam looked up from his computer. "Close the door and sit down."

Ryan took a deep breath to boost his courage to proceed. "Okay, Sam, everything has been cool so far with the Banetti accounts. I know they pull in a large chunk of dough for the firm. And I have no problem with the work itself."

Shaking his head, Sam interrupted, "And you, Ryan, have definitely benefitted from that large chunk of dough quite handsomely, right?"

Dismayed, Ryan accepted, "Yeah, you're right. I admit that." Then he gained control. "But here's the thing you don't know about…" Ryan seemed hesitant about mentioning what he came to tell Sam.

Sam waited a couple of seconds. When Ryan didn't continue, Sam said, "Well? Go on. What is it?"

Ryan looked around the room, then blurted, "I'm being followed."

Sam suddenly came to attention, forehead wrinkling. "You're being followed? When? By whom?"

"That's just it. I don't know who, and I don't know why. Honest! I haven't breathed a word about anything having to do with Banetti except to Melanie. I can't keep secrets from her. She's my fiancée. But, like I say, I'm being followed by—"

Sam jerked upright. Did he hear Ryan correctly? He raised his hand in the air, palm facing outward. "Wait a damn minute. Stop right there! What exactly did you tell Melanie?"

Ryan suddenly felt nervous and started picking at his cuticles. "I… I just said I was a… a little worried with some of the activities in which one of our clients was involved."

Sam's face turned red. "You said what?"

Ryan knew Sam was livid, but he really didn't know why. He didn't understand why he couldn't tell his fiancée things about his work. After all, they were going to be married soon. And he definitely hadn't mentioned any names. But he felt defensive, as if he had made a huge mistake. "I… I didn't go into any detail or anything. I just said this client wasn't the most honest guy."

Sam shook his head back and forth, taking a worried, deep breath. "Ryan, Ryan, what have you done?"

"What do you mean? I didn't give her any names or

anything like that. I'm not stupid. Besides, she's my fiancée. I can't keep things from her."

Shaking his head again, Sam mumbled, "I'm not so sure about that stupid part anymore."

They were quiet for a few seconds, each with their separate thoughts scrambling in their heads. The silence was making Ryan nervous, and he needed Sam's advice. "Anyhow, so what do I do about this car following me?"

Sam twisted his lips and began tapping the desk with his forefinger. "Do you know what kind of a car it is? Did you get the license plate number? Can you describe the driver?"

"Well, it's always a recent model black SUV with tinted windows. I haven't been able to catch the plate number or a glimpse of the driver. They don't follow close enough for me to get a look. But I'm absolutely sure they're following me. They usually hang a couple of cars behind me, but I know they're there. Could be they want me to notice them; I don't know."

"Hmm," was all Sam said as he put both elbows on the desk and covered his mouth with his right hand.

Ryan waited for Sam to say something else. When his boss didn't speak, Ryan again asked, "What do you think I should do about this?"

Sam took his hand away from his face. "I don't know… I don't know." He clasped his hands together, elbows still on the table and began shaking his forearms slowly back and forth, lips puckered. Finally, he leaned back on his chair and replied, "Let me think about this a while. I'm going to mention it to Padgett." He paused. "Two things here. It's either the FBI or Banetti's guys. Either way, it can't be good. If it's the FBI, what made them decide to follow you? Did they discover something we don't know about and are trying to spook us? If it's not the FBI or some other government agency but some of Banetti's men, then *why* would they be following you? If Banetti has a problem, why hasn't he brought it up to Carl and me?" He paused again. "Something stinks here."

Ryan shook his head. "Like I said, I did nothing wrong. I'm sure of that."

Sam glared at him. "Are you absolutely sure about that, Ryan? Saying what you said to Melanie wasn't the smartest thing, you know. The only reason my wife Alyssa can talk about Banetti is because she works on his accounts as well. And we never discuss anything about him in public. As for Carl's wife Leanne, she knows nothing whatsoever about Banetti or any of our clients." He stared at Ryan. "In the future, you don't mention Banetti's name or *anything* about him to *anyone*. I mean *anyone*. Not your fiancée, not your mother, not your priest or pastor, not even God. Do you understand?"

Ryan looked wretchedly sorry. "I understand. I won't mention anything to Melanie about work from now on."

Sam arose from his chair. "Let's table this for now. I'll discuss this with Carl. As far as you're concerned, just keep your mouth shut and your eyes open. Keep alert. If you can catch the plate number of that car that's following you or anything else about it, all the better. And let me know immediately."

Ryan also stood up. "Okay. I'll be on the lookout." He stopped at the doorway. "Sorry about all this, Sam."

As he exited, Sam replied, "You should be."

While Ryan had been in his office, Sam had not indicated how serious he thought this matter was. But with Ryan gone, he admitted to himself he was very concerned. Why would either the FBI or Banetti's men be tailing Ryan? Surely, his talking to his fiancée wouldn't get back to Banetti. And that type of vehicle, a black SUV, had to be either some government activity or Banetti's men. This could be a real problem. A real serious problem.

After several seconds, Sam picked up the phone and left a message on Carl's cellphone. "Hey, Carl, as soon as you're back from court, I need to talk to you. I'll be in my office. It's important."

Chapter Seven

*Early Saturday morning, after the fire.*

After talking to the two paramedics who transported Alyssa Nagy to the hospital, Stacey Atkinson drove her partner and herself back to police headquarters. They needed to discover more details about the Nagy family. Was it possible that they had a child? Did the name "Sammy" refer to her husband or perhaps her son? Firefighters had confirmed only two bodies were found in the burning building. No other bodies were found, neither adults, children, nor pets.

Detective Hamilton began speculating aloud. "It just doesn't seem right. If the kid is safe, where is he? If he isn't safe, still, where is he? And if the kid is dead, why didn't they find his body in the fire?"

Atkinson pulled into the parking lot at headquarters, and the two detectives went directly to Chief Rutherford's office. After Hamilton knocked on the door, the chief responded, "Come in."

Hamilton spoke first. "Chief, you know that fire on the north side where the couple was found shot before the house was lit up?"

The chief had been reaching for a folder on the side of his desk. "Of course, I know. The one on Fifth Avenue. Why do you think I'm still here in the middle of the night?"

Ignoring the sarcasm, Hamilton continued. "Yes,

the Nagy residence."

With the folder in his hand, the chief asked, "What about it? Do we know who shot them yet?"

"No, it's too early to get evidence on that, but we have reason to believe that the Nagys may have a kid, a boy, even though the rescuers found no child's body at the fire site. Do you know if he has been found yet or anything about him?

Stunned, the chief put down the folder and promptly admitted, "No. I know nothing about any child. How do you know this?"

Atkinson told him about their conversations with both the 9-1-1 dispatcher and the paramedics. "They all insisted she said 'Sammy,' not 'Sam,' like you'd call a child, not an adult."

The chief reached for his phone and called the policeman on duty at the hospital and put the speaker function on so Atkinson and Hamilton could hear the responses directly. "Sergeant Morrissey, are the families of the burned victims still at the hospital?"

Morrissey replied, *"Yes, chief, they're all in the chapel right now."*

"You need to find out immediately what they can tell you about the name 'Sammy.' Was Mr. Nagy called that, or could that be the name of another individual, maybe a child. Interrupt them, no matter what."

*"Yes, chief."*

Chief Rutherford waited on the phone for Sergeant Morrissey's return.

While they waited, Hamilton shook his head. "Damn! How could we have missed this? Let's hope we're wrong."

A few minutes later, Morrissey came on the line.

*"Chief, the Nagys had a son they called Sammy. Neither Mr. Nagy's brother nor Mrs. Nagy's sister know anything about the boy's whereabouts. In fact, they don't seem to know much about the boy at all."*

The chief looked puzzled, but replied, "Okay, I'm gonna send Hamilton and Atkinson over to talk to them. Don't let them leave the hospital until the detectives arrive."

The chief hung up his phone. Shaking his head, he addressed the detectives, "Apparently, there is a boy. Seems odd, but nobody in that chapel knows much about him. Get over there and talk to the relatives. Find out what's going on. We have to find this kid, ASAP."

While driving to the hospital, Atkinson wondered aloud, "What's going on? The aunt and uncle of a little kid can't supply any information about him?" She shook her head. "I find that very strange."

Hamilton was deep in thought. "Agree." He leaned back on his seat and glanced up toward the top of the car. "We're in big trouble if we don't find out where that kid is. Hopefully, he's just at some neighbor's house." He paused. "In fact, let me get some guys to check the houses in the area of the fire. See what the neighbors know about the kid."

Atkinson replied, "I don't think those neighbors are gonna be too happy with being awakened so early in the morning."

"That's too damn bad, isn't it? A kid's life is at stake here. You see where *we're* at in the middle of the night, don't you? We aren't in our cozy beds dreaming of lollipops and roses, are we?"

"Yeah, you're right about that. I sure could use a little nap right now."

Hamilton took his phone out. "Besides, most of the neighbors are probably already awake with that fire and all its commotion right on their block." He called headquarters, telling the dispatcher to send a unit to knock on doors in the area of the fire in order to get any information on the boy and his whereabouts.

After the two detectives arrived at the hospital, they went directly to the chapel. Inside, a few individuals were seated in a front pew, consoling each other. The detectives introduced themselves. "Folks, I'm Detective Willard Hamilton." He turned to his partner, "And this is Detective Stacey Atkinson. We're investigating the deaths last night of Mr. and Mrs. Samuel Nagy."

After looking around at all those seated in the room, he immediately began explaining why he and Atkinson were there. "It has come to our attention that Mr. and Mrs. Nagy had a young child, a son. We need to find him ASAP. At this time, this is our primary concern. I know you all are currently dealing with deep sorrow and emotions regarding the deaths of your loved ones. Later, you may be called in for questioning more specifically about the circumstances and the deaths of those two individuals. However, for now, the child is our priority." He again looked around the room. "I understand none of you have any idea where he is, but what can you tell us about the boy?"

No one spoke directly, but the detectives noticed elusive glances back and forth between the family members. Their behavior seemed unusual, but he waited patiently for someone to explain.

Finally, a stoic looking older woman with fluffy white hair who'd been sitting on the right side of the chapel admitted, "I'm afraid we don't know much about the child, detective."

Confused, Hamilton looked around at all the pallid faces in the group. "I'm sorry, ma'am, aren't you people the family of the Nagys?"

Hesitating, the woman responded, "Yes we are, but you see, most of us have been estranged from Sam and Alyssa for many years now."

With his face clearly showing his stunned reaction, Hamilton wanted more information. "Okay-y? Then let's start by finding out who you are, and why nobody can tell me about this child."

The ambivalent family members began to introduce themselves, starting with the woman who had first spoken to Hamilton. "I'm Patricia Karis, mother of Alyssa."

The woman sitting to the left of Mrs. Karis introduced herself and the man next to her. "My name is Madelyn Winthrop, and this is my husband, Corey. I'm Alyssa's older sister."

The man on the opposite side of the aisle stood up. "My name is Adam Nagy, and this is my wife, Naomi. I'm Sam's older brother."

Both Atkinson and Hamilton stared at the group for several seconds. Then Atkinson questioned, "You mean to tell us that all of you are aware there is a child, but nobody here knows anything about him or his whereabouts?"

Looking embarrassed, they all nodded their heads but said nothing.

Hamilton threw his arms into the air. "What the hell? Will one of you people please explain how that is possible? How the hell none of you seem to even care about this kid?"

For a few moments, the relatives continued to stare at Hamilton. Then Adam Nagy cleared his throat. "Ah-hem. Uh, you see, detective, it's like this." He hesitated as if he didn't want to continue with his explanation. "It's not that we don't care about the boy. Of course, we want you to find him. It's just that our families haven't been close for several years. We knew Sam had a son, but my wife and I have never met the boy."

The detectives' mouths dropped open as they gazed at Adam Nagy. Atkinson shook her head and focused on the man standing before them. "Mr. Nagy, normally I would say your family's differences are no concern of mine or the police department. However, in this situation, a child is missing. His life is at stake. He may be in serious danger. So we need to know what's going on here. Can you be a little more specific?"

Adam Nagy glanced over at Alyssa's family before speaking. "Well, as far as my brother Sam is concerned, my family wanted no part of his life. I don't know if you officers are aware, but Sam was a very wealthy attorney. Naomi and I are church-going Christians who try to follow God's plan for us. Ever since my brother went into the law practice with that—" His face took on an ugly grimace. "—that shyster, money-hungry lawyer, Carl Padgett, our families have drifted apart. Sam no longer cared to have any relationship with my wife and me either. He was too busy making money and defending wealthy deadbeats and criminals to bother with us."

Adam Nagy sat back down in his seat, taking a deep breath and clutching his wife's hand.

Detective Hamilton took over questioning him. "When was the last time you saw your brother, Mr. Nagy?"

Adam lifted up his chin as he recalled the last time he had faced his brother. "It was at my mother's funeral about four-and-a-half years ago."

"Did you have any discussion or conversations with him at that time?"

Adam shook his head and scoffed, "Oh, yes I did— if you want to call it a conversation."

"What do you mean? What did you talk about?"

He appeared very uncomfortable as he described his last dealings with his brother. "Where do I start? Uh, I'm embarrassed to say we had a big argument right in front of Mom's casket in the middle of the funeral home with all our friends and relatives watching and listening. Well, before she got sick, Mom told me she had gone to dinner at selfish Sam and Alyssa's huge, showy house when Alyssa was pregnant with their child. Mom was so excited for them. And for herself. You see, Naomi and I had two girls at the time, and this child of Sam's would be Mom's first grandson. Mom was in good health then. But shortly after that dinner, she was diagnosed with pancreatic cancer and went downhill fast. When Sam found out about Mom's cancer, he claimed he couldn't deal with her illness. It was too emotional for him."

Nagy's face flushed, and his eyes seemed to radiate fire. "*He* couldn't deal with it! What exactly does that mean? *He* wasn't dealing with it—Mom was." He swiftly shook his head. "The jerk!"

Looking embarrassed about his emotional outburst regarding his dead brother, he continued his outrage in a somewhat calmer fashion. "Sam proceeded to tell me that his wife just had a baby, and the baby wasn't sleeping well at night. Plus, he was working on a big criminal case that took up most of his time. What with the baby and work, he had no time or patience for our mother or what she was going through."

Adam Nagy stared at the detectives. "Can you believe that? No time for his own mother when she was very ill with only months to live? During her entire illness, I doubt if he even saw her three times. What a jackass! He told me if she needed money, just let him know. Sure, his money would solve everything. Mom didn't need his money; she needed *him*." Adam shook his head again and clamped his mouth tightly closed as he turned his face away from the detectives. After a slight pause, he added, "Detectives, I'm sorry my brother and his wife are dead, but truthfully, they have been dead to my family for a long time. As for the boy, I wish I could help you out there. I surely don't wish any ill will toward him."

Even though she was stunned at the venom in Adam Nagy's voice regarding his recently deceased brother, and not wanting to give any opinion on that relationship, just for clarification, Atkinson asked, "So you've never seen your brother's boy, and you know nothing about him or his current whereabouts. Is that correct?"

Instead of looking at the detectives, Adam Nagy stared straight ahead at the chapel's small altar. "That's correct. I've never seen the boy, and I know nothing about him—period." Then he looked back at the detectives. "Actually, when I learned of Sam and Alyssa's deaths, I just assumed the boy was safe somewhere. It never even crossed my mind that he would be missing. Sam and Alyssa had a boat load of friends. When the police told us about the fire and their deaths, I thought the boy was with one of them."

Naomi Nagy clasped her husband's hand and leaned

on his shoulder. Her eyes couldn't hold back the tears from streaming down her cheeks. Detective Atkinson decided to get Naomi's opinion about the boy. "Mrs. Nagy, do you have anything to add to your husband's statements? Was your relationship with your brother-in-law's family the same as your husband's?"

Naomi grabbed a tissue from the box on the small table beside her, dabbed at her eyes, and wiped away the tears on her cheeks. She turned toward the detective. "I-I liked Alyssa—at first. Actually, I introduced her to Sam. We were in the same sorority at Youngstown State. Sam was still attending Moritz College and was home for Christmas break. Adam and I invited the two of them over for dinner, and they hit it off immediately. They got married not long after Sam passed the bar." She paused. "So, yes, Alyssa and I were friends. But once Sam and Carl Padgett's firm started dealing with more criminal elements than innocent clients and defendants, and Alyssa started working for the law firm, my friendship with Alyssa began to wane. I too spoke to her the last time at Mama Nagy's funeral, but it was very brief and distant. It was like we were mere strangers and had never been good friends at all."

Atkinson asked, "Did you talk about her son in that conversation?"

Naomi briefly hesitated. "Yes. Yes, we did. She told me he was a colicky baby, and she was not getting much rest. She invited me to visit her to see the baby."

"Did you take her up on her offer?"

"Of course not. After the big blow-up between Adam and Sam, I thought it best to end our friendship permanently."

Atkinson wanted to know a little more. "How did

you feel about that?"

"Well, I admit I was a little sad. We had been such good friends for a few years. But I had to think of my family first." She glanced over at her husband. "My husband and our girls."

Again, just to verify, Atkinson asked, "So at this time, you know nothing about the child or where he might be?"

"No, detective, I don't. That was the last time I spoke to Alyssa. Like my husband, I just assumed their boy was safe with a neighbor or someone in Alyssa's family."

Then both detectives turned to face the three people sitting on the other side of the chapel aisle. Hamilton asked, "Mrs. Karis, can you tell us about your relationship with your daughter?"

Patricia Karis, the older woman facing him, straightened her body against the back of the cushioned chair. "You might say I've had the same non-relationship with my daughter as Adam Nagy had with his brother. My daughter, Alyssa, has been estranged from me since shortly after she married Sam." She looked down at her folded hands resting atop her tailored black slacks. "However, the relationship that I *didn't have* with my daughter was totally her doing, not mine."

"What do you mean, Mrs. Karis?"

She brought her folded hands up to her mouth. After a few seconds she took a deep breath and replaced them on her lap. "The only way I can describe it is that Alyssa became a different person once she married Sam Nagy. It was as if I didn't even know my own daughter any longer."

"Can you be more specific, ma'am?" asked

Atkinson.

After a few additional seconds, Mrs. Karis responded, "Yes, I can." More hesitation and another deep sigh. "I'm going to preface this by saying that my daughters lived a comfortable lifestyle. I don't think they ever wanted for anything material. Douglas Karis, my late husband, was a very wealthy man. He was a brilliant businessman and invested his money wisely. And he took good care of his family as well. So when he died suddenly at the age of fifty-two of a massive heart attack, my girls and I were unprepared for his passing. I was forced to be thrown into the business world when all I ever knew was how to plan an event or coordinate our household staff. For a while, taking care of all our family's business affairs took every second of my waking hours. Otherwise, all that hard earned wealth my husband had attained would've been thrown away, and we would've ended up penniless. I know that is no excuse, but the way Alyssa turned out may have had a lot to do with those circumstances. I had to completely change my lifestyle and take over all of Doug's business dealings and duties, his investments, and the people who worked for him. I no longer had time to be the mother I was before his death. By then Alyssa was in her teens. She became wild and unruly, never listening to my disciplinary rules or tactics. And, like I said, I didn't have the time or energy to enforce them like I should have."

She paused and looked over toward her daughter, Madelyn, who gently touched her mother's arm. "Thank goodness, Maddie was older, more mature, and a different type of personality. She tried to help with Alyssa, but Alyssa was a very stubborn, willful young lady. She knew all the answers, and none of them led her in the right direction. In the middle of all this turmoil, she met Sam Nagy. At first, I thought he might be able to harness her wildness and help her to see the evils of her ways." Again, she hesitated, shaking her head. "But I was wrong."

Patricia Karis looked straight ahead at the chapel and breathed several deep breaths. The detectives waited. Finally, she looked back at them. "The big blowout came after she and Sam came back from their Paris honeymoon. I was at our office downtown in the middle of a critical conference with my accountant and the VP of our investment firm. We were discussing a very vital issue when suddenly, without warning, Alyssa burst into the conference room, thrashing her arms and scattering all the papers in all directions."

"Did you ask her what was wrong?" Hamilton asked.

"She was upset about the fact that she couldn't access her trust fund. She assumed it would be available when she was twenty-one. However, her father had had the presence of mind to make it unavailable to her until she was twenty-eight years old. She actually thought I had the capability to release the trust fund to her, but that wasn't the case at all. Doug had set no exceptions to the age condition. My hands were tied. Although, looking back, if I had that power, I don't know if I would've released the money to her anyhow."

Mrs. Karis paused again, shaking her head. "But that's a moot point now, isn't it? She did get her money when she turned twenty-eight, but just as she had told me that day, she never spoke to me again. She completely cut me out of her life, and I'm sorry to say, out of my grandson's life also."

Madelyn clasped her mother's hand and leaned her head on her shoulder.

Detective Hamilton asked Mrs. Karis, "Then you did know about the child?"

"Oh, yes. I knew about him, but I wasn't allowed to see him. I would call their home or their office, but I was never permitted to talk to Alyssa. I left message after message, begging her to let me see the boy, but I never got any response. Eventually, she blocked my number."

"So you never even saw the boy?" asked Hamilton.

Mrs. Karis sadly shook her head. "No, I never saw him. I sent him birthday presents, Christmas presents, but I have no idea what became of them, whether she let him have them or not. Whether she told him they were from me. Whether she even told him he had a grandmother, I don't know."

Detective Hamilton frowned. Then he addressed Madelyn Winthrop. "What about you, Mrs. Winthrop? What was your relationship with your sister and her family?"

Madelyn dropped her mother's hand and clasped her own together. "Ours was also a strained relationship. Alyssa did tell me when she was pregnant with the baby, and I received a birth announcement. And once when he was about six months old, we had lunch together, and she brought the baby. I tried to get her to let my mother see him, but she was totally unreasonable about it. As kids, I knew Alyssa was stubborn and vindictive, but I thought she'd grow out of it. Instead, as she got older, she became worse. For a while we would talk to one another on the phone, but eventually, she stopped calling me and also stopped taking my calls." She shook her head and became quiet. Then she added, "I really don't know why.

We never had an argument or anything like that. She just stopped all communication with me. So I gave up trying."

The room was silent for a few seconds. Then Detective Atkinson stepped back so she faced all the relatives in the room. "Do any of you happen to have a picture of the boy?"

Everyone stared at her with vacant eyes, having no answer to her question. Then Madelyn Winthrop reached for her purse on the floor. "Wait a minute! I think I do have a picture of him. It isn't recent, but it may help you." She opened her purse and spent a minute looking for it, unzipping and zipping compartments, opening up small packets within the purse. Finally, she removed a snapshot from a small leather pouch. "Here it is!"

"Let me see it." Immediately, Patricia Karis grabbed it from her daughter. As she held it in her hands, tears emerged from the corners of her eyes. She stared at the photo for several seconds before passing it on to Detective Atkinson. With her voice shaking, she turned to Madelyn. "I-I never saw that picture before."

Madelyn also was crying. "I didn't want to show it to you, Mom. I knew it would upset you too much."

"I know, dear. I know. I understand." Both women removed tissues from their pockets and wiped their eyes.

Detective Atkinson looked at the picture of the boy. In the photo, he appeared to be about two years old with round, chubby cheeks and blond, curly hair. His engaging smile made his large, clear blue eyes sparkle. She handed it to Hamilton. He too viewed it for several seconds, then asked, "Does anyone know how old this boy is today? In this picture he looks about two or three."

Patricia Karis looked up, still patting her eyes. "He's

five years old. His birthday was the eighth of July."

Hamilton then mentioned, "So this picture is a few years old."

Madelyn Winthrop agreed, "Yes. That was the last picture Alyssa sent me."

He glanced at the picture one last time. Before placing it in his shirt pocket, he asked, "Do you mind if I keep this for a while? I'll return it to you as soon as possible."

Madelyn replied, "Sure, detective. I'd just like it back eventually. You understand."

Then Hamilton addressed Madelyn's husband. "Mr. Winthrop, do you have anything to add to anything that has already been said?"

Corey Winthrop looked up from consoling his wife. "No, I don't. I never had many dealings with Sam. We didn't run in the same circles. I'm a building contractor, a successful one, but not in the same financial league as Sam and Alyssa. A few years ago, Maddie would mention her sister now and then, but lately she hasn't talked about her at all. That family just hasn't been part of our lives, actually ever."

After Atkinson and Hamilton exhausted their questioning, they both took out their business cards and distributed them to each of the family members in the chapel. Atkinson said, "Please, if you think of anything that might help us find the child, get in touch with us immediately. We fear for this child's safety. Currently, we have a whole crew combing the neighborhood around the house, hoping we'll get some information about his whereabouts. He could be in grave danger. We don't know if he was hurt in the fire, if he was kidnapped by the assailants, or what happened to him. So if you hear anything or think of anything else, no matter how important you think it may or may not be, please contact either Detective Hamilton or me."

Pat Karis stood and faced the detectives. "I'm so sorry we couldn't be of more help. Since we were not part of Sam and Alyssa's lives, we all assumed the boy was safe somewhere. We now know that was a stupid assumption. We'll do anything you want us to do to help find my grandson."

\*\*\*\*

After the detectives left the chapel, Pat Karis rose to her feet. "Maddie, let's go."

Madelyn also stood. "Where are we going, Mom?"

"We're going to help find Sammy."

"But, Mom, it's in the middle of the night. How can we do anything?"

Pat looked at her watch. "No, it's morning. And I don't care what time it is. All of us," She moved her arm around the room, taking in everyone. "It's time we got off our asses and did something to find my grandson."

Chapter Eight

*Saturday morning, about 4:00 a.m., after the fire*
Detectives Atkinson and Hamilton left the hospital chapel, both confused and surprised at the testimonies of the family members of Samuel and Alyssa Nagy. How could they have no knowledge concerning a five-year-old child, their own grandson and nephew? Will Hamilton had three grandchildren of his own. They might not be five years old; in fact, they were in their teens, one even in his twenties. But they had always been a part of his life despite the disagreements he often had with his son-in-law. Nothing would keep him from those kids. So it was not only very strange but also difficult for him to understand how this little Nagy boy's family could not know *anything* about him.

Stacey Atkinson had two beautiful nieces, children of her older brother. They were a huge part of her life also. Once a month she had the girls overnight with a sleepover. They would do fun things during the day, like seeing a movie, going shopping, buying pizza and streaming something on TV, or going to local music venues. She enjoyed every minute spent with them. So how could this little boy's family not know a thing about him? What a shame for the boy and his extended family.

Detective Atkinson started the car's engine and looked toward Hamilton. "So what's next, boss?"

Hamilton looked at his watch. "What say we have

some breakfast?" He hesitated. "Then I think it's time to talk to this Nagy guy's partner."

Atkinson looked at the clock on the dashboard. "It's Saturday morning. Guess we'll have to go to his home, not his office. Maybe wake him up."

Scrunching his forehead, Hamilton glanced over at her. "You got a problem with waking the guy up on the weekend?"

She put the vehicle into gear and gave it some gas. "Not at all." As she pulled out of the parking lot, she asked, "How about that fast food place up the street?"

"Sounds good to me. Probably not much open around here this time of day."

They had a quick breakfast sandwich and coffee at the restaurant. While eating, Atkinson looked up the home address of Carl Padgett, Sam Nagy's partner. "He and his family live in Canfield."

"It figures. That law firm is very successful."

"Oh? You know something about it?"

"Yeah, I've had to talk to Padgett a few times. Some of that firm's clients are not such upstanding citizens. I've even had to testify in court a couple of times against an offender he represented."

"How about Sam Nagy? Did you ever have any dealings with him?"

"No... I saw him around the courthouse a couple of times but never spoke to him or knew any of the parasites who contributed to his coffer."

It was almost five in the morning when they pulled into the Padgett's driveway. They walked up to the front door, and Hamilton pressed the doorbell. They could hear it echo inside the home. No one came to answer the door, so he pressed the buzzer again, hearing it echo a second time. He waited another minute before pressing it a third time. Finally, the detectives heard someone on the other side of the door unlocking a bolt.

When the door opened a few inches, a woman with messy, honey blond hair and hazel eyes still half asleep gawked at them. In a groggy voice, she muttered, "Uh, may I help you?"

Both detectives pulled out their badges and introduced themselves. Hamilton spoke first. "Mrs. Padgett?"

The woman's eyes opened wider; the detectives noticed she stood up straighter. "Yes, I'm Leanne Padgett. What is this about?"

"We need to speak with your husband," Hamilton said. "May we come in?"

"What is this in regard to, detective?"

"Please, ma'am, can you just get your husband? It's very important."

Hesitating, she slowly opened the door wide enough so the detectives could enter the house. She wore a fleecy, powder blue robe wrapped around her slim body and delicate, matching blue slippers on her feet. "Come this way."

They entered a huge hallway with gleaming marble floors and a spiral staircase in front of them. Mrs. Padgett led them to a room off to the left. "Please have a seat while I wake my husband."

Instead of sitting, the detectives walked over to the white brick fireplace against the far wall. Atkinson whispered to Hamilton, "Guess we woke her up. Guess they don't know about the fire yet."

"Yeah, gonna be a bit of a shock to them."

Five minutes later, Carl Padgett walked into the

room wearing a burgundy velour robe. His feet were encased in tan leather slippers. Striped pajama bottoms covered his long legs below the robe. A rather imposing tall man, he seemed to command authority. He completed tying his robe then raked his hand through his disheveled hair.

"Detectives? Please have a seat. What can I do for you?" He eyed them suspiciously as he sat down on a gray, high-back recliner on the opposite side from them.

Hamilton and Atkinson ignored his offer to sit. Hamilton began to explain their reason for awakening this man so early on a Saturday morning. "Mr. Padgett, we're here to talk to you about your partner Samuel Nagy."

Padgett looked confused. "What about Sam? I don't understand."

Hamilton continued, "I regret to inform you that last night, there was a fire that destroyed the Nagy home, and—"

"Oh, my God!" interrupted Padgett. "Are they all right?"

"No, sir, Mr. and Mrs. Nagy perished in the fire."

From the living room entranceway, Leanne Padgett let out a deep scream, "Oh, my God!"

Carl Padgett's body stiffened; his face transformed into a horrified mask. "What! No! That can't be!"

"I'm sorry to say, but I'm afraid it's true," Hamilton added. Then he gave Padgett a few seconds to take in the news. Padgett bent his body, placed his elbows on his knees and his head in his hands. The detectives could hear him breathing heavily.

Hamilton gave the man a few more seconds to absorb what he had just heard. However, they were not only there to tell Padgett about the fire, but their primary concern at that specific time was to find out about the Nagy's son. "Sir, I'm so sorry for your loss, but there is something important we need to ask you immediately."

Padgett took his hands away from his head and looked up at Hamilton. His face was moist and pale. "What is it, detective?"

"Well, sir, we understand that the Nagys had a five-year-old son, but the boy apparently was not found in the house. No one seems to know where he is. I was wondering if you could give us any information regarding where we might find him."

From the look on Padgett's face, the detectives could tell that he was shocked and bewildered. "Sammy wasn't in the house? Sammy isn't dead?"

Hamilton continued, "Only Sam and Alyssa Nagy were found in the house. The boy wasn't there, and we have no idea on his whereabouts. We have checked neighbors, friends, and families. No one seems to know anything about him. We were hoping that you could shed some light on where he might be."

Padgett slowly shook his head. "I-I know nothing about where he would be." He lifted his head slightly and put his right hand on his mouth. Removing his hand, he asked, "You said you checked with the families? I know both Alyssa and Sam were estranged from them. B-b-but I have no idea where the kid could be." He shook his head again. "I'm sorry, detectives."

Atkinson and Hamilton glanced at each other. They both took out their cards and handed them to Padgett. Atkinson explained, "Sir, you probably will be contacted later for more questioning regarding the Nagys, but our concern right now is the boy. Here are our cards in case you think of anything else."

Padgett stood up, took the cards, and then asked, "Why might I be contacted again?"

Atkinson responded, "The fire was of a suspicious nature; both the fire department as well as the police are looking into the situation."

Padgett was confused. "Suspicious nature?"

"Yes, sir."

"Do you mean it was intentionally set?"

Atkinson looked at Hamilton, who nodded his approval. She said, "Yes. Both Alyssa and Samuel Nagy were shot to death before their home was set on fire."

## Chapter Nine

*Monday, 5:50 p.m., twelve days before the fire*

When Attorney Carl Padgett finished with his court case appearance and tapped on his partner Sam Nagy's partially opened office door, Sam was working on a new larceny case he had procured that morning. The accused was as guilty as hell, but he had money enough to hire the firm. That was all that counted. Carl pushed the door open and walked over to one of the chairs in front of Sam's desk. He sat on the chair and breathed a heavy sigh. "Whew! That was some trial today. You'd never believe that freakin' Judge Morrison. That man should've retired years ago. He's a senile, cantankerous, old fart and a discredit to his profession."

Sam looked up from his papers and pushed back his chair so he could address Carl. "Yeah, I had him on a case last week. What a twit! So how did your case go today? Did you win?"

Carl's mouth morphed into a large grin as he nodded his head. "You bet we did. Luckily, we had the evidence against the state's claim. So we came out looking like roses."

"Great," added Sam. "Another big bank deposit. Congrats."

"Yeah, not too shabby." Then Carl's face took on a more serious demeanor, and the smile disappeared. "Say, I got your phone message after court. What's going on?

You sounded concerned."

Sam leaned forward, pushed the files on which he was working off to the side, and propped his elbows on the desk while clasping his hands together. "We might have a problem."

Carl's voice took on a cautionary tone. "What kind of a problem are we talking about here, Sam?"

"Well, at this point, I'm not exactly sure."

Carl tilted his head and gazed at him questionably, waiting for an explanation.

Sam cleared his throat. "Ryan tells me he's being followed."

"What're you talking about? That's absurd."

"I wish it were. But according to Ryan, a black SUV has been tailing him for the last couple of days."

"Did he take down the plate number or see who was in the vehicle?"

"Apparently not. The SUV always keeps a safe distance behind him, and the windows are tinted."

Carl shook his head. "Who the hell could be following him and more importantly, why?"

Sam's voice became very guarded. "I figure it's either government or one of Rocco Banetti's men."

"I'm confused. Why would you think it would be either one of these?"

"As far as the government goes, I'm not sure. Maybe they somehow found out something about one of Banetti's questionable syndicates or offshore bank accounts and are going to look into it. Maybe they think they can get some information from Ryan." He paused. "I don't know."

After settling back in his chair, Carl responded, "Yeah, I suppose that's a possibility." He too paused for a couple of seconds. "Maybe we should talk to Rocco about this. Perhaps he knows something we don't know. He could be keeping something from us."

Sam leaned toward Carl. "Before we do that, there's something else you should know."

Carl's cautionary expression changed to one of suspicion. "What is it?"

Sam had no choice. He knew he had to tell Carl that Ryan had revealed information on Banetti to his fiancée. Carl's hot-headed nature gave Sam concern as to how he would handle the situation. For the sake of the firm, it had to be done.

"It appears that Ryan has mentioned to Melanie that he is working on a client that isn't exactly up and up."

Carl jumped out of his seat and pounded his fist on Sam's desk, causing papers to flutter and pen and pencils to bounce and roll. "What the hell! What is wrong with that damn kid?" He began to pace back and forth in Sam's office. "He knows better than that."

"Carl, I don't think we ever specifically said he shouldn't mention anything about Banetti or his affairs to Melanie. Hell, she wasn't his fiancée when he joined the firm. So we probably didn't think to specifically talk to him about it when he got engaged."

Carl continued to pace. "The kid should've known better. That's all I'm saying. He's smarter than that. We shouldn't have had to even mention to him to keep his mouth shut when he got engaged. It's a given."

Sam countered, "Think of it, though. This is the woman he plans to marry. He probably thought they shouldn't have any secrets from one another. Don't you remember when you were madly in love?"

With a snort, Carl gave him a sideways look. "That

was way too long ago for me to dredge up in my memory."

"Just the same, maybe we should give him the benefit of the doubt. He didn't give her Banetti's name, just an insinuation."

Carl took his seat again. "But we told him specifically to speak to *no one* about *anything* he worked on, didn't we?"

Sam admitted, "Yes, we did. I won't deny that."

Carl raised his right hand, shaking it back and forth. "You think I tell Leanne everything that goes on around here?" He chuckled sarcastically. "No way! If she knew some of the things about this business, she'd divorce me before I had a chance to take my next breath." He paused. "You too, right?"

Pursing his lips, Sam nodded. "You're definitely right about that. Even though Alyssa's up to date about the partnership, she knows nothing about some of our clandestine activities. That's for sure."

Despite the seriousness of the situation, both men smiled, thinking about some of their extra-curricular, secret affairs and deeds.

But their smiles faded quickly, and Sam added, "Well, I reamed Ryan out and told him not to say anything else to Melanie about work or anything work related. And I told him to keep trying to get the plate number of that SUV. Do you think we should do something else at this time?"

Carl sat back in the chair and tapped his closed lips with his forefinger. "Let's sit on this for a day or so. We have a meeting with Banetti next week. We'll see if he says anything either in a threatening way, or maybe asks a question about Ryan. Maybe then we'll have a clue how to handle this."

Carl got out of his chair, and Sam stood up. Carl asked, "You still up for golf at the country club in the morning? Weather is supposed to be accommodating."

"Hell, yeah. I'm looking forward to beating your ass again."

Carl walked out the door, pausing and turning toward Sam. "We'll see about that, pal."

**Chapter** Ten

*Saturday, 5:15 a.m., after the fire.*

In the quiet of the dark library, Thin Lizzy suddenly awakened from a deep sleep. Briefly, she forgot about the small boy still asleep beside her. As her eyes shot over to his tranquil form, it all came back to her. Oh, yes, she had a problem, a big problem. Glancing up at the windows on the other side of the building, the gloomy sky pressed against the pane. She quietly rose and walked around the bookshelves filled with the huge volumes until she came to the librarian's desk nearby. A small, illuminated, digital clock rested on its corner, displaying five-fifteen. She would soon need to flee from the library to avoid any employees coming into work that morning. Normally, this was not a problem. She would simply grab all her stuff and hustle out of the building, finding a new place to temporarily stow all her gear and wander around town for the rest of the day.

But she wasn't alone now. There was the kid. What could she do with him? She knew nothing about him. It had been difficult for him to even give her his name. Why was he still in those pajamas? Why no shoes or slippers? And why did he look so nasty and dirty? She had to get some answers before making any kind of decisions about what to do with him. The best solution was to make sure he got back home. But where was his home, and why did he leave it in the first place? No little kid his age should be wandering around the city in the dead of night. Something was terribly wrong with this situation.

She went back to the corner where the boy lay, still sound asleep. She knelt on her knees on the thin carpet and lightly nudged his shoulder. "Hey, boy. Hey, Sammy. Ya gotta wake up. I have ta talk ta you, and we gotta get outta here."

He stirred slightly, and his eyes fluttered but remained closed.

She gently shook him again. "Come on, kid. You gotta wake up. You gotta talk ta me."

Finally, he flickered his eyes until they opened a crack. When he saw Thin Lizzy staring at him, he jerked upright, eyes bulging, and scooted away from her, gluing himself to the wall, terror on his face.

Thin Lizzy was startled by his abrupt actions. She raised her hands. "It's okay! It's okay. You remember me, don't cha? I'm Thin Lizzy. Remember?"

Confused, Sammy gawked at his surroundings, turning his head from side to side. For a few seconds, he was fortunately unaware of his current predicament and what had happened to him the previous night. But it came back to him in full force, striking him like a sledgehammer. Yes, he was in the big library with this peculiar lady. Yes, he had walked a hundred miles to escape whatever had happened at his home, which he wasn't quite sure. He was sure of the fire. But his mommy and daddy? This was worse than any bad dream he'd ever had. He began to whimper.

Thin Lizzy was bewildered. How could she calm this little guy down enough to make sense of his predicament? They had to get out of the library—and soon. Still on her knees she rested back on her calves and tried to calm him. "It's okay. It's okay. Yer safe now, kid, uh, Sammy. Whatever happened to ya, yer safe now. I'm not gonna let anybody hurt cha."

She wasn't so sure if this were actually possible, but she needed answers, and they needed to vacate the library very soon. Hesitantly, she reached over and touched his leg. "I'm not gonna hurt cha. Remember? I saved ya from gettin' run over by dat car. Remember?"

He finally began to relax just a little. His eyes shrunk back to normal, and he turned a little more toward her. He simply said, "Oh, I forgot."

She felt so sorry for the kid, even though she was unaware of the circumstances that had suddenly transported him into her world, one with no place for any child, let alone one as young as he was. But she had to make the best of it and figure out what they should do next. "I didn't mean ta scare ya, kid, but I wanna aks you some questions so's I know what ta do which you. Okay?"

He calmed down a little more and nodded his head. "Okay."

Where should she start? "Uh, first, where do ya live?"

"I-I live at 2255 Fifth Avenue, but—" He suddenly stopped talking, stared at the dark carpet, and began to sob again. "B-but my house burned all down. I don't know what happened to my mommy and daddy." He hesitated. Then, "And those men had guns, and I heard loud bangs. Like on TV. And Mommy didn't come and get me from my hiding place like she said she would."

Thin Lizzy's eyes and mouth opened wide. She couldn't believe what the boy was telling her. A fire!

Men with guns! "Ya mean yer house was on fire?"

Still with his head down, he nodded.

She brought her legs out from under her and stared at the boy, the condition of his pajamas, his face, and his injured feet. "Ya mean you were in yer house when it was on fire?"

He again nodded his head without looking up.

She rustled her butt over the floor to sit next to him. "That's why yer so dirty, huh?" He had mentioned men and gunshots. What could this mean? "Did ya see da men with da guns?"

He nodded his head again.

"Did dey see you?"

Again, the head nod.

Painfully, not wanting to know the answer, she asked, "Who did dey shoot?"

He lifted his head. "I don't know. I was in my hiding place when I heard the bangs."

"Yer hidin' place? Where were ya hidin'?"

"In the bathroom upstairs way back in the closet."

Sometimes since the incident that devastated her life so many years ago, Thin Lizzy often had a hard time understanding things. Sometimes she became confused. But it was perfectly clear to her from what the boy told her that something horrible had happened to him, making his situation very serious and tense and causing him to run away from his burning home.

She bent over, put her hand on his knee, and gently lifted his face with her other hand. "Do ya think you can start at da beginnin' and tell me everything dat happened?"

He looked at her with hopelessly sad eyes. "Okay."

She waited.

He coughed slightly and began, "Uh, Mommy, Daddy, and me, we were playing my new card game in the living room, and we heard this big loud boom. And two big men came into the living room. They pointed guns at us. Then Mommy shoved me and told me to run and hide. So I did. I ran up the stairs and hid in the bathroom closet, and I crawled under a big blanket. Then I heard this noise. Bang! Bang! That's when I was really scared, but I stayed in my hiding place 'cause Mommy said she'd come and get me. Then I heard somebody walking up the stairs. I thought it was Mommy, but it wasn't. They turned on the light, and this big shadow came over to the closet. Then I stayed as still as I could, and I didn't even breathe. But the shadow opened the door and grabbed the blanket. I thought for sure he was gonna kill me, but then somebody yelled something, and the shadow left."

He stopped narrating and took a deep breath.

Thin Lizzy compassionately looked at him. "Do ya think you can tell me what happened next?"

Another big sigh, and he took a couple more deep breaths. "Mommy told me she'd come and get me, but I was having a hard time breathing in that closet, so I got out. But the bathroom was really smoky, and I still couldn't breathe very good. I didn't know what to do, so I went downstairs to look for Mommy. But when I got in the kitchen, Mommy wasn't there, and a big fire was in the dining room, so I wanted to go outside. Then I went to the back door, but I burned my hand really bad on the handle, but I opened it anyway." He stopped talking and looked at his injured hand.

When he turned his hand upright, for the first time, Thin Lizzy saw the angry, red skin on his palm. She gently grasped it. "Oh, my Gawd! You poor li'l boy!" She swiftly crawled over to the trash bag with her stuff in it and began routing through it. "I have ta wrap yer hand so's you don't get no more dirt in it."

She pulled out what appeared to be a ragged, dingy pillowcase. Then she got on her feet and walked away from Sammy. "I'm gonna get some scissors over dere."

In the darkness of the library, it was difficult for Sammy to see where Thin Lizzy had gone. Soon she returned, holding a pair of scissors. She picked up the tattered pillowcase and cut it into strips. Then she knelt down near Sammy and gently took his injured hand. She looked into his eyes, "Is it okay if I wrap dese around yer hand? It'll make it feel better."

Sammy nodded his head.

Thin Lizzy carefully wrapped the rags around the little hand to protect it from further damage. She had a feeling of Deja vu as she completed the task. Had she done something like this before to her child?

"There! Does dat feel a li'l bit better now?"

Sammy nodded his head again.

"Okay, can ya maybe tell me what happened after ya hurt yer hand?"

Again, he nodded his head before continuing, "Then I got outside and I could breathe better. Then I heard sirens, and they were really, really loud. I was so scared. I didn't know what to do, so I just started walking and walking and walking. Then I saw Wick Park and I sat on a bench for a while 'cause I was so tired, and I fell asleep. But this scary man woke me up. He didn't hurt me, but he was really scary. When he went away, I fell back to sleep, but then I heard more noise, and some big boys were sitting on a table talking real loud. I got scared of them too, so I got out of the park and walked until I couldn't walk no more." He looked at her and sadly frowned. "That's when you found me."

All Thin Lizzy could think about was what this poor little kid had gone through the night before. No wonder he was a mess. The kid probably walked a couple of miles. And with no shoes and a burned hand. She felt such compassion for him.

But she couldn't spend any more time thinking about what had happened to him. Her thoughts focused on what to do with him now. She was in a huge predicament. She knew they had to get out of the library, but where could they go? She couldn't parade around town with him. And then there was all her stuff. She had to find a new place to put it. It couldn't stay in the library. That lady in the blue clothes would probably throw it away, thinking it was garbage. But she couldn't put it back under that abandoned car either. She was sure they would be towing that car away very soon. And the boy's feet? He can't walk very much with no shoes. What was she going to do?

Several minutes had passed since she had looked at that clock on the desk. It was probably after five-thirty. That meant she had to be out of the library in about an hour or so. She had to make a decision now.

First things first. The kid was now awake enough to move on. "Okay, uh, Sammy. Here's what we're gonna do for now." She began rummaging through her bag of stuff again. "Now, I gotta protect yer feet a li'l bit like I did yer hand, but we gotta get outta here real quick too." She grabbed a tattered sleeveless shirt from the bag. With her teeth, she enlarged a small hole in the cloth and began ripping it into pieces.

Then she touched his leg. "I'm gonna wrap dese around yer feet." She took a few minutes to cover his tiny feet with the rags as best she could. Then she took the remaining strips from the pillowcase and bound them around the shirt rags to hold them in place. Next, she routed in the food bag for some Styrofoam or cardboard that wasn't too messy from the food inside it in order to create some make-shift shoes for the boy. She found a Styrofoam container with two bread rolls in it. She turned to the boy. "You wait right here. I need ta find a pen." She got up and walked toward the desk on the other side of the room.

Sammy wasn't sure what the woman was doing. Why did she need a pen? Was she going to write something somewhere? But not knowing what else to do, he remained on the floor, waiting for her return. Besides, she was really trying to help him, wasn't she? He had no one else. He had to trust her.

When Thin Lizzy reached the desk, having retrieved the scissors previously, she knew the drawers were unlocked. She found a ream of paper in a side drawer and removed a couple of sheets from it. From the pen holder atop the desk, she took a ballpoint pen. Taking the pen and paper back to the corner where the boy was waiting, she first wrapped the two bread rolls in the paper to keep them from getting hard and replaced them in her food bag. Then she cut the lid off the Styrofoam container. Holding it up to Sammy's foot, she said, "I'm gonna measure yer foot, so keep it straight."

Using the pen, she traced around his foot as best she could. She did the same with the bottom part of the Styrofoam on the other foot. When she had both feet traced, she carefully cut out the drawings. She held them up to show Sammy. "There! These should help."

She laid the cut footprints aside and looked back in her bag of stuff. She pulled out a pair of mismatched, heavy thermo-type men's socks. At the inside bottom of each sock, she placed one of the cut-outs of Sammy's feet.

"Here, put dese on yer feet. Dey'll help protect dem until we can find somethin' better for you." Thin Lizzy had been saving those socks for the colder weather, but the boy needed them now.

He took the heavy socks and pulled them onto his feet making sure the cut-outs were flat on the bottom of the strips of rags that Thin Lizzy had previously put on his feet. The socks actually came up past his knees. Sammy tucked his pajama bottoms into the stockings to help hold them on his legs.

The two of them stood up. "How do dose feel on yer feet?"

Sammy took a few steps to try out Thin Lizzy's shoe project. "Uh, I guess, okay. My feet still hurt, but not as much."

Thin Lizzy reached over and picked up her rock. "Well, maybe we can find somethin' else later on." She handed the rock to Sammy. "Here, you hold dis. I'll carry my stuff and our food."

Sammy took the rock, but he was so confused. He didn't know where she was taking him, what she planned to do with him, and just what was happening to him. The one thing he did know was that he had to pee. Should he tell the lady? As he started to follow her, he blurted, "Uh, Lizzy Lady, I have to pee, okay?"

Thin Lizzy hadn't even thought about this possibility. Of course, the kid would have to pee. She stopped and turned around to face him. "Okay. We'll stop at da bathroom on our way out. Can ya hold it until we get downstairs?"

Sammy nodded his head.

They walked over to the desk to replace the pen and scissors, and then Thin Lizzy led them down the wide staircase to the main level. Both Sammy's feet and right hand felt a little better.

Thin Lizzy showed Sammy the location of the bathroom where she had hidden the night before. "Here, you go in dere. I have ta put dis flashlight back. If ya get done before me, you wait right outside da door. Okay?"

Sammy nodded his head again as he struggled to open the heavy bathroom door. Thin Lizzy left to replace the flashlight.

The bathroom was dark. Sammy felt against the wall for the light switch. He found it but was barely tall enough to click it on. He stood on his tiptoes and finally was able to press the switch upward. The light was blinding. He had to remain still until he could focus enough to see. Then he placed the stone next to one of the sinks and went into the first stall to relieve himself. He felt much better afterwards. Coming out of the stall, he went to a sink to wash his hand, being careful not to get the rags on his right hand too wet.

As the water streamed out of the faucet, he stared at it, transfixed. He was really in a predicament. His mind was simply too immature to handle what he was facing. He wasn't equipped to even come to terms with what had happened to him since the night before. He too was just as confused as Thin Lizzy. But what choice did he have? His daddy always told him if he was in trouble and needed help and Mommy and Daddy weren't around, he should find a policeman or a teacher and ask them for help. But where could he find a teacher or a policeman? Aside from those scary people in the park, Thin Lizzy was the only other person he had seen since he escaped the fire. In his young mind, he realized he had to trust whatever she had in store for him. He was just a kid, He didn't know how to take care of himself. There was no one else.

Suddenly, the bathroom door opened. "Are you okay, Sammy?" It was Thin Lizzy. "You weren't outside da bathroom. I got scared."

Sammy shook his head to get himself back to reality. He continued to wash his left hand as best he could. Grabbing a paper towel, he dried it while Thin Lizzy waited by the door.

"Okay, let's go now," she said as he threw away the damp towel.

Sammy picked up the stone he had placed on the floor next to the sink and followed Thin Lizzy out of the bathroom. She turned off the light and led them to the door she used to enter the library, pushing it open and holding it until he was outside. He stood waiting as she moved herself and her two big bags out the door and then closed it tightly. "Follow me," she said. They approached a couple of bushes on the side of the building. "You tuck dat rock underneath dat bush. We'll get it back tonight so's we can get back in da library."

He did as he was told. He had no other alternative. Then he followed the lady around the outside of the library as she slung her bags over her shoulder and walked over to the sidewalk. His feet hurt, but the added padding helped somewhat to protect them. The lady walked slowly, and he was able to keep up with her.

They walked along the street among many big buildings. He vaguely remembered seeing these when his mother had taken him to the library to get his books. But they looked so much bigger when he was walking next to them than when he was riding in his mother's car. He remembered asking his mother what all those buildings were. She had told him they were the local university. Then she had to explain to him what a "university" was.

After walking a couple of short blocks, Thin Lizzy and Sammy crossed the street and turned onto a pathway to the buildings of the "university." She led him over to a bench along the course and said as she strode toward it, "Let's sit here and eat some food. I'm hungry. Are you?"

Sammy hadn't thought if he was hungry or not. He supposed he was. He had been too confused and upset to think of food. But now that she mentioned it, he was a little hungry.

After they sat, Thin Lizzy put both her bags down beside her. She reached into her food bag and pulled out some chocolate cake. It was smashed and crumbled when she handed it to the boy. The white frosting was intermingled with the dark cake. It looked very messy. Sammy glanced up at Thin Lizzy, confused how he was supposed to grab this clumpy mass. She stared back at him. "Go 'head. Take it. It'll be good. Just taste it."

Hesitantly, Sammy took the glob with his left hand and began to eat it. As he ate, he needed to use his right hand to assist the left hand. Consequently, his bandages, his left hand, and his face became coated with clots of frosting and cake crumbs, but it was good. He hadn't been aware of how hungry he really was.

Thin Lizzy had pulled another squashed piece of cake out of her food bag and was also munching contentedly on it. "Mmm, good, huh?"

Sammy nodded his head as he delightfully chewed the messy clump and devoured every bit of it that wasn't sticking to his face. Then he licked clean the fingers on his left hand, but continued to hold his sticky, bandaged, right hand in the air.

After Thin Lizzy had finished her piece, she walked over to a grassy area behind the bench and bent down. Sammy watched her, wondering what she was doing. First, she rubbed the palm of her hands on the dewy grass to clean off the cake from her hands. Then she rubbed the grass again to moisten her hands, next rubbing her face to remove the sticky residue from it. After finishing her own cleanup, she rubbed the bottom of her shirt on another area of the grass to moisten it. She stood back up and walked over to Sammy. Taking the moist corner of her shirt, she proceeded to wipe the remains of the cake and frosting from Sammy's face. Then she stood back and looked at him. "Dere! Nice and clean now. Now, you go clean yer hands on da grass.'"

Wide eyed, Sammy had sat watching Thin Lizzy as she performed all these strange tasks. When she had wiped his face with her shirt, he sat perfectly still. He didn't know what to think. This was the strangest lady he'd ever met. But the longer he was with her, the more comfortable he became. And her strangeness helped him forget about the bad things that had happened to him the night before and what might happen next. At least, he wasn't alone anymore. He was beginning to trust this weird lady. Maybe she really would help him find some answers. He got off the bench, walked over to the grass, and also rubbed both his hands, including the strips of rags, on the moist, green surface.

When he returned to the bench and sat back down, Thin Lizzy again reached into her food bag. She pulled out a plastic bottle filled with about two-thirds of water. "Want a drink?"

He was thirsty after that cake. He grasped the bottle and took several gulps before handing it back to her. Then she too took a long drink before replacing it in her bag.

After satisfying their hunger and thirst, they sat quietly on the bench, each in their own unusual thoughts that less than twelve hours ago they had never imagined would have entered their minds. But here they were, a woman on the street without any kind of home or family whose mental capacity had been tragically compromised years ago and a small boy whose short life had experienced an event so tragic and so traumatic that he couldn't wrap his young brain around it. Both of them were struggling to figure out what to do next.

*Chapter* Eleven

*Friday, after 11 p.m., 8 days before the fire.*

Ryan Nesbitt had rented a room at the Delite Motel out on Market Street. It wasn't fancy, but it was clean. The last time Melanie came to his dingy apartment, she told him she would never meet him there again. "I'm afraid to even drive anywhere in this neighborhood, Ryan. I see gangs of sleazy characters on the street corners every time I come here. And I swear there are more stray dogs roaming the streets than they have at the dog pound. You've got to move somewhere else."

They had been discussing moving in together so they could spend more time with each other, but Melanie would never move into Ryan's miserable apartment even though it would be so much easier than meeting at the Delite Motel all the time.

Ryan agreed with Melanie. His apartment was in a neglected neighborhood on the south side, which was not the safest place to live. As for Melanie, she still lived in Canfield with her father and younger brother. She also wasn't sure how her father would accept her moving in with Ryan. Her dad, Salvatore Carlini, liked Ryan, figured he had a decent job with a promising career ahead of him, but he was an old-fashioned man who considered it a sin for unmarried couples to live together.

So Ryan and Melanie's moving in together was put on hold for a while. Just like their wedding date. That too was still up in the air. Ryan wasn't sure why. It seemed Melanie hedged the topic every time he brought it up. He was ready, and she said she was also, but she always had some excuse. Sometimes she couldn't make up her mind if she wanted a summer wedding or a winter wedding. What difference did it make? A wedding was a wedding. Then she was worried about who to ask to be her maid of honor. Ava would be upset if she asked Mia, but Mia would be livid if she chose Ava. Ryan told her to have both of them be maids of honor, but that was a no-no too. She told him nobody would do that. He finally stopped bringing up the subject of a wedding date. When she was ready, she'd have to tell him.

Thus, Ryan agreed with her that he should get another apartment, but he didn't see the point in moving out of his place and then moving again after their wedding. "I want to, babe, but it'd be such a hassle to move twice, once now and once when we get married."

Melanie agreed, "Yeah, that's true, but why don't you get a place for the two of us, and then I'll move in after we're married. I'll help you find it. We can go looking this weekend."

That had been their plan. When they went apartment shopping, they had found a few places they liked but had not made any final decision or any commitment yet on one of them. In the meantime, they spent their nights together at the Delite Motel. Besides being clean, it was close by, inexpensive, and definitely in a better part of town than the location of his apartment. The motel room had all they needed: a queen-size bed, a sanitized bathroom with a shower and fresh, white towels, even a small fridge where Ryan had placed their six pack of beer, and best of all, for Melanie's sake, safety and privacy.

They were cuddled, lying naked on the bed after a steamy two hours of sexual bliss. Melanie had her head resting on Ryan's chest. Ryan continued to gently kiss her dark, silky hair as it flowed over his arm. They had been silent for a while after their copious activity. Ryan was the first to break the silence. "You know I love you, babe, don't you?" He expected the same response from her.

But Melanie didn't answer immediately. Then she raised her head and her shoulders in order to look into his eyes. "Of course, I do, and I love you too, but..." She hesitated.

Ryan's forehead wrinkled as he stared at her. "But *what*?"

Melanie pulled away and sat next to him on the bed, wrapping the sheet around her breasts and under her arms. Ryan also raised himself to a sitting position, propping against the bed's headboard. He waited for her answer.

Not looking at him but staring straight ahead, Melanie finally acknowledged, "It's just that, well, you... you are just always so... so private and secretive about things."

Surprised, Ryan defended, "What are you talking about? I tell you everything. You even know all the stupid stuff I did as a kid. Remember? I told you how Jason and I ate those raw crickets in the tree house in his back yard. And what about when I told you the principal of Austintown Middle School caught us skinny-dipping at Lake Newport in Milk Creek Park?" He paused. "Need I go on?"

She acquiesced, "Well, yeah, that stuff you told me

about, but what about now? What about your family? What about your job? You don't tell me anything about your work. For all I know, maybe you're lying to me about working for those attorneys. Maybe you just pretend to go to work every day. One guy did that to me, you know. I met him at this party one night. He told me he was a financial advisor for some big firm in Cleveland. He was a sharp dresser and was the perfect gentleman, so I believed him. Turns out he lied to me. He didn't know anything about finance or how to handle money. Guess where he worked."

"Where?"

"In the service department at the car dealership. Can you believe that? He never smelled like oil or gas or anything, and his hands and fingernails were always clean and well-manicured, but wow, was I surprised."

"How did you find that out? Did he tell you?"

"Ha! Hell, no, he didn't tell me. My car was making this weird noise, so I took it into the dealership to have it looked at. Wouldn't you know, who would walk out of the garage in a greasy blue uniform but this dude? You can't believe how shocked I was. He saw me staring at him and tried to look the other way, but I knew it was him."

"So did you see him after that?"

"Are you kidding? Definitely not. I called him that night and told him I didn't appreciate being lied to like that. He could've told me he was an auto mechanic. I wouldn't have minded, but to lie about it? No way!"

Ryan wondered how much truth was in her story. She was too classy of a girl to date an auto mechanic. He was fairly sure of that. However, he had to defend himself in this discussion. "Well, I really am an attorney, and I work for a legitimate firm. You can stop by any time to see for yourself, Padgett & Nagy, LLP. That's the name of the business. He shook his head. "And you're wrong about me not telling you anything about my family. First of all, you met my mom, Maureen. You saw what she's like. She's so wrapped up with God and religion she barely knows I still exist. Besides, she lives near Cleveland. I don't see her much anymore. So there's nothing much to say about her. And my dad? Well, he's been out of the picture since I was a teenager. I don't know anything about him myself. As for my sister, Brittany and I were never close. She's ten years older than me and has lived in Oregon somewhere in some kind of commune or something. I haven't heard from her in years. So there again, there's not much to tell." He gave her a knowing look. "What about you? What about your family?"

Tearing up, she protested, "I told you my mom died when I was thirteen. You know my brother, right? You met him a couple of times. You saw what a jerk he can be. And my Dad? You met him too, didn't you?"

"Yeah, yeah. I did meet him, just that one time."

"Well, then, you know he's not well. He had that accident at work, and after my mom died, he gave up on both my brother and me. I practically had to raise Nicky myself."

Ryan didn't respond, so Melanie continued, "Look at what I tell you about all the other teachers at the school where I teach. You know as much of the gossip as I do—who's cheating on their husbands; who's pregnant and doesn't know who the father is, who's so old the kids are constantly pranking her without her even realizing it. And the kids in my classes? You know who's dating

106

who; who broke up with who and why; who's on drugs. You know everything I know. Don't you think you could share a little with me? After all, I'm your fiancée."

Ryan was conflicted. She was right. She had told him about her family and her work. All the good and the bad gossip. But he knew deep down he had to keep his work confidential. He tried to appease her and reminded, "Just the other day I told you about that client of mine, the one that was into a lot of illegal activities. Remember? You know I can't divulge anything more than that. It's against the confidentiality clause in my contract."

"Well, yeah, I know. But I'm your fiancée. I like to know what you do at work. Who am I going to tell? I'll keep anything you tell me private. You know that." She curled up against him, grabbed his face in her hands, and kissed him passionately.

He responded with his entire body as they slide down under the sheet and snuggled next to each other for another bout of erotic pleasure. "Oh, Mel, I love you so much!"

Afterwards, Ryan knew he had to talk to her, tell her more. He didn't know why she had such power over him. Maybe some other day. Not tonight. Maybe.

He cuddled against her sexy body, and they both fell asleep.

Chapter Twelve

*Saturday, about 6 a.m., after the fire*

After concluding their conversation with Carl Padgett, Atkinson and Hamilton drove back to police headquarters. They were surprised to find the chief still in his office, looking stressed. "Have you learned anything new, detectives?"

Hamilton answered, "Nobody seems to know a thing about the boy. We questioned both sets of relatives as well as Sam Nagy's partner, but we got nothing. And the officers canvasing the neighborhood have yet to come up with any leads."

"Actually, the families of the boy came in to talk to me," the chief added. "They're planning to distribute flyers and start a volunteer search in the area. Mrs. Karis, the boy's grandmother, is footing the bill, so the city won't have to pay for it. I've assigned Sergeant Mosley to help them, and I've also put out an Amber Alert for the boy. The family told me you have a picture of him. They can use it on their flyer."

"Yes, I do." Hamilton reached into his pocket and pulled out the picture that Madelyn Winthrop had given him. "It's a few years old."

The chief took it from Hamilton. "Hmm, cute little kid. Maybe we could get that sketch artist to do some age progression on it. It shouldn't be too hard for her. He's just a couple years older, right?"

Hamilton agreed, "Yeah, that's what I figured, too."

Atkinson said, "Here, chief, I'll take it and get it to the sketch artist to see what she can do with it. Then I'll make some copies."

After looking at the photo for several more seconds, he handed it over to the detective. She left his office to carry out her task.

While they waited for Atkinson's return, Hamilton queried, "So what's next, chief? We've talked to the families; we've talked to Sam Nagy's partner; and we've been told by the officers who canvased the neighborhood of the fire that no one has seen the boy or knows anything about his whereabouts."

The chief noted that Hamilton's eyes were drooping, and his clothes were rumpled. He actually looked like the chief himself felt after being up for so long. "I'm gonna go home for a quick nap. I suggest that you and Atkinson do the same. We'll give the family time to get those flyers distributed this morning and with the help of Mosley, coordinate the volunteer effort. I'd say be back here at noon, and we'll assess the situation then."

Taking a heavy breath as he stood, the detective agreed, "Sounds like a plan. See you back here at noon."

**Chapter** Thirteen

*Saturday, about 6 a.m., after the fire.*

Thin Lizzy and Sammy sat on the bench along the walkway of the university. Sammy glanced over at Thin Lizzy, who was staring straight ahead. He knew this lady didn't have to help him, but it seemed like she was willing. How much could she do? She lived in the library. Nobody lived in a library. And her clothes? She was dirtier than him. How come she looked that way and smelled that way? And that cake she had given him to eat? She just grabbed it out of that big trash bag, all smashed and squashed. Where did she get it? A restaurant wouldn't sell her pieces of cake that looked as messy as those pieces.

Oh, well, what else could he do but to stay with her and hope she could find his mother and father for him? And take him home. But deep, deep in his mind, he had a huge scary feeling about his home and his mommy and daddy.

As Thin Lizzy stared into space on that campus bench, her confused mind went in all directions. She knew she could barely care for herself. She couldn't be responsible for another person, especially a little kid. How could she feed him? How could she keep him safe? So much bad stuff happened on the streets. It was hard for her to avoid any of it even on her own. But she had to help this boy. She had to protect him. He had no one else. Only her. She had to find a way to do it.

Thin Lizzy literally shook herself out of her reverie and stood up quickly. "Okay, Sammy, da first thing we got ta do is find a place ta hide my bags so nobody can find dem."

Her eyes circled around the campus for an answer. No, she couldn't hide them here. Too many people would be walking around the campus in the next few days. Then she remembered that she used to hide her stuff near the church next to the art museum. That's what she'd do—at least for today.

"Okay, Sammy, I thought of a place ta hide my bags. It's not too far. You won't have ta walk too much." She lifted her bags, slung them over her shoulder—she was used to this—took hold of his left hand and trotted in the direction of the art museum just up the street on Wick Avenue.

Sammy latched onto Thin Lizzy's hand. Though his feet were hurting, he slowly walked beside her through the campus to another huge building that he had also visited once before with his mother. He remembered being very bored as he and his mom meandered around all the big rooms in the art museum with just a bunch of pictures on the wall. There were hardly any places to sit. Sometimes there was a bench in the middle of a room, but that wasn't enough for all the people who were walking around. And some of the pictures were funny-looking with just colors and scribbles, no people or trees or houses or anything. His mother said he would enjoy it, but he didn't at all. It was so boring. Although, afterwards, they went to lunch, and he got a hot dog and French fries. *That* was the fun part.

Thin Lizzy and Sammy walked through the parking

lot of the museum to the back of the church next to it. Way back beyond the building itself, a fence with high weeds stood several yards away. Thin Lizzy carried her bags to a tree about a yard away from the fence. She placed her bags between the tree and the fence, then pulled the weeds out from under her bags so they would stand up again and block the sight of the bags from anyone passing by. She hoped the branches and leaves from the tree would also keep the food a little cooler to avoid spoiling too quickly. She didn't want to feed Sammy any spoiled food. He had enough problems with which to deal without making him get sick too.

After being freed of the burden of the bags, she could now concentrate on what to do about Sammy. "Let's go around and sit on da steps of da museum, kid, so I can think."

They walked to the front of the art museum and sat on the large, cement steps leading to the entrance. That was fine with Sammy, for his feet were hurting him.

Thin Lizzy sat on the steps, moving her head back and forth, twisting and moving her lips, also back and forth. Sammy didn't want to interrupt her. He knew his life was in her hands. She was all the help he had. He definitely wanted her to find an answer. He was so lost, and he had to depend on someone else. It had to be her.

As for Thin Lizzy, she was trying to think of all the people she knew who might help her. Since she had been on the street, she had always tried to keep a low profile and avoid trouble of any kind. She did okay—most of the time. She had no friends, really. There was Aggie Bee, about the only person she remotely considered a friend. Could she trust her? She wasn't sure. But it was different now. She no longer was alone. And she needed help. What could she do? Who could help her?

Chapter Fourteen

*Early Monday morning, 4 days before the fire.*

At five-thirty Monday morning, Rocco Banetti sat at home in his casually opulent, slate breakfast nook, partaking of his second cup of strong, black coffee. He had finished his healthy breakfast of a vegetable omelet and twelve-grain toast. He searched the morning news on his tablet as he sipped the robust brew. Occasionally, he glanced out the wide picture window next to him at the expansive backyard landscaped with flowery plants and lush hedges and his sparkling, Olympic-size pool staring back at him. If his wife Stella was good for anything, it was making sure the landscaping on the property remained pristine and the pool was kept crystal clear.

As he was about to take another sip of his coffee, in the distance, he heard the dim sound of the doorbell chime. Hell, who was coming to his house this early in the morning? Olga must have ordered a delivery from the specialty store. She needed to tell them to come around to the side door so he wouldn't be disturbed.

Moments later, the housekeeper, entered the breakfast nook. In her Slavic accent she said, "Mr. Rocco, sir, two men at front door to see you."

Banetti straightened his posture. "Two men to see me?" He looked at the time on the kitchen clock. "At five-forty in the morning?"

"Yes, sir. Two men."

"Who are they?"

"They say they from United States Department of Justice."

With a jerk, he put his coffee cup down on the table, sloshing the liquid out of the cup and onto the tabletop. "The Justice Department?"

"Yes, sir."

This was not good. Why hadn't Nagy or Padgett warned him about this? Why the hell were these men showing up at his house barely after five in the morning? He had to keep his cool, but he also had to act innocent yet authoritative. "Well, show them into the library. I'll be there momentarily."

Immediately, he took out his phone. Nagy and Padgett were probably still in bed, but he didn't care. This was urgent. Quickly, he texted both men.

*–The DOJ is in my library. Why the hell didn't you warn me?–*

He was surprised to see Sam quickly responded.

*–Say nothing. Tell them they need to contact us.–*

Then that was the plan. He'd be cordial but wouldn't say anything to incriminate himself.

When he entered the library, he found two men standing next to the window, staring out at the wide expanse of his property. Banetti went over to greet them. In a cheerful voice, he offered, "Good morning, gentlemen. What can I do for you so early this morning?"

Both men turned with the sound of his voice. They were dressed in impeccable, dark navy suits, muted design ties, and stark white shirts. The taller man spoke in a deep, commanding voice, "I'm Special Agent Terrance Corcoran. This is Special Agent Trace

Forrester. We are with the U. S. Justice Department."

Banetti responded in that still cheerful tone, though he was anything but cheerful, "The Justice Department, huh? That's interesting. You must have the wrong address. I'm Rocco Banetti. Are you sure you're here to speak to me?"

Special Agent Corcoran answered, "Yes, sir, we are here to ask you some questions."

Showing his smooth, cocky attitude, Banetti acknowledged, "You are here to ask me some questions? I can't imagine what those might be, but please, have a seat so we can get on with this. I need to get to my office soon."

He sat on the sleek leather high-back chair next to the window. The two DOJ agents sat in two similar chairs across from him. Once seated, Agent Corcoran focused on Banetti. "We understand that you are the CEO of REB Enterprises."

It wasn't a question, so Banetti said nothing but had a slight, sly grin on his face.

Corcoran continued, "Can you tell us about the offshore bank accounts that you have in various foreign countries, including Switzerland, Singapore, and the Cayman Islands?"

Banetti continued to grin despite the tense feeling slowly growing in his body but still said nothing.

Corcoran waited a few seconds for Banetti to answer. When he did not, Corcoran took out a sheet of paper and asked another question, "Can you explain how all these shell corporations listed on this paper are connected with you and REB Enterprises?" He stood and started to hand the paper to Banetti, who raised his hand and refused to accept or look at it.

Before Corcoran could ask another question, Banetti interrupted, "There is no need for either of you to ask me any further questions. I will not answer anything without my attorney present."

Banetti arose from his chair. "If you'll give me your cards, I'll see that my attorney gets them." He glanced at both men before saying, "You have a good day, Agent Corcoran and Agent Forester." Then he casually walked out of the library, buzzing Olga on his phone. "Olga, please see that these men exit my home."

As he went upstairs to his home office, he saw Olga rushing toward the library to lead the agents to the front door. In the dim light of dawn, he watched from the office upstairs window as the men got into their dark SUV and drove away from his property. He took a deep breath, tried to calm down, and immediately called Sam Nagy. He didn't care that it was only six in the morning.

Sam answered the phone on the first ring. Before even greeting Banetti with a banal *hello*, he quickly queried, *"What did they want?"*

The anger in Banetti's voice darted through the phone like an electric current. "Hell, man, they asked me about my offshore bank accounts and shell companies. What's goin' on here, Sam? How the hell do they know anything about me?"

*"Rocco, I don't know. This has nothing to do with us. You know we run a very tight ship here. This is not coming from our end."*

"Well, then, where *is* it coming from?"

*"There must be a leak or a hitch somewhere in one of your organizations. I don't know."*

"What about that kid that works for you? Nestor or Nesbitt or something? Can you trust him?"

*"Yes, of course, I trust him. He's been working on your accounts for a couple of years now with no problems, right? He's a good guy, sharp and dependable. I can assure you this wouldn't be because of him."*

Banetti wasn't so sure he believed Sam about that kid. "Well, what'll I do now? I got the damn men's business cards. Are you gonna contact them or what?"

*"What time will you be in your office this morning?"*

"I'm gonna leave in five minutes, but I have a board meeting at eight-thirty."

*"Okay. I'll meet you there at seven, and we can discuss this."*

\*\*\*\*

An hour later, Rocco Banetti was in his corporate office at his desk when Louise, his secretary, who had come in early at his request, buzzed him. "Your attorneys are here to see you, Mr. Banetti."

Banetti, who was still unsettled from his encounter with the agents from the DOJ earlier that morning, confronted the two attorneys before they even sat on the chairs on their side of his desk. "What the hell is going on here? I can't believe those guys came to my house, my private residence at five-thirty in the morning."

Sam Nagy assured him, "Rocco, just like I told you on the phone, this has nothing to do with us. We have a firm hand on everything going on concerning you and your companies, and I am confident that nothing has been discussed or leaked to anyone from our end. I know you're upset, and we do have to nip this in the bud immediately. That's why Carl and I are here."

Padgett interjected, "Do you have the cards from the DOJ agents?"

The two business cards lay on his desk. He pushed them forward. Padgett picked them up, studied them for a moment, and passed them on to Nagy. As he glanced at the cards, Nagy uttered, "Hmm, I've heard of this Forester dude before, but not this Corcoran."

Padgett appeased, "Rocco, we'll get in touch with these two agents and see what they're after. However, in the meantime, it would be wise if you would check with your own top guys to see what they know internally, within your various entities. I know you're very efficient and control all your companies with an iron hand, but with the kind of businesses you have, there's always a chance something can go wrong, or someone will turn out to be not who you expected them to be. If the DOJ is looking, that means they have a reason, and of course, that definitely gives you cause to be concerned. Like I said, we'll talk to these agents to get a clue what they know and what they want from you."

The attorneys arose from their chairs. Banetti got out of his and came around his desk. "Alright, gentlemen, I expect to hear back from you very soon. This crap has got me worried. I don't like to be a worried man. It there's a problem on my end, I'll take care of it, I expect you will do the same."

Padgett said, "We're gonna fix it, Rocco. You can take that to the bank."

A few minutes after the attorneys left, Banetti buzzed Louise. *"Yes, Mr. Banetti?"*

"Louise, get in here. We have a couple of meetings to plan."

Chapter Fifteen

*Saturday, about 6 a.m., after the fire.*

Attorney Carl Padgett sat back down in the chair in his expansive living room. The information the two detectives gave him had thrown him for a loop. First, when they said the fire was suspicious, his mind froze. But when the female detective said Sam and Alyssa had been shot to death, Padgett couldn't catch his breath. He knew immediately who was behind this. The shooting of Sam and Alyssa could only mean one thing. Banetti. It had to be Banetti and his men. No one else. After learning from Sam a couple of weeks ago that Ryan Nesbitt was being followed by a black SUV, Padgett was a little concerned. Then he and Sam's meeting with Banetti last Monday regarding Banetti's visit from the DOJ really heightened Padgett's apprehension. And the next day, he and Nagy had talked to those DOJ agents and learned the evidence the DOJ had on Banetti had been obtained by the agency itself. It did not come from anyone in Carl's law firm, not even Ryan. He was positive of that.

So whatever the DOJ had learned had to come from Banetti's organization, not his firm. But this fire with Sam and Alyssa dead... Not just dead but shot to death! Padgett was terrified. He had to think, but his brain was still muddled with sleep and the tragic news about Sam and Alyssa. And little Sammy. What could they have done with him? Well, that wasn't his concern right now either. He had to think of his own well-being and safety.

He stood up and called out, "Leanne, where are you? Come here! We need to talk right now!"

Leanne, who had gone back to bed, awakened quickly from a drowsy sleep to hear her husband bellowing her name from downstairs. She hadn't removed her robe when she had lain back down. She slowly got out of bed, put her slippers back on her feet, and yelled, "I'm coming, I'm coming. What is such an emergency? I want to sleep for a few more hours."

When she entered the living room, Carl's face was as white as mashed potatoes. She noticed also that he was actually trembling. This had to be bad. She quickly went to him and grabbed his arm. "What is it? What's the matter? You look terrible."

Carl was breathing heavily. "Leanne, are our passports up to date?"

Leanne thought this was a strange question since just last year they had been to Paris. "Of course, Carl."

"Well, find them right now. Then I want you to pack."

She was flabbergasted. "Pack? Where are we going? I can't go anywhere. I have that charity dinner tomorrow and—"

Carl stood and tightly grabbed her shoulders. "Listen to me and listen well. Our lives are in grave danger. We have to leave the country immediately."

She jerked backward. "What are you talking about? Leave the country? You're insane!"

"I don't have time to explain or answer any of your stupid questions. Just do as I say. Find those passports. Pack large suitcases for both you and me. I'll get all our cash out of the safe and make the travel arrangements."

"B-but where are we going?"

"I don't know yet, but far away from here."

## *Chapter* Sixteen

*Saturday, around 9 a.m., after the fire.*

Thin Lizzy and Sammy had remained on the steps of the art museum for quite a while. Sammy waited to see what the lady planned to do next. He wasn't in any hurry. He was tired, and his hand and feet were hurting in spite of what Thin Lizzy had put on them. Besides all that, he had no idea what to do, where to go, or who could help him. After all, he was just a little kid.

He couldn't even make a telephone call. He had no cellphone. Sometimes his mommy would let him play games on her phone, but she said he was too young for one of his own. At least if he had one now, he could call… Who would he call? He knew his own telephone number at his house and his mommy and daddy's cellphone numbers, but who else? He knew his friend, Corbin's, number. At least, he thought he remembered it. 330-744… He forgot the other numbers.

While the two of them sat quietly on the steps, Thin Lizzy pondered their dilemma. What was she going to do with the kid? Not only tomorrow or the next day, but right now. How could she walk around town with him, her being a street person, a vagrant, with no money, no home, nothing to call her own but a bag of rags and a bag of garbage? And the boy in those dirty pajamas and no shoes? She was smart enough to realize they would be stared at by anyone who saw them. That would be enough of an issue, but what if somebody called the cops on them? What then? They'd probably think she kidnapped the kid or something and put her in jail. Then what would happen to the boy? No, she had to think of *something*. But what?

The boy was such a good kid. He did everything she asked. And what horrible things had happened to him! She felt so sorry for him, giving her more resolve to help him in whatever way she could. But how? She looked down at him, calmly sitting next to her, not complaining about his feet or hand, not crying about the terrible situation he was in, just patiently expecting and waiting for her to make some type of decision on his behalf. He trusted her to help him. She had to find a way to do just that.

She sat up rigid and straight. *I have ta do somethin'. I have ta trust somebody. De only person I know dat I trust even a li'l bit is Aggie Bee. So I guess I have ta find her.* She stood. "Come on, Sammy. I got a plan."

Immediately alert, Sammy turned his head toward her and quickly stood up. Thin Lizzy offered her hand to him, and he latched onto it. "Where are we going?"

She smiled down at him. "We're goin' ta church."

Wide eyed, Sammy glanced down at his dirty pajamas and shoeless feet. His mom had taken him to church a couple of times. Both of them were dressed in their best clothes. His mommy looked like a princess when she put on one of her colorful dresses and her fancy shoes. And he had a gray suit she told him he had to wear. It was not very comfortable. He also had to put on his scratchy, white shirt with a tie like his daddy wore, only smaller.

He hated it when she made him go to church. It was

so boring, sitting on the hard bench while that man in front of him dressed all in black kept talking on and on forever, sometimes yelling at everybody. A couple of times, Sammy started to fall asleep, but his mom nudged him awake. He almost forgot where he was. So he wasn't too happy about Thin Lizzy taking him to church. But what could he do about it?

Yes, Thin Lizzy had an idea. Her friend, Aggie Bee, loved church. She spent a lot of time at the church on the corner of Rayen Avenue. It wasn't too far from the art museum. Thin Lizzy hoped that Aggie Bee would be there this morning. She would ask for her help.

The Blood of Jesus Pentecostal Church was located in an old stone building built more than a hundred years ago. Its history had seen a number of Protestant denominations over those years. Now, though old and in need of serious repairs, it was a haven for many of the street people, where they often found needed assistance as well as spiritual guidance. Its doors seemed to always be open to help anyone. Aggie Bee had invited Thin Lizzy several times to join her on Sunday mornings, but Thin Lizzy never felt comfortable accepting her invitation. However, now she needed help.

Even though it was a Saturday morning, as Thin Lizzy and Sammy approached the stairs leading up to the large wooden double doors that were almost devoid of paint, powerful singing with a piano accompaniment resonated from within. At the top of the stairs, Thin Lizzy dropped Sammy's hand to use both of her own to yank at one of the massive front doors. As it creaked open, Thin Lizzy gently prodded Sammy forward through the doorway into the narthex of the church. She entered directly behind him. Ahead of them at the front of the large sanctuary, a group of about twenty men and women clad in an array of clothing in various degrees of cleanliness, style, and shabbiness were gathered around a rotund woman in a red sweat suit playing the piano. All were singing at the top of their lungs, "*Halleluiah, halleluiah, Jesus is king.*"

Thin Lizzy didn't want to interrupt their singing, so she guided Sammy to a pew in the back of the church, waiting for the group to complete their hymn. As she sat quietly listening to the music, she spied Aggie Bee standing close to the piano, animated and powerfully and clearly singing her praises. She knew Aggie Bee loved to sing, and she had a beautiful voice. Sometimes when they would walk together, Aggie Bee would softly sing her hymns as they wandered the streets of town. Thin Lizzy enjoyed listening to her, just as she was now enjoying this peculiar choir's vocal talents. Even Sammy was awestruck and attentive as the choir roared out their notes. She patiently waited for a break in the music.

When the practicing choir completed their hymn, in unison they all shouted, "Praise the Lord!" Thin Lizzy felt Sammy's tiny body suddenly jerk, startled by the outcry.

Some of the choir members then began talking among themselves. Others piled their tattered hymnals atop the piano and walked toward the exit, bidding their goodbyes to those remaining. Thin Lizzy got out of her seat. Taking Sammy's hand, she led him to the front of the sanctuary where Aggie Bee was talking to one of the other women who had been singing. When Aggie Bee noticed Thin Lizzy approaching, she immediately stopped talking and stared at Thin Lizzy and Sammy, her mouth open as wide as an apple and her eyes as large as walnuts. "Thin Lizzy! What da—whatchu doin' here? Who dat li'l one?"

Thin Lizzy said in a cautious voice, "Can I talk ta ya for a li'l bit, Aggie Bee?"

Aggie Bee was utterly speechless—for a couple reasons. Thin Lizzy had always refused to come to church with her, even though she'd asked Thin Lizzy to join the choir. When they walked together on the streets, the two of them would often sing together. They were about the same age, so they both were familiar with many of the same popular songs from their younger years. Thin Lizzy had a pleasant voice too, but she wouldn't join the choir or even come to the church services. Imagine Aggie Bee's surprise at seeing her friend—inside the church and walking toward her.

But the sight of her friend was not the biggest shock. That child. That soiled, disheveled little boy. What on earth was she doing with a small, unsightly boy? She had never told Aggie Bee why she was on the streets, although she oftentimes had hinted at once having a child of her own years ago. Aggie Bee didn't ask questions. It was not her business. Street people were private people who normally kept their personal matters and their past issues to themselves. But this child couldn't be ignored. Thin Lizzy had no children. So who was he, and where did he come from?

Therefore, when Aggie Bee saw the two of them standing next to her, she was so confused that she hadn't heard a single word Thin Lizzy had spoken. Instead of answering whatever question it was, Aggie Bee stooped down in front of the boy and blurted, "Thin Lizzy, who dis?"

Sammy was frightened by Aggie Bee's sudden

aggressive motion. He jumped back, dropping Thin Lizzy's hand. Thin Lizzy, noting his fear, turned to him and took his hand again. "It's okay, Sammy. She don't mean to scare ya. She gonna help us."

Aggie Bee stood back up, raising her hands in the air. "Oh, oh, li'l guy. I don't mean ta scare ya! No siree!"

"He's gone through a lot, Aggie Bee." She looked down toward Sammy. "Isn't dat right, Sammy?"

Aggie Bee looked apologetically at Sammy and spoke in a softer voice, "So yer name is Sammy, huh?"

Sammy shyly muttered, "Yes, ma'am."

Aggie Bee looked over at Thin Lizzy. "My, he sure a polite li'l lad, ain't he?"

Thin Lizzy had come to the church for a purpose. "Can I talk ta ya, somewheres private?"

Since the sanctuary was quite large, Aggie Bee said, "Let's go back in da corner. Nobody gonna bother us dere." She led them back away from the others. Thin Lizzy followed, still holding Sammy's hand.

Aggie Bee sat down at the end pew with hands folded on her lap and her back against the corner so she could look toward Thin Lizzy, who sat next to her, still leaving enough room so she could face the woman. Sammy climbed up next to Thin Lizzy, also looking toward Aggie Bee. Thin Lizzy placed her left hand on Aggie Bee's folded hands. "I need yer help."

Aggie Bee simply shook her head. "Go on."

"Ya see, we in a li'l bit a trouble here."

"Yeah, I see dat. I knowed you ain't got no li'l boy. So who dis kid?"

"It's a long story, but dis is Sammy, and his house burned down last night."

Aggie Bee slapped her hand over her mouth and

popped her eyes wide open. "What!"

"I'm gonna tell ya all I know."

Thin Lizzy explained how late last night she found Sammy, dirty and terrified, in the middle of the street. She revealed how the big SUV almost ran him over before she grabbed him and rushed the two of them to the curb. She told how she then took him into the library to spend the night. Aggie Bee knew Thin Lizzy had been spending the last couple of weeks in the library, so she wasn't surprised when Thin Lizzy informed her of that part.

Thin Lizzy continued, "I didn't know until dis mornin' what happened ta him 'cause last night he was too tired ta even talk. Ya see, he walked and walked and didn't even know how far he walked. And he didn't have no shoes or even slippers on his li'l feet. Dey're all cut and sore now."

Aggie Bee shook her head and sniffled, "Oh, my, oh my!"

"Dis mornin' he tells me dat his house burned down, and he don't know where his mommy and daddy are."

Aggie Bee interrupted. "Who was watchin' him in da house? Wasn't his momma and poppa wit him?"

"Dat's the thing. Ya see, before da fire started some bad men broke in da house, and Sammy's mama tole him to hide. So he hid upstairs in a closet. Dat's when he heard some gunshots, and—"

"What! Gunshots?"

"Yeah, and den da bad guys came lookin' for him, but dey didn't find him. And when dey were gone, he smelled da smoke and couldn't breathe real good, so he got outta his hidin' place and got outta da house. Den, he said he was so scared he just kept walkin' and walkin' until I found him in da street."

Aggie Bee began moving back and forth and wringing her hands. "Oh Lawdy, Lawdy!" She looked around Thin Lizzy at Sammy. "You poor, poor li'l boy!"

Sammy simply stared back at her with his sad, blue eyes and no expression on his face.

Thin Lizzy asked, "I hate ta aks ya, but do ya think you can help us somehow? I don't wanna walk around wit him 'cause, ya know, Darkman and Mojo, ain't no tellin' what dey might do. I'm scared a dem."

Aggie Bee nodded her head. "Yeah, I know, I know. Umm, lemme think." She looked up and pursed her mouth into a small circle. After a while, she lowered her head, taking a deep breath. "I tink we gotta talk ta Preacher Anton. He ain't in right now, but I knowed he gonna be back dis afternoon." She stood up. "Come wit me. We got some old clothes in da basement we savin' for da rummage sale next month. How 'bout if we see if we have any li'l boy clothes and shoes, so's he can get cleaned up a li'l bit?"

Aggie Bee led them down a long hallway to a large metal door. She opened it to a wide set of stairs. Turning on the lights, she led them down the staircase to a spacious room. In one corner were boxes and boxes of clothing. In another were piles of old furniture in various conditions of wear and tear, some looking usable, some questionable, and some even in pristine shape. Folding tables and chairs were stacked against the walls on the opposite side of the big room. Aggie Bee walked over to the clothing boxes. "I tink some a dese are sorted. Uh, lemme see…" She routed through several of them, moving them out of her way as she progressed, until she found what she was looking for. "Here it is. Come over here."

Thin Lizzy and Sammy joined her as she dragged a box into the open area.

Searching through the box, Aggie Bee pulled out a pair of gray sweatpants that looked to be about a child size six or seven. "Here, dese should do ya. Maybe dey be a li'l big, but you can roll 'em up on da bottom." She handed them to Sammy as she continued routing through the box for something else.

Sammy hesitantly took the pants, folding them over his arm.

Aggie Bee continued her task and soon drew out a long sleeve T-shirt with light blue and black horizontal stripes. Holding it up, she said, "Dis okay for his shirt." She handed it to Thin Lizzy, who gave it to Sammy. Sammy grabbed it and placed it over his arm on top of the sweatpants.

Aggie Bee stood up. "Now we got to find some shoes for ya." She left the box of the boys clothing, placing the items she had discarded neatly back into the box. Then she stood up again, looked over the many other boxes before she exclaimed, "Ah, dere it is."

She moved a few cartons out of her way and walked over to a rather large box filled with shoes of all sizes. She dragged the box of shoes over to where Thin Lizzy and Sammy were standing. As she hauled it closer, she said, "We have ta find a pair a shoes dat'll fit ya 'cause ya can't go anywhere without shoes." She stood up. "Thin Lizzy, how 'bout you gettin' one a dose foldin' chairs so da boy can sit down and we'll try some a dese shoes on his feet?" Aggie Bee continued to scrounge through the shoe carton, putting those too large or too small out on the floor. She eventually pulled out two different sizes of sneakers. "Here, try dese on him. See which one fits da best."

Thin Lizzy explained, "He got real heavy socks on right now, and I put some rags and stuff inside 'em to kinda protect his feet."

Aggie Bee twisted her mouth. "Take da socks off. Let's see what's dere."

Sammy sat on the chair that Thin Lizzy had set up for him, and she carefully removed the long, heavy stockings. The Styrofoam pieces tumbled to the floor, leaving only the rags tied around Sammy's injured feet.

Aggie Bee came over to examine the boy's feet. Shaking her head, she could see spots of blood on the rags. "Let's leave da rags on yer feet but ditch da Styrofoam. We better put da socks back on him ta help protect da feet. Maybe a pair a dese shoes will fit him." She handed Thin Lizzy both pairs that she had taken out of the box.

Thin Lizzy tried the first pair on Sammy's feet. When he stood up to walk in them, they were flopping up and down.

"Dose won't work," proclaimed Aggie Bee. "Try da other pair."

Sammy sat back on the chair. Thin Lizzy removed the first pair of sneakers and tried on the second pair. The first pair had shoelaces while this pair had self-fasteners. She fastened the strips and Sammy stood up and walked around a little.

"Dat's much better," pronounced Aggie Bee. "Dose'll work just fine." She began placing the discarded shoes neatly back into the heavy box and dragging it back to its original spot.

Thin Lizzy folded the chair and also returned it to its

place against the wall. She picked up the Styrofoam pieces and threw then in a large trash can in the corner of the room.

Bewildered, Sammy stood looking around, holding his newly acquired secondhand clothes over his arm and his slightly worn sneakers on his feet.

Chapter Seventeen

*Tuesday, 8 a.m., 3 days before the fire.*

Several top representatives from each of Rocco Banetti's legitimate companies and organizations were present at the mandatory meeting held in the large conference room at REB Enterprises corporate offices. There were no excuses, no exceptions. You were at this meeting—or *else*.

At midnight the night before, a different, clandestine meeting was held at an undisclosed, secret location. Present at that meeting were those whom Banetti called his kingpins, head honchos of all the criminal elements of Banetti's holdings.

Banetti demanded answers from all. Why did the DOJ knock on his door at five-thirty on a Monday morning? He grilled every team member at both meetings, individually and as a group. Each member was given the task of checking and rechecking every associate, every aide, and every single peon under their command to investigate and identify any leaks in their part of the organization.

Someone was after Banetti, and he needed to find out who and why before it was too late. Each attendee at both meetings was required to expel by any means necessary any person deemed questionable or unfit in any way to do their job correctly. Of course, those names also had to be turned over to Banetti so he could subject any additional punishment he considered appropriate for the transgression.

After both meetings, Banetti felt that he had a handle on the situation as far as his organization was concerned. His executives and kingpins would take care of any problems within the various legitimate and illegal companies and groups. He only hoped that his attorneys at Padgett & Nagy, LLP had done what they needed to do within their firm.

At precisely 11:15 a.m., Rocco Banetti and his chief of security, Benny Ricci, stomped into Padgett & Nagy, LLP's downtown office. Chloe Gannon, the receptionist at the law firm, looked up from her desk. "May I help you, sir?"

"I'm here to see Carl and Sam."

"What is your name, sir?"

"They'll know who I am."

"Please have a seat while I contact them."

"I'll stand but be quick about it."

Chloe acted immediately. "Mr. Padgett, there are two gentlemen here to see you."

*"Send them back to my office, Chloe, and tell Sam to join us here ASAP."*

Without further conversations, she arose from her desk and escorted the two men back to Padgett's office. On her way back to the reception area, she knocked on Sam Nagy's door. "Mr. Nagy, Mr. Padgett requests that you join him in his office immediately."

Sam, knowing that Banetti was expected, pushed what he was working on aside and joined the men in Padgett's office.

A small conference table was located on the side of the room. When all four men were seated at the table,

Banetti began, "So what did you find out from the DOJ?"

Both attorneys looked very grim. This was not going to be good news. Padgett replied, "Well, I got in touch with the two agents immediately after I talked to you and set up a meeting for yesterday afternoon. I'm afraid they have some damning information on some of your offshore bank accounts and a few of those shell corporations. They wouldn't give me too many details, but they said enough to know this is serious business, Rocco."

Banetti sat stoically in his seat while Padgett informed him of the bad news. He could feel the nerves and cells in his brain revolting to the accusations and worming their way to a solution. "What can we do about it? How can we stop this?"

"I don't know. This has gone too far." Padgett shook his head. "Did you check with all *your* people? Do they know anything about how this happened? As we told you previously, this did not come from our end."

Banetti replied, "I took care of my team." He looked from Padgett to Nagy, then back again to Padgett. "Are you sure you've taken care of yours?"

Swiftly, Padgett answered, "Of course, we have. As we've told you several times, anything about you or your entities is seen by only a very few people, all of whom can be trusted explicitly to maintain your confidentiality. Your records are safe and secure here. There are no leaks."

Sam, who hadn't said much so far, asked Banetti, "Have you been in contact with any of your banks about their receiving requests to confiscate any of your bank records?"

Banetti's eyes shot daggers at Sam. "No, is that

something I should be expecting?"

Sam answered, "It's something they can do if they find it necessary."

Banetti stood, as did Benny Ricci. "We're done here." He stalked to the door, opening it. Before going out, he turned and pointed his finger. "I'm warning both of you... None of this better happen. Put a stop to it now!"

**Chapter** Eighteen

*Saturday, near noon, after the fire.*

When Thin Lizzy, Aggie Bee, and Sammy left the basement of the Blood of Jesus Pentecostal Church, Aggie Bee suggested, "How 'bout we let Sammy wash up a li'l and change into his new clothes. What do ya think, Sammy?"

The boy nodded shyly and followed the two women up the stairs where Aggie Bee showed him to the men's restroom. "Can ya do it yerself?"

He opened the door. "Yes, ma'am."

Thin Lizzy nodded. "We'll be waitin' right out here for ya."

No one else was in the restroom. First, Sammy relieved himself at one of the urinals. Afterwards, with a paper towel squirted with liquid soap, he washed his face and left hand at a sink, trying to keep the right hand as dry as possible. Sloshing water on his face to rinse, he then took another couple of towels to dry.

Still alone, he removed his very dirty pajamas, pulled on his new sweatpants and T-shirt and felt a little better right away. It wasn't that he minded being dirty. Plenty of times, he and his friends, Corbin and Jace, had gotten sweaty playing ball or just running around having fun. But that was different. He didn't mind that kind of dirt. But these pajamas? They reminded him of things he wanted to forget.

After putting the socks and shoes back on his feet, he rolled the pajamas in a tight ball, tossed them into the trashcan, and left the restroom to join the two ladies.

Aggie Bee and Thin Lizzy were still waiting. Aggie Bee asked, "Ya do okay in der, Sammy?"

"Yes ma'am."

Then she led them to a room attached to the church kitchen. "Let's have some food," she said. "It's just about lunchtime. I gotta help clean da church in a while, but I'm hungry now. Maybe by da time we be done eatin', Preacher Anton be here."

About a dozen other people were gathered in the room, sitting at long, scarred tables eating sandwiches and chips with water bottles placed beside their food. Some were dressed in clean, neat clothing while others wore unkempt clothes similar to Thin Lizzy's.

She stopped and stared at the gathering. Surprised, she asked Aggie Bee, "Uh, does da church feed all dese people all a time?"

"Oh, no, not all a time, but today all a us, we gonna give da church a good cleanin'. Dese people are gonna help clean for free meals, and Preacher Anton, he gonna give 'em some money for helpin' out."

"Oh, can I help and get some money, too?"

"I-I guess so. Wait till Preacher Anton come in. I'll aks him." She hesitated. "But I knowed he ain't gonna mind me givin' ya somethin' ta eat. 'Specially dat li'l kid." She directed them to an empty table. "Let's sit here. I'll get our food."

Aggie Bee came back with a tray filled with sandwiches, chips, and water. She placed it on the table and passed the items out to each of them. Then she sat down to enjoy her meal.

Sammy slowly unwrapped his bologna and cheese sandwich and took a bite of one of the halves. He was definitely hungry, but he had never tasted this type of lunchmeat before. It was different, but it was good. Soon he finished that half and after taking a sip of his water, he picked up the other half to devour it. So many thoughts ran through his head. He was so worried about his mom and dad, yet he was equally worried about what would happen to him. He trusted Thin Lizzy and maybe this Aggie Bee lady, but still... He couldn't come up with another idea. He *had* to trust these weird ladies and hope that they could find answers for him.

When they finished their lunches, Aggie Bee mentioned, "I think Preacher Anton is in his office now. Let's go talk ta him."

The church offices were down the hall leading to the back of the church. Preacher Anton's office door was open, and he was sitting at his desk, looking over some papers when Aggie Bee rapped softly on the door, "Preacher Anton?"

He was a large man with large facial features — bulbous nose, full lips, bushy eyebrows that partially hid his black marble eyes, and clear skin like melted milk chocolate. With the sound of the knock, he looked up. "Sister Aggie. Come in; come in."

Aggie Bee entered the office, followed closely behind by Sammy and Thin Lizzy.

Preacher Anton raised his woolly eyebrows and sat up rigidly when he saw the boy. "And who do we have here, sister?"

There were only two frayed chairs in front of Preacher Anton's desk. The two women took those seats. Sammy stood next to Thin Lizzy's chair, resting his left hand on its arm. Aggie Bee explained, "Dis here's my friend, Thin Lizzy, and dis boy is Sammy."

Preacher Anton relaxed in his chair as his eyes urged an explanation. He nodded his head toward Thin Lizzy and the boy. "And why might your friend and this young man be here to see me?"

Aggie Bee decided, "Preacher Anton, I'm gonna let dem esplain da situation ta ya."

Thin Lizzy was not used to talking to strangers, especially those in authority. However, she knew it was her task to relay to him why she and Sammy were in his presence. With her voice stuttering, she replied, "Uh, I found Sammy in da middle of da street last night and I grabbed him when a big black car was gonna hit him." She paused to catch her breath. "He was lost so I took him to stay wit' me and now we're here 'cause I needed help and thought Aggie Bee maybe might help us."

Preacher Anton was keenly aware the homeless were oftentimes hesitant about giving out any information about themselves or their situation. But he was good at his job. He looked compassionately at Thin Lizzy. "May I call you Lizzy?"

"Yes."

"So, Lizzy, you found this boy last night. Can you tell me where you found him?"

She was so nervous. "Yes."

He waited, but she didn't continue, so he prodded, "Lizzy, where did you find Sammy?"

"Uh, on Wick Avenue near da library?"

That was all she said, but Preacher Anton needed more information. "Did he tell you where he came from, where he lives?"

"Yes."

141

He waited, but she didn't continue. Maybe he'd have better luck with the boy. First, he asked Aggie Bee, "Aggie, could you get a folding chair out of that closet for Sammy? He looks a little tired."

Aggie Bee immediately arose and retrieved a chair, setting it up next to Thin Lizzy. Sammy moved out of the way and then climbed onto the chair.

After Sammy was settled in his seat, Preacher Anton folded his hands together, leaned forward, resting his elbows on his desk, and looked toward Sammy. "Young man, can you tell me your name?"

Sammy was sort of surprised. No one had ever called him a young man before. His mom and dad called him "Sammy" all the time. His teacher, Mrs. Eckhart, always called him "Samuel." Other people called him "boy" or maybe, "kid," but never "young man." For a second, he wasn't sure this preacher was actually talking to him. But since he knew the man was not talking to Aggie Bee or Thin Lizzy, he must be talking to him. He answered clearly, "Sammy."

The preacher looked at him tenderly. "Do you have a last name, Sammy?"

"Yes, sir, Samuel Rooney Nagy, Junior."

"Hmm, that's quite a name for a young lad. How old are you, Samuel Rooney Nagy, Junior?"

"I'm five years old."

"My, you seem like a bright boy for your age."

"That's what my mommy and my teacher says, but I'm not as smart as Corbin."

"Why do you think Corbin is smarter than you?"

"Well, he knows everything about football and baseball and basketball, everything. When he's at my house, he talks and talks to my daddy about all that stuff.

Sometimes I think my daddy likes Corbin better than me."

"I'm sure your dad loves you very much and wouldn't trade you for any other kid, not even Corbin."

Sammy lowered his head. "Well, maybe."

"Do you know why your mom and dad named you Samuel Rooney Nagy Junior?"

Sammy blinked away the tears that had started to form. "Yeah, my daddy is Samuel Rooney Nagy Senior. He told me that my grandpa's name was Rooney."

"That's very interesting."

Preacher Anton thought he had loosened up Sammy a little, and he wanted to get some answers. "So, Sammy, can you tell me what happened to you last night and why Lizzy found you in the middle of the street?"

Sammy raised his head, eyes moistened with tears, and mouth turned down at the corners, but he began to tell Preacher Anton about his traumatic experience. "Last night Daddy, Mommy, and I were playing cards in our living room…"

He told Preacher Anton the entire series of events from being in his living room until Thin Lizzy found him on the street. Then he added the parts about sleeping in the library, eating cake for breakfast, and trashing his dirty pajamas in the men's room waste basket.

Preacher Anton was speechless. This poor little lad. What he had gone through these past several hours! He had never had a situation like this with which to deal. But that didn't mean he couldn't find answers. This boy had been through enough trauma. He had to help him. "Well, Sammy, you are not only a clever boy, but you are a very brave boy. I am so sorry you had to go through what you did last night, and I'm going to find out some answers

143

for you."

Then Preacher Anton turned to Thin Lizzy. "Lizzy, you also are a very brave person. Thank you, so much, for saving this boy's life and keeping him safe. That took a lot of courage."

"Awe, no sir, I ain't brave. I just couldn't let him get killed by dat car."

"No, Lizzy, you are brave. Not only did you save him from the car, but you kept him safe through the night. Who knows what kind of harm would've come to him if you hadn't found shelter for him." He looked at both Aggie Bee and Thin Lizzy. "I know you ladies are very aware how dangerous these streets can be, especially at night. I want to thank both of you for bringing this issue to my attention."

The ladies simply nodded their heads.

Preacher Anton stood up. "Now, I've got to look into this matter and find some answers. In the meantime, for as long as it takes me to deal with this, I want the three of you to stay in the church. You can sleep in the basement tonight. You'll be safer here than in the library or in the alleys downtown."

"Preacher Anton?" Aggie Bee interrupted. "I come here today ta help clean da church. Ya think Thin Lizzy and Sammy can help, too?"

"By all means. That's a great idea. There's lots for everyone to do. And I should be able to give you some information later today after I check with some authorities in the area."

Before they left Preacher Anton's office, Sammy folded up his chair and replaced it back into the closet.

Chapter Nineteen

*Tuesday, 4:00 p.m., 3 days before the fire.*
Ryan Nesbitt had been out of the office for most of the day, lining up witnesses for a new case he was working on, so he was unaware of Rocco Banetti's visit with the managing partners earlier that day.

When he returned to the office at four o'clock, he asked Chloe, the receptionist, if Carl and Sam were in. She told him they were in a private meeting and did not want to be disturbed. Ryan then went to his own office and finished up a small amount of paperwork he had left behind that morning. At five o'clock, he departed the office for the day to go home and freshen up, planning to meet his fiancée for dinner later that evening. Even though they'd spoken on the phone every night, they'd not seen each other since last Friday. Both had spent the weekend out of town: Melanie, on a field trip in Columbus with her history class students and Ryan, in Toledo, following up on some information regarding his new case. They were not able to get together until that evening.

On that Tuesday, Ryan left the parking lot and drove the interstate on his way home. As he usually did, he was driving in the middle lane when he noticed that damn black SUV following directly behind him, not three cars away as had been the norm. Every night this week, it had been behind his car but more at a distance, even though he took a different route home each night. He couldn't figure out how they found him each time. They must've been waiting somewhere near the parking lot where he had a reserved space. Maybe they were actually waiting in the *same* parking lot.

As he grasped the steering wheel, his hands started to sweat when he noticed in the rearview mirror that SUV getting closer, seeming more aggressive than usual. Maybe the driver thought he was just traveling too slowly on the left and simply wanted to pass his vehicle. Ryan wasn't in any hurry. He wasn't meeting Mel until eight-thirty, so he quickly glanced to the right to be sure the lane was clear and then put on his turn signal. Inching his car over to the right-hand lane, he noticed that the SUV was also changing lanes to the right instead of passing him on his left, as he had expected.

Ryan sped up a little, going over the speed limit by at least fifteen miles per hour. However, the SUV also increased its speed to maintain a very close distance behind him. What the hell was going on?

He was now speeding dangerously too fast for the heavy traffic on the interstate, and the SUV couldn't be more than inches from his bumper. He was terrified and couldn't go any faster. Traffic was too heavy. He had to do something, and he had to do it immediately before he hit the car in front of him. He looked to his right; the berm on his side of the road was clear, so he veered the vehicle onto it, barely missing the barrier on the far right. Up ahead, something was in front of him on the road berm. It was an unmoving, abandoned vehicle. He had no place to go. The barrier continued on his right with the terrain on the other side of it sloping into a couple of trees. His option was to either hit the abandoned vehicle or ram his car into the road barrier.

Taking a deep breath, he pressed the brakes to the floor and opted for the barrier.

Chapter Twenty

*Saturday, around 1:00 p.m., after the fire.*
After leaving Preacher Anton's office, Aggie Bee led Thin Lizzy and Sammy back to the sanctuary. "Our job is gonna be ta wash da pews. Sammy, how 'bout if you wait here while Thin Lizzy and me get some buckets and rags."

He didn't want to be alone in that big church. "Can I come with you? I can carry stuff, too."

"Yeah, why not?" responded Aggie Bee.

The three of them trudged down the hall to the janitor's room. Several other people were already there, getting supplies for their chores. A man in a blue uniform was handing out whatever supplies were needed for each particular job. If necessary, he also doled out instructions.

Behind the uniformed man was his helper, Lacey Gracey, another of Aggie Bee's friends. "Hi, Lacey Gracey," greeted Aggie Bee. "How ya doin' today?"

"Hi, Aggie Bee, I'm doin' just fine. How 'bout you?"

"Well, we need two buckets full a soapy water and lotsa rags. We gonna clean da pews today."

Lacey Gracey filled two large, red buckets with the required water and sanitizing soap mixture and handed them to Thin Lizzy and Aggie Bee. "The rags be over in that round bin. Take what you need. You have fun."

"Oh, we sure gonna," Aggie Bee laughed as they walked over to the bin. "Can ya grab us a big handful a rags, Sammy?"

It was a large, green bin filled with various types of rags. Sammy reached in with his whole body and pulled out a huge armful. Aggie Bee chuckled again. "Dat should do it for us."

They spent the afternoon cleaning the wooden pews with Thin Lizzy starting on one side of the sanctuary, Aggie Bee on the other. Sammy followed Thin Lizzy with a dry rag to wipe the water off the seats once they were washed. It took them several hours to complete the task. By then, it was near supper time. As with lunch, the church planned to provide supper also for all the workers.

The three pew cleaners took their supplies back to the janitor's room, emptying the remaining dirty water into the large utility sink and placing the soiled rags in a big red barrel. Then they made their way back to the dining area outside the kitchen, which was set up for the evening meal. At least a dozen men and women were already seated around the tables eating, while another two dozen filed into the room and got in line to retrieve trays of food from the kitchen serving window. Aggie Bee got in line in back of Stoney, another street person whom she knew. Sammy stood behind Aggie Bee and Thin Lizzy behind him.

As the line began to fill up in back of them, Thin Lizzy noticed that her nemesis, Darkman, and his sidekick, Mojo, were about six people behind her. Sweat started to drip down her forehead, and her hands began to shake. She didn't want those men to see Sammy. Who knew what they would do? She tried to shield him as they moved forward, hoping they were far enough away that they wouldn't notice the boy.

As they advanced toward the serving window, Sammy tried to reach up for his tray, but he wasn't tall enough. The young woman handing out the food smiled at him. Thin Lizzy grabbed the tray for him and asked, "Can ya put my food on his tray too, and I'll carry it?"

"Sure," said the woman, as she placed all of Thin Lizzy's food on the same tray.

The three left the line and carried their food to the last table on the right side of the room against the outside windows, Thin Lizzy, still trying to shield Sammy from the view of her intimidators, placed the tray on the table and pulled out a chair for Sammy. They sat facing the windows with their backs toward the other tables and the line of workers waiting for their food.

Thin Lizzy thought she had been successful in hiding Sammy from those bad men. However, as she started to put a spoonful of stew into her mouth, she heard a gruff, deep voice say, "Ah, Thin Lizzy, who you got here? Who dis li'l boy, huh?"

To her dismay, Darkman and Mojo took seats across from them at the same table and kept staring at Sammy—exactly what Thin Lizzy had hoped to avoid. Her heart sank to her feet. Then it felt like her heart was going to jump out of her chest. *Dey can't do anything ta us. We're in da church. Preacher Anton will protect us*. At least she hoped that would happen if those men started threatening them.

Aggie Bee, more accustomed to Darkman's aggressiveness, looked up from her stew. "Mind you own beeswax, Darkman."

He laughed out loud. Mojo looked out of the corner of his eye and snickered. Then addressing Thin Lizzy again, Darkman gloated, "Dat ain't yo kid, right? Who you steal him from, huh?"

Sammy stopped eating and focused on the ugly, dark man. He felt an instant fear of him. He wasn't sure why. Yes, he had that ugly face with a big, big nose and lips that looked like a rotten apple, His eyes were these teeny, little ones like black bugs. And his face had weeny, little holes all over his cheeks and chin. But it wasn't just the way he looked that frightened Sammy. It was everything—his face and especially those eyes. His voice that sounded like the bark of that big, mean dog who lived behind him. And he was big, like the bears Sammy had seen at the Pittsburgh Zoo. Even though he was hungry, Sammy was too terrified to take another bite of the food. He put his spoon down on the tray and latched onto Thin Lizzy's hand. She had also stopped eating.

Darkman picked up his spoon and began to eat his stew, but after every bite he glared at Sammy, then Thin Lizzy. Sammy tried to eat more of his food, but the stew had a hard time getting past his throat. He took smaller bites, hoping that would help as the man kept looking at him with those mean eyes.

The conversation between those at the table did not develop any further. It appeared that Darkman had said all he wanted to say. But why did he continue to look at Sammy? This concerned all three of them—Aggie Bee, Sammy, and Thin Lizzy. Aggie Bee finally blurted, "Why you keep lookin' at da boy, Darkman. He ain't none o' yo business."

"Hey, skank, I can look at anybody I wanna. You

ain't a gonna stop me."

"Well, maybe I will."

"And how ya gonna do dat, bitch?"

"I'm gonna tell Preacher Anton you didn't even do no cleanin' of da church, but you be eatin' his food."

Darkman stared maliciously at Aggie Bee. "Yo better not do dat if ya knows what's good for ya."

"Is you threatenin' me, goose-head?"

Darkman pushed himself out of the folding chair, knocking it against the wall behind him. He reached across the table, grabbed Aggie Bee's wrist, and twisted it in a vise grip.

She screamed, "Eeekk! Help!"

A few men at the next table jumped up. One yelled, "Darkman, let her go."

Like knives soaring across the room, Darkman's eyes riveted on the man who spoke. "Yo gonna do somethin' 'bout it, Stoney?" He still clenched tightly onto Aggie Bee's wrist.

Stoney and the tall man next to him, known as Figaro, darted around their table toward Darkman. They grabbed his shoulders and tried to loosen his grip on Aggie Bee. As they struggled, suddenly, Preacher Anton scurried into the room. "What's going on in here?"

The entire room grew silent. Darkman dropped Aggie Bee's wrist. Stoney and Figaro moved back against the windows. Darkman's chair crashed to the floor. No one spoke for several seconds.

"I asked what's going on here," Preacher Anton repeated.

Still no one spoke. Several more seconds passed.

Sammy looked at the ugly man who had grabbed Aggie Bee's wrist. The man was staring at Preacher

Anton now. Then Sammy glanced to the side at Aggie Bee. She was rubbing her injured wrist; and he saw tears in the corner of her eyes. Without thinking, he pushed his chair back and stood as tall as he could. He pointed his index finger at Darkman and spoke in a strong, clear voice. "That ugly man hurt Aggie Bee."

Even Preacher Anton was speechless. Out of all the people in the room, only the small boy had the courage to come forward. He stared at Darkman. "Is that true? Did you hurt Aggie?" Then he took a second to think. "What are you doing in this church, anyhow? Why are you eating at our table? I know you were not one of my workers today. This food is for those who have helped clean the church, not for those who have come here to cause trouble. It's very clear you're not here to serve the Lord." He paused to focus on Mojo. "Or your friend next to you. I want you both to leave the Lord's house immediately."

Just as Preacher Anton spoke, three large, muscular men came through the doorway and stood behind him. Preacher Anton continued, "You either leave peacefully, or my brothers will show you the way out." Another pause. "Your choice, men."

Darkman's beady eyes looked like they were on fire. He didn't immediately speak. With the slight nod of his head, he motioned for Mojo to get out of his chair. The room was silent again. With the sound of their footsteps clomping against the tile floor, the two men walked slowly toward the door, passing close by Preacher Anton and the three men who had joined him.

Before exiting the room, Darkman pointed toward Aggie Bee, Sammy, and Thin Lizzy. His bellowing voice almost shook the room. "I'll get you, bitch, and that brat, too."

**Chapter** Twenty-One

*Wednesday morning, 2 days before the fire.*

Muddled and confused, Ryan Nesbitt woke up in a strange, dark room with a piercing headache; in fact, his head felt like it was the size of a basketball. Where was he and what had happened? A dim light oozed in from the large window on the far side of the room. It was either early morning or late afternoon. He could see medical machines on his right side with wires and tubes attached to him on various parts all over his body.

He raised his head as much as he could, the pain penetrating more intensely. He looked at his right arm—covered in a hard, plaster blue cast. Then he tried to raise his body by propping his left elbow on the bed, but he didn't have the strength to be successful. Plus, the pain grew more excruciating with each movement. He lay back on the pillow and tossed the lightweight blanket from his body, becoming aware of another blue cast on his right leg. His headache was so severe that he reached with his left hand to his forehead only to discover it too was shielded in a generous white bandage.

Then instantly, it came back to him with such a force that caused his stomach to churn. He remembered leaving work on Tuesday afternoon and then hitting the freeway barrier. All at once, he realized he wasn't dead. He was actually very lucky to still be alive. But it looked like he had really done a number on his body. Did anybody know he was here? His mom? His sister Brittany? Melanie? His boss?

Just when he was about to press the button on a remote device attached to the side of his bed, he heard conversations coming from the hallway. The door opened; his mother, Maureen, and Melanie came into his room.

"Oh, thank God, you're awake," his mother wailed. "We were so worried about you, son."

Melanie rushed over to his bedside and gently kissed him on his cheek. "Oh, Ryan, baby!"

Ryan's mind was still hazy and overwhelmed. He didn't need to acknowledge them because at that moment Melanie moved out of the way to allow a nurse who had also entered his room to begin her duties. "Good morning, Mr. Nesbitt. I'm Renee, your nurse. I'm so glad to see you're finally awake. How are you feeling this morning?"

"Uh, not so good."

"Well, no wonder. You did some nasty things to your body yesterday." She lightly patted his shoulder. "But we're gonna get you as good as new in no time."

Nurse Renee was a sturdy woman with hair the color of cinnamon candy, probably in her fifties and dressed in sky blue scrubs. She began checking the machines keeping track of his vital signs. She took his blood pressure and his temperature. Then she touched his shoulder again. "Do you think you feel like eating something for breakfast this morning? I'll get a cafeteria staff member to come in and take your order. We're glad you're awake, and we're gonna get you back on your feet as soon as possible."

The nurse left the room, and Melanie pulled her

chair to Ryan's left side. She took his hand and held it to her cheek. "Oh, baby, I'm so sorry this happened to you. It's all my fault. I'm so, so sorry." And she began to sob uncontrollably.

Ryan was confused. Slowly, he was remembering the details of his car accident. He had been alone in the car. That black SUV behind his vehicle was threatening him. To avoid hitting any other vehicles, he rammed into the barrier off the side of the road. How was that Melanie's fault? But at that point, he didn't have the strength to question her. He didn't have the strength to say much of anything. He just wanted to sleep.

He closed his eyes again and forgot all about his accident and his current body condition—and what Melanie had said.

## Chapter Twenty-Two

*Saturday evening, after the fire.*

After Darkman and Mojo's exit from the church dining hall, the other diners remained very quiet. Still standing near the doorway where he had banished those two men, Preacher Anton encouraged, "Go on, everyone. Continue eating your supper. You will have no more disturbances from the likes of those devil worshipping men." He looked around the hall. "In fact, it is time for me to join you." He walked over to the serving window. "Sister Serena, may I have a bowl of stew, please?"

Serena handed him a tray of food. Preacher Anton carried it over to the place vacated by Darkman. One of the large men who had stood behind him at the entrance removed the trays of food left behind by Darkman and Mojo. Another of those men replaced the fallen chair so Preacher Anton could sit. Before he did so, he said to one of his men, "Brother Jaleel, would you take away Sister Aggie's spilled food and replace it with a clean tray?"

When Aggie Bee's food tray had been replaced, Preacher Anton then requested, "Let us pray and thank the Lord Jesus for this bountiful meal."

Everyone bowed their heads.

Preacher Anton closed his eyes, tilted his head back, and raised his hands. "Lord Jesus, thank you for this magnificent and bountiful harvest you have provided to this special flock of yours. We are thankful for every morsel you have given us. Today we ask your blessing on all of these workers and keep them safe from the wrath of the devil." He lowered his arms and head. "Amen."

Those in the room responded in unison, "Amen."

Sammy, who had mimicked the action of everyone else in the room as the prayer was given, was in awe of this man standing across from him. In a way, he reminded him of his daddy—big and strong and able to fix stuff. Look how he was able to make that bad, ugly man leave the room. Maybe he didn't need to be afraid of that ugly man anymore. Now he had three people to help and protect him—Thin Lizzy, Aggie Bee, and Preacher Anton.

Preacher Anton sat down at the table and began to eat his stew. He took a bite of stew and a bite of his slice of bread. Then he addressed Sammy, "Young man, I told you in my office that you were a very brave boy. Now I'm saying that you are also honest and courageous. I'm proud of you, especially after all you have gone through since yesterday. And you stuck up for your friend, Sister Aggie, when no one else would. That took a lot of guts."

Sammy felt proud of himself that this strong man would say all these nice things about him. "Thank you, sir. Darkman was hurting Aggie Bee. I had to tell you even if it was tattling."

"Well, Sammy, when someone is being hurt by someone else, that is not considered to be tattling. You were protecting her from further harm."

Everyone in the hall had gone back to eating their food. Sammy resumed his meal also. When Aggie Bee had finished hers, she asked Preacher Anton, "Preacher, did ya happen ta get a chance ta look into what we can do 'bout Sammy yet?"

Preacher Anton put down his spoon. "I made a few phone calls. I called the police department, but the chief was not available. I also tried to get in touch with the Mahoning County Children Services downtown, but they were closed today. I'll try the police department again tomorrow. In the meantime, I want the three of you to stay in the church until I get some answers. You'll be safe here. We'll set up some cots in the basement for you to sleep on tonight.

As the men and women in the crowded room finished their meals, they began departing from the church. Preacher Anton and one of his men, Brother Isaiah, directed Aggie Bee, Thin Lizzy, and Sammy back to the basement. Brother Isaiah removed three cots from the storage area and set them up for the trio.

"You should be safe and comfortable here for the night," assured Preacher Anton. "Tomorrow, we'll find some answers about this young man." He glanced down at Sammy. "You get a good night's sleep, Sammy."

Aggie Bee and Thin Lizzy searched through one of the rummage sale boxes for bedding to place on the cots. When they found three sets, they brought them to the cots and began to make the beds. Sammy started spreading a sheet on his cot. "I know how to do this."

Aggie Bee stopped tucking in her sheet. Raising her eyebrows she peered at Sammy. "How you know how ta make a bed, boy?"

He continued to tuck in the corners of the sheet. "Madelina, she's our housekeeper. She showed me how. Mommy was really proud of me when I showed her I could do it. And my bed at home is lots bigger than this bed."

Aggie Bee responded as she finished her cot. "Well, Sammy, I'm proud a you, too."

When their cots were all made up, the three of them retired for the night. It had been a very busy day for all of them, but Sammy was especially tired after his ordeal the night before and all that had happened to him since then. His young mind was excessively filled with what he had experienced. It needed to take a break. He immediately fell asleep after he took his shoes off and rested his head on the pillow.

****

The Blood of Jesus Pentecostal Church locked its doors at eleven every night and opened them at six each morning—as long as someone of authority was on the premises. That evening before leaving the building, Brother Isaiah had locked the doors promptly at eleven with three people sound asleep in the basement.

Around three a.m. Sunday morning, a muffled clatter reverberated from the back of the church. Only the two men climbing through the broken window heard the sound they had made when Mojo used a rock wrapped in a soiled shirt to break the glass. They carefully and quietly got through the opening, brushing shards of glass from their sleeves.

"Where do we go now?" whispered Mojo.

"I dunno," answered Darkman. "We got to look around for dat bitch and dat big-mouth brat. I knowed dey here somewheres."

Without speaking and walking as softly as possible, the two intruders looked throughout the church—the sanctuary, the dining hall, the empty offices. They couldn't access Preacher Anton's office because it was locked. Mojo muttered, "Do ya think they might be in

161

there?"

Darkman held his ear against the door to listen to any sounds. When he straightened up, he replied, "I don't think so. Let's look some other places. If we don't find 'em, we come back and figure how to break in Anton's office. Dat Anton, he somethin' else, ain't he. He think he a preacher man. Ha! He just like you and me. He growed up right down da street from me. Who he think he kiddin'?"

Mojo chuckled, "Yeah, I bet you beat his ass when he was a kid, right?"

"Damn straight 'bout dat, man."

They continued looking throughout the church, checking the sanctuary a second time, searching through all the aisles. "Nobody here. Let's look in da basement. I bet dey dere," suggested Darkman.

They returned to the hall leading to the basement door. Darkman cautiously opened the door. It made a slight swishing noise as it was freed.

The large space below was very dark except for minor light from the streetlights outside filtering through the small, squatty windows located at ground level. The shoddy men grasped` the railing tightly as they tiptoed down the staircase. At the bottom of the stairs, they hesitated so their eyes could adjust to the darkness. After a few seconds, Darkman tapped Mojo on the shoulder and pointed to a cot about ten feet away from them. There on the cot beneath a blanket lay the boy. The men advanced to that cot.

In one swift motion, Mojo bent over the boy and clamped his hand tightly over Sammy's mouth to keep him from making any sound. Darkman grabbed the blanket on top of Sammy and swiftly wrapped it around the boy. Easily lifting him off the cot, he propped him over his shoulder, and he and Mojo sprinted toward the stairs, scurrying up them.

Since Mojo no longer had his hand clasped over Sammy's mouth, Sammy was now wide awake but totally confused. He was tightly wrapped up in something and was unable to move his arms. He began to kick his legs and bellow, "Oh, oh, help! I can't breathe! Help!"

Awakened from sleep, both Aggie Bee and Thin Lizzy immediately perched up on their cots. They too were confused. It was so dark that they were unable to register what was happening. Thin Lizzy finally reacted. "Sammy? Sammy? Where are you?"

By that time, Darkman had reached the top of the stairs, threw open the door, and they were escaping down the hall toward the back entrance of the church.

Aggie Bee heard the opening of the basement door. Her eyes searched for the source of the noise, and with the dim hallway light above shining through the opening, she was able to ascertain two large figures rushing out98 the doorway, one carrying a bundle on his shoulder. She jumped off her cot and yelled to Thin Lizzy, "Dey got da boy. Let's go!"

She and Thin Lizzy hurriedly slipped on their shoes, found their way to the unlit staircase, and darted up them. In the hallway, they saw the two dark figures leaving the church through the back door. They hurried after them. By the time they got to the door, opened it, and looked around the parking lot, they saw no one.

The culprits were gone. And so was Sammy.

## Chapter Twenty-Three

*Wednesday afternoon, 2 days before the fire.*

Ryan Nesbitt woke up for the second time since the accident and found Melanie still by his bedside.

"Mel?" he moaned.

From her seat on the visitor chair, Melanie jerked upright. "Ryan! You're awake. Oh, baby. I was so scared. I thought you were gonna die."

Gazing around the room, Ryan pondered, "Wha-what time is it?"

Melanie took her phone out of her pocket. "It's three-twenty. Aren't you hungry? You haven't had anything to eat all day."

"Uh, I gu-guess so."

"Some lady was in here this morning, asking what you wanted to eat. Your mom ordered stuff for you, but then you fell back to sleep. They took the food back after a while. Do you want me to get them to bring you up something?"

"Uh, I g-g-guess so."

"Okay." She came around the bed, grabbed the remote devise hooked to the safety rail, and pressed the nutrition number. "I'm calling for Ryan Nesbitt in Room 6014. Can you send up his lunch?" There was a pause. "Thank you." She replaced the remote and went back to her seat.

"Where's my mom?" Ryan asked.

"Oh, after you woke up the first time, and she saw you were okay, she left. She said she'd be back later."

"You're still here?"

"Yes."

"How come you didn't leave?"

"I don't know. I guess I'm still worried about you."

He was silent for a while. Then unexpectedly, he asked, "Why did you say this morning that you were sorry, and this was all your fault? What are you sorry about? You didn't make me crash my car. How could that be your fault?"

Melanie head jerked toward him. "Did I say that this morning? I don't remember."

"Yes. Yes, you did. That was sort of odd."

"I-I don't remember. If I said it, I don't remember why. All I know is that I'm so glad you didn't die. I really don't think I could live without you now. I mean it, Ryan. I really love you." She got out of her seat kissed him gently on the lips, cautiously hugging him.

He smiled. "I love you too, sweetheart. I'm glad I didn't die too."

Her face showed a knowing grin as she lightly tapped his arm. "Oh, you! Always joking. Of course, you're glad you didn't die."

They both chuckled, even though it hurt him to do so.

A nurse pushed the curtain open and entered Ryan's room. "Mr. Nesbitt, you're awake. Good to see you smiling. How are you feeling?" She began to check his vitals on the machines.

Ryan dolefully responded, "Not so good. Every bone in my body aches."

"No surprise there. You broke several of those

bones."

"When am I gonna be able to go home?"

"You'll have to talk to the doctor about that. He was in earlier, but you were sleeping. He'll be back tomorrow morning, but I'm sure you'll be in here at least a few more days. Then you're going to need physical therapy. So you'll be out of commission for several weeks."

"Oh. Will my arm and leg be normal after the physical therapy?"

"That's a question for the doctor. The orthopedic specialist will also be in to see you tomorrow. You can talk to him about that."

After the nurse finished her chores and left the room, Ryan shook his head, "Damn! I can't believe this."

"What do you mean?" asked Melanie.

"I-I don't understand. I-I was on the freeway, just driving to my apartment after work. Remember? We were gonna meet for dinner. Then all of a sudden, this black SUV starts tailing and harassing me. I tried to get away from it, but it was impossible in all that heavy traffic. So I did the only thing I could've done if I didn't want to ram into other cars on the road. I went onto the shoulder and hit the barrier abutment." He frowned. "I didn't know what else to do. And now look where I am." He focused his eyes on Melanie. "I didn't know what else to do, babe." Tears welled up in his eyes. "I didn't want to crash into any of the other cars."

Melanie moved closer, firmly but gently clasping his hand. "Oh, Ryan, it wasn't your fault. You didn't have a choice. You probably saved the lives of other people. I'm just so glad you're gonna be okay. I love you so much." She too began to cry.

He removed his hand from hers and swiped his

knuckle across his eyes to dry the moisture before it trickled down his cheeks. "Mel, I need to tell you something."

Melanie straighten her body in the chair to prepare herself for what seemed like some secretive, ominous knowledge or confession about to be revealed. Her question was caught in her throat. "What, Ryan?" She barely was able to release her words as the perspiration accumulated on the back of her neck.

"I-I probably should've told you this before, but I didn't want to worry you."

"Go on. What?"

"A black SUV has been following me for a couple of weeks now, but it never threatened me like it did yesterday. It just stayed a few cars behind me, but I knew it was following me. I told my boss about it, and he just said to keep an eye on it and let him know if I could get the plate number or see who was driving. Well, it never got close enough for that. And yesterday... Well, I just needed to get away from it because I knew I was in big trouble."

She let out a huge breath. "Oh, oh, Ryan. You should have told me."

"I didn't want to worry you. I thought they would eventually stop following me or maybe confront me somehow." He scoffed disdainfully, "But I sure didn't think they were gonna run me off the road."

She again reached over and gently hugged him.

As she was sitting back on her chair, a young woman came into the room, carrying Ryan's tray of food. "Mr. Nesbitt, here's your lunch. I hope you enjoy it." She put the tray on the over-bed table and exited the room.

Melanie stood up. "Hey babe, I have a couple of

errands to run. Do you mind if I take off while you eat? I'll be back in about an hour or so."

Ryan took the lid off his steamy plastic plate and glanced down at a thin, crusty slab of meat and gooey, watery macaroni and cheese. "Sure, hon. Take your time. I think I'm gonna take a nap after I choke this stuff down." He wrinkled his nose as he reached for the fork with his left hand. Eating was going to be a challenge.

Melanie kissed him on the cheek. "Okay, I'll be back soon." Before she walked out the door, she turned and added, "Oh, by the way, while you were sleeping, I called your office and told them about your accident. They were worried and wondered why you didn't go in to work this morning. The receptionist said she had tried to call you several times. She also said she'd tell your bosses what happened and what your room number is."

"Oh, thanks, hon. I didn't even think about letting them know."

"No problem. Love you." And she was gone.

Ryan, being right-handed, tried his best to eat the bland food using his left hand. After a few bites, he gave up and went back to sleep.

He was dozing off when he heard the rustle of the curtain around the bed. He opened his eyes to see Sam Nagy, standing nearby. Sam gasped. "Oh, my God, Ryan! How did this happen? Chloe said Melanie called to say you had been in a bad accident. She didn't go into many details. I'm sorry I didn't get here any sooner, but I came as soon as I could."

Ryan flinched. "Sam, I-I think somebody's trying to kill me."

"What? I thought it was a car accident."

"Well, it sort of was, but…"

As Ryan explained the details of his traumatic experience, Sam listened intently, his face showing no emotion. When Ryan had completed the recounting of his accident, Sam took a deep breath and sat on the chair next to Ryan's bed. He didn't speak immediately, but when he did, his voice had a worrying sound to it. "This has got to be the work of Banetti's men."

Ryan disclosed, "That's exactly what I thought. But why? Why would the man want to hurt me? I've done nothing to him. I've kept everything about him and his business a secret from everybody."

Sam reminded, "I didn't want to bring this up, but that's not entirely true, Ryan."

"What do you mean?"

"Remember what you revealed to me in my office a couple weeks ago?"

"You're talking about Melanie and what I said to her? But I didn't mention any names at all. There is no way she would know anything about..." He stopped short of mentioning Banetti's name to Sam, Then he said, "You know who. No way."

Sam shook his head. "Something isn't right about this entire situation." He paused. "I believe you, Ryan. I do. And that's what's so confusing. This had to be *his* men." He paused again. There's something else, too."

"What do you mean," asked Ryan.

"Well, I haven't had a chance to talk to you about this, but the DOJ visited him at his house the other day."

"The feds? Oh, my God! What do they know?"

"They know something. I'm not sure what and how much. They didn't tell us much. I think they're just testing the waters right now, searching and asking questions, but I bet it won't be long before they take some kind of action."

"Do you think they'll come after us?"

"Possibly… Yes, possibly." Another pause. "But for damn sure your accident isn't the work of the DOJ or the FBI. They can be unscrupulous, but they would have no reason to hurt you physically in any way."

Sam stood. "I have to get back to the office." He looked at his watch. "I'm seeing a client in a half hour. I'm not sure what we're gonna do about this. I'm gonna have a serious talk with Carl." He lightly patted Ryan's arm. "Is there anything you need? Anything I can get you?"

Ryan frowned, "No, Mel will be back later if I need anything. I'm kinda tired now anyhow. But, if you figure any of this out, Sam, will you let me know?"

"Sure, kid, I will."

Chapter Twenty-Four

*Early Sunday morning, after the fire.*
When Aggie Bee and Thin Lizzy discovered someone had taken the boy, they were at a loss what to do. Aggie Bee was fairly certain that Darkman and Mojo were those obscure figures she'd seen carrying Sammy out the back entrance of the church. Who else would do a terrible thing like that? Those men were pure evil, and Aggie Bee didn't want to even think what they planned to do to the boy. She had to get help—and fast.

While looking out the back door of the church and seeing no sign of the kidnappers, Thin Lizzy shrieked, "Dey're gone. What are we gonna do? Dey'll hurt Sammy. I know it."

"Take it easy, Thin Lizzy. We'll think a somethin'." Aggie Bee took a deep breath. "Dere's a telephone in da kitchen and a list on da wall with some important phone numbers. Preacher Anton's number is dere, I'm sure. We'll call him."

"Will he be mad at us for wakin' him up?"

"I don't know. I don't think so. Dis is real important. We got to get help."

In the kitchen, Aggie Bee turned on the overhead lights. The phone was attached to the wall next to the serving window. A list of telephone numbers in a plastic sleeve was tacked beside the phone. She looked up the number for Preacher Anton's cellphone, lifted the receiver, and punched in Preacher Anton's number.

After several rings, a gruff, sleepy voice answered, *"Uh, uh, Preacher Anton Morris here."*

"Preacher Anton, dis is Aggie Bee at da church."

*"Uh, Aggie Bee, it's three fifteen in the morning."*

"I know Preacher Anton, but we got an emergency here. Two men broke into da church, came down da basement, and stole dat li'l boy, Sammy. We don't know what ta do."

Preacher Anton was now fully awake. *"What? They took the boy? Do you know who the men were?"*

"I ain't positive but I'm purty dang sure it was dose good-for-nuttin's Darkman and Mojo."

*"Hmm."* The line was quiet for a few seconds. *"I'll be there in twenty minutes, and Aggie Bee?"*

"Yes, sir?"

*"The phone number for the police is on the list next to the phone in the kitchen. Call them and tell them what happened."*

"Yes, sir."

Aggie Bee hung up the phone, looked on the phone list again for the local police, and punched in their number.

*"Youngstown Police Department."*

"Hello, my name is Agnes Washington. I'm at da Blood a Jesus Pentecostal Church on Rayen Avenue. A li'l boy name Sammy was kidnapped."

*"Do you know who kidnapped the boy?"*

"I think I do, but I ain't positive."

*"I'll send an officer there immediately. He should be there in fifteen minutes."*

"Thank you, ma'am."

After Aggie Bee got off the phone, she turned to

Thin Lizzy. "Let's go unlock da front door and turn some lights on. Da police'll be here in a coupla minutes."

They hurried to the front of the church where Aggie Bee unbolted the lock on the door. The two women waited impatiently for the officer's arrival. They barely spoke to each other as they paced back and forth in the narthex of the church. Every time Aggie Bee passed the door, she opened it to see if the police officer had arrived yet. Finally, she saw the police car park in front of the church. She opened the door wide, holding it open with her body while the officer exited his vehicle and walked up the church stairs.

"Oh, thank you, thank you fer comin', officer. Preacher Anton is on da way. Please come in da church."

Inside, the officer gave the women a strange look before introducing himself. "I'm Officer Jerry Llewelyn." He was dressed in a white shirt and navy-blue pants with a gun and belt attached at his waist. He removed a small tablet and pen from his shirt pocket. "Please give me your names."

"I'm Agnes Washington, and dis is my friend, huh…"

Thin Lizzy interrupted, "Elizabeth Thorpe."

"Uh, okay, ladies, first of all, do you have permission to be in this church at this time of night?"

Immediately, Aggie Bee answered, "Oh, yes sir, yes sir. Preacher Anton tole us we could stay here tonight. He be here soon. You can aks him for yerself."

The officer looked from one woman to the next. "Uh, okay. I'll take your word for it until I speak to this Preacher Anton. For now, who can tell me what happened here?"

Knowing Thin Lizzy did not do well speaking to

strangers, especially those in authority, Aggie Bee initiated, "Officer, dis li'l boy named Sammy was kidnapped about a half hour ago. We was all three sleepin' in da basement when two big guys came and grabbed him off his cot. Dey bundled him in his blanket and took him out da back door. We woke up and tried ta catch 'em, but dey was gone when we looked out da door."

"Do you know how they got into the church?"

"Yes, dey broke a window in da back."

The officer suggested, "Tell me about Sammy. Is he your son?"

"Uh, no, officer. Lemme esplain." Aggie Bee did her best to tell the officer a quick version of how Thin Lizzy had found Sammy and how they had ended up at the church.

Officer Llewelyn listened intently to Aggie Bee's explanation, then he concluded, "Hmm, ladies, I need to make a phone call." He took out his phone and immediately called police headquarters. "This is Officer Jerry Llewellyn calling in from the Blood of Jesus Pentecostal Church. I think I have a lead on that boy who's been missing since Friday night. Send reinforcements right away and get in touch with the detectives who've been on the case. Tell them we may have a break."

Aggie Bee and Thin Lizzy stood transfixed as they listened to the officer's phone conversation. The faces of both the women turned to frozen masks of surprise. This policeman knew about Sammy. He probably knew where he came from and where he belonged. Thin Lizzy felt a slight burden lifted from her. At last, she was going to have some help. But hopefully, because of Darkman, it wasn't too late for Sammy.

The officer hung up his phone and addressed the women, "A couple of detectives have been working on a case involving a missing five-year-old named Sammy. I'm thinking maybe your Sammy could be that missing boy. The police and the community have been searching for him ever since it was discovered that he was missing." He hesitated. "Now while we wait, let's go to the back door, so I can take a look at the window where the kidnappers came into the church."

Aggie Bee led the way to the back of the church. Officer Llewelyn walked over to the broken window. He removed a pair of latex gloves from his trouser pocket and put them on his hands. From his other pants pocket he took out a small flashlight. Shining the light on the window, he examined it thoroughly. The women saw him take a small piece of dark plaid material off a section of the broken window. Removing a small plastic bag from his pocket, he placed the fabric into it. Then he walked over to the door, opened it up, and stepped outside. The women saw him walk around the back of the church for a couple of minutes. Then he got on his cellphone again and talked to someone.

When he came back to the doorway, he said to the women, "The detectives in charge of this case will be here in about forty-five minutes. Let's go back inside and you can tell me about the men you think kidnapped the boy."

**\*\*\*\***

When Aggie Bee, Thin Lizzy, and Officer Llewelyn got back to the sanctuary, they sat in the back pew discussing the chain of events of the kidnapping in more detail. He also quizzed them about how Sammy came to be in their protection.

Preacher Anton arrived and heard voices coming from the church sanctuary, walking back to see the ladies and a police officer in deep conversation. They stood as Preacher Anton approached. He held out his hand to the police officer. "Officer, I'm Preacher Anton Morris. I'm in charge of this church. Do we know what has happened to the boy?"

Officer Llewelyn arose and shook his hand. "Sir, I'm Officer Jerry Llewelyn. I've called in two detectives who are working on a case involving a boy who has been missing since late Friday night. I expect them here within the hour. Maybe this boy who was kidnapped is the boy who is the object of this citywide search. We've had over two hundred volunteers searching for him, all coordinated and paid for by his grandmother. She's also got flyers posted throughout the city. This is the first positive lead we've had on his possible whereabouts."

Hearing this news about a grandmother, Thin Lizzy thought about Sammy. He has a grandmother. Somebody will love him if his mom and dad aren't alive. That revelation helped put her mind at ease.

Then Officer Llewelyn motioned toward the women. "These women have told me about the two men they suspect took the boy while they slept." He looked down at his notebook. "Uh, a man they call Darkman and one they said is Mojo. They didn't know their real names. Can you tell me anything about these men?"

Preacher Anton slowly shook his head. "Those men are two bad dudes, especially Darkman. In fact, we had what you might call a serious difference of opinion with him and his crony last evening in the dining area. He was harassing these ladies and the boy, and I had the two men removed from the church."

"Do these men often come to functions at the church?"

"Not at all. In fact, I was surprised to see them here. I think they were trying to sneak a free meal. You see, yesterday, several from the homeless community were helping to give the church a good cleaning, and we offered free meals as well as some cash to those who worked. Darkman and Mojo tried to get in on the free food part, but when they caused the disturbance, I couldn't let them stay."

"Do you happen to know their real names?"

"I only know their reputation but not their names."

"Do you have any idea where they might be found?"

"That I don't know either. It could be anywhere around town."

Aggie Bee interrupted, "Sometimes I sees 'em hangin' out on Market Street. Dere's some boarded-up buildin's around dere. Maybe dey took Sammy dere."

Officer Llewelyn nodded his head. "Let me call headquarters and send some men to that area. Ma'am, is that the lower part of Market Street near downtown?"

"Yes, sir."

The officer went into the narthex to make his call. Preacher Anton looked at the women. "This has been a terrible experience for you. How are you ladies holding up?"

Aggie Bee fretted, "Oh, Preacher Anton, we so worried 'bout poor li'l Sammy. Dose men are so mean. We afraid dey gonna hurt him."

"I'm concerned too. At least the police are on it now. We'll just have to hold tight and hope they find him soon."

A heavy knock on the front door caught everyone's attention, and the door suddenly opened. A tall, heavyset man in navy pants and a gray button-down shirt entered with a woman who barely came up to his shoulders and wearing loose fitting jeans and a thin, pale-yellow sweater. They walked directly into the sanctuary.

Officer Llewellyn introduced them. "These are Detectives Will Hamilton and Stacey Atkinson. They've been trying to find Sammy since Friday night." He motioned toward Preacher Anton. "This is Preacher Anton Morris. He's in charge of the church. I'll let him introduce the ladies."

Preacher Anton spoke, "This is Agnes Washington and Elizabeth Thorpe. Elizabeth is the woman who found the boy late Friday night. I'll let her tell her story."

"Let's wait on that," Detective Hamilton said. "Our concern now is finding the boy as soon as possible. We can go over all the details after he is rescued and is safe." He looked around the area where everyone was sitting. "Now, is there a more convenient place where we can talk?"

"Come with me." Preacher Anton led them to a large room with a long, battered wood table in the middle and an array of chairs in various degree of wear and tear surrounding it. Everyone took a seat except the two detectives.

Detective Hamilton began, "Now, who can tell me about the kidnapping."

Aggie Bee glanced around the room at everyone and then raised her hand. "Uh, sir, uh, detective? I guess I'll tell ya what happened. It started in da kitchen when me and Thin Lizzy and Sammy were eatin' our stew, and—"

"Hold it! Who is Thin Lizzy?"

"Oh, sorry sir" She pointed to Thin Lizzy sitting next to her. "Dat's what we calls her. Uh, I guess her name be Elizabeth."

"Okay," Detective Hamilton said. "You can continue."

"Well, as I was a-sayin', we was eatin' our stew when Darkman and Mojo comes in and sits across from us and starts—"

"Hold it! Who are Darkman and Mojo?"

"Oh, oh, sorry again sir. Dey be da guys I tink took Sammy."

"Uh, okay, I'll try not to interrupt you again, Ms. Washington."

"Well, we was eatin' our stew and Darkman started harrassin' us. Den, he grabs my wrist and is twistin' it and hurtin' me. Den Preacher Anton comes in da dinin' room and Darkman stops, and Sammy tells Preacher Anton what happened. Preacher Anton makes Darkman and Mojo leave, but when he walk out da door, Darkman say he gonna get us."

Hamilton asked, "So did he come back later or what?"

"Well, Preacher Anton, he let us sleep in da basement last night, me, Thin Lizzy, and Sammy. In da middle of da night, I tink dey comes back and takes Sammy from his cot. I sees two dark shapes goin' up da steps and out da door. One of dem have a bundle over his shoulders. I hear Sammy screamin' for help. I tink he is in da bundle. Thin Lizzy and me, we hurry after dem, but by da time we gets up da stairs dey be gone. Dey go out da back door. We look but we don't see 'em nowheres. So's we den calls Preacher Anton who tole us ta call da poo-leece. So's dat's what we did."

Detective Atkinson had been taking notes on Aggie Bee's statement. She then asked, "How did the men get in the church? Was it locked?"

"Yes, ma'am. Preacher Anton, he make sure every door be locked at eleven o'clock. Dey breaks da window in da back of da church and climbs through it."

Detective Hamilton turned to Officer Llewelyn, "Officer, did you check out the point of entry."

"Yes, I did." He arose from his seat. "Would you like to take a look?"

"Yes, I would. How about if all of you remain here while Detective Atkinson and I check this out? We'll continue when we come back."

The three police officers left the conference room. On their way to the broken window, Officer Llewelyn removed a plastic bag from his pocket. "This is a piece of clothing that was caught on one of the sharp points of glass on the broken window."

Detective Atkinson took it from Llewelyn, looking at it intently. "Hmm, this may prove an important piece of evidence. Good work, Llewelyn."

The two detectives took pictures of the window. They walked outside and looked around the area. When they came back into the church, Hamilton said, "We'll have the crime scene crew come out to look for further evidence. I have doubts they'll find much. As for fingerprints on the doorknob, there are probably several prints on it, but who knows if any belong to the kidnappers?"

Atkinson got on her phone and contacted headquarters to get the crime scene inspectors on the premise. Then the three officers returned to the conference room. Detective Hamilton spoke to everyone, "I'm gonna ask all of you to go to police headquarters to make formal statements." He addressed Thin Lizzy, "Ms. Thorpe, the detective will ask you to tell her how you found Sammy Nagy. Will you be able to do that?"

Thin Lizzy, who had been nervously wringing her hands, looked up. "Yes, sir."

Officer Llewelyn drove Aggie Bee and Thin Lizzy to headquarters in his police vehicle. Preacher Anton took the church van in which he had driven to the church earlier. Each person was placed in a separate small interrogation room to tell their account of the kidnapping. Preacher Anton repeated to the detective questioning him the disagreement with Darkman in the dining area last evening. Then he mentioned the phone call in the early hours from Aggie Bee and his immediate departure for the church.

As for Aggie Bee, she talked about her friendship with Thin Lizzy. Then she told of her complete surprise when Thin Lizzy arrived at the church during choir practice with a small boy beside her. She told how Sammy looked when she saw him, soiled pajamas, no shoes, bulky men's socks covering his injured feet and a large part of both legs. She described the clothing they had collected for him that he was wearing when he was captured. She also talked about how the boy and Thin Lizzy helped to clean the church pews. She then got around to talking about the confrontation in the dining area, Darkman's attitude, his painful grasp on her wrist, and his eviction from the church by Preacher Anton. Lastly, she told of the actual kidnapping of Sammy while they were sleeping in the basement.

The detective taking her statement asked several questions about Darkman and Mojo. She told them all she knew about them, which was very little other than how mean and cruel they were. When the woman detective asked her if she had any idea where the men might have taken Sammy, she again mentioned the abandoned buildings on Market Street.

While Aggie Bee was relaying her account of the kidnapping to one detective, Thin Lizzy was in another room telling another detective, Detective Rose Kemp, the full version of her connection with Sammy, starting with the moment she saw him standing in the middle of the street in the dead of night with that huge black SUV barreling toward him. For fear of some type of retribution and punishment, she left no details out of her narrative. During her lifetime, her perception of the law had not always been positive, and her level of fear always soared when she was around them.

Since the incident that had happened years ago, Thin Lizzy's communication skills had been compromised. Sometimes she had a difficult time conveying her thoughts and experiences. But she knew this was extremely important in helping the police find Sammy. She had to put her distress and trepidation aside and tell this detective everything she knew in the best way that she could. It was slow at first, but the detective was very kind and patient. She didn't try to rush Thin Lizzy but gave her time and encouragement throughout the recitation.

It took almost two hours for the entire interview. Both Detective Kemp and Thin Lizzy were exhausted afterward. Upon the completion of the interview, the detective said, "Ms. Thorpe, I think you deserve a big cup of steaming coffee and one of those glazed donuts waiting for you in the break room." As they walked out to the reception area where Preacher Anton and Aggie Bee were still discussing their experiences with other detectives, Detective Kemp announced, "In the break room, coffee and donuts for everyone."

## Chapter Twenty-Five

*Wednesday, late afternoon, 2 days before the fire.*

Rocco Banetti was about to leave his office. He had sent Louise home early. She had a baby shower to attend for her expectant granddaughter, who was due on Halloween. As he got up from his chair and was reaching for his jacket, Benny, his security chief, entered the office. Banetti sat back down on his chair. "Well? What's the news?"

Benny sat at one of the chairs in front of Banetti's orderly desk. "One broken arm; one broken leg; a concussion, some internal injuries including a bruised kidney."

"So he's gonna live?"

Benny nodded.

"Good." He leaned back on his chair. "So he went off the highway all on his own then?"

"Yep, it appears that way. A lot of traffic. He didn't have much choice."

"Good."

Banetti leaned forward with his elbows on the desk. "And the squad?"

"Long gone before the cops or paramedics showed up."

"Good."

"Any eyewitnesses?"

"None coming forward so far."

"Good."

After a pause, Banetti leaned back on his chair. "Nice work, Benny. Very nice work."

\*\*\*\*

Melanie Carlini left the hospital with her emotions on a roller-coaster. When she originally agreed to this covert assignment from her Uncle Rocky, she never imagined it would go this far—or in the direction it took. First of all, she never thought she'd develop such deep feelings for Ryan, nor did she believe they'd actually fall in love.

Sure, she reported back to her uncle on what Ryan had told her, but never in her wildest dreams did she expect harm to come to Ryan. A serious car accident! What the hell! He could have been killed! Was that the plan from the beginning? And that was why she was so confused.

If this was just a game, like she and Uncle Rocky had discussed, what was he keeping from her? Nobody was supposed to get hurt. Maybe it truly was just an accident. Maybe Ryan just got unlucky and was driving with a bunch of crazy other drivers on the road. Maybe... But she had to talk to her uncle—just to be sure.

The building was locked when she arrived at REB Enterprises, but she could see lights on in her uncle's third floor office. She took out her phone and called him. "Uncle Rocky, it's me. Can you let me in? I have to talk to you."

He told her he'd be right down. She stood outside the door, pacing back and forth and wiping her tears away. When he opened the door, she rushed past him into the lobby. "Why! Why, Uncle Rocky! You said you wouldn't hurt him. You said it was just a game!"

He grabbed her shoulders. "Calm down, sweetheart. Calm down." He put his arm around her and led her over to a long, sleek couch on the side of the reception area. "He's gonna be okay. Nothing serious or life-threatening. You have nothing to worry about. He'll just be laid up for a couple of weeks. That's all."

She pulled away from him and stared at him in horror. "Nothing serious? Are you crazy? He could've been killed. You said you wouldn't hurt him."

Banetti's face turned to stone. "I never said I wouldn't hurt him." Then his gaze softened again. "Look, sweetheart, he went too far. If he talks to you about me and my businesses, who knows who else he told about my affairs. This Ryan kid can't be trusted. He knows too much and that makes me nervous and him dangerous."

"But he'd never talk to anybody else about you. Just me. He promised. Besides, as much as I goaded him about it so many times, he never even whispered your name. Never."

Banetti snickered, "Baby, you can't believe that he never talked to anyone else. I definitely don't believe that. He's a snake. I can't trust him. Don't be naïve. Eventually, he would've told you everything." He hesitated, wondering if he should say more. He decided to clue her in on the seriousness of the situation. "You know who visited me the other day?"

While wiping away her tears with her knuckle, she looked up at him. "Who?"

"The DOJ, the Department of Justice. Now, don't you think it's strange that they'd be coming around asking me questions not long after he started spilling his guts to you?" He shook his head. "It's no coincidence,

Mel. Believe me."

Melanie's eyes opened wide. "Oh, shit, Uncle Rocky. I didn't know."

"Of course, you didn't. And I wouldn't have mentioned it to you, but you need to know the seriousness of what's going on here. I can't allow my own attorneys to try to ruin me, can I?"

She was calmer now. "B-but you won't hurt him anymore, right?"

Banetti slightly raised his head and tightly clamped his jaw. "I hope I don't have to, sweetheart. I hope I don't have to."

Both were quiet for a while. Then Banetti arose from the couch. "Let me buy you dinner, now, kiddo."

She finished drying her eyes with a crumpled tissue she withdrew from her jean pocket. "No, I have to get back to the hospital now. I promised Ryan I'd be right back."

He offered his hand, pulled her up from the couch, and put his arm around her narrow shoulders. "You know, you have a dilemma here."

Narrowing her eyes, she tilted her head to look at him. "What do you mean? What kind of dilemma?"

They walked toward the exit door. He opened it, and gently pushed her out ahead of himself. "He doesn't know about me. If you're that serious about this dude, what's gonna happen when you tell him I'm your uncle?"

She abruptly stopped and turned to him. "I don't know."

## Chapter Twenty-Six

*Very early Sunday morning, after the abduction.*

Sammy Nagy was scared. Real scared. Every part of his body trembled, and his heart boomed against his chest. He struggled to think about all that had happened since the two scary men burst into his house. Then the gunshots. Then the fire. Then his nomadic escape, not knowing where to go and what would happen to him. Then Thin Lizzy.

At first, she was so scary, but he soon realized she was actually kind and willing to help him. If it hadn't been for her… Well, he didn't want to think about that. Then he met Aggie Bee and Preacher Anton. They were nice to him too, giving him new clothes, food, and a little bed to sleep on. He thought he'd finally be safe, and soon he'd be able to go home. Yet deep down, he knew he couldn't go back to his real home. And he was afraid for his mother and father. What had happened to them? He wouldn't think about that either.

Just when he thought he was going to be okay and would be safe again somehow, those two men—Darkman and Mojo—suddenly appeared. Thin Lizzy had warned him they were mean and nasty. She tried to stay away from them, but they came right into the church. They sat directly across from him and made him very nervous. Then Darkman hurt Aggie Bee, but nobody would tell Preacher Anton what was wrong. So he had to tell him. He thought when the preacher made those men leave that he would never, ever see them again. He was sleeping so peacefully on that little bed in the basement when, *whoosh*, somebody wrapped him in that itchy blanket. He screamed for help as loud as he could. Then he felt he was being tossed into the air like a ball before being dumped onto someone's big shoulders. Then an awful smell filled his nose and he really had trouble breathing. After that, he thought he might vomit.

He felt himself being carried and bounced up the stairs while he screamed for help. After a few seconds, he thought they took him outside, because then he felt the cool, night air ooze through the blanket wrapped around him. Within a couple of seconds, he thought he was plopped into some type of cage. He wiggled and squirmed, trying to free himself of the itchy blanket, but the more he struggled, the more tangled up he became.

Apparently, the cage he was in must've had wheels because it began to move. His body bounced and jostled up and down, feeling like his arms and head were bumping up against a wire fence, like the one around his school playground. Up and down, up and down—on and on, forever and ever.

When it seemed like the bumping would never stop, it got worse. It then felt like the cage he was in was thrown and bounced down a bunch of stairs. Bump! Bump! Bump! After coasting a little, everything stopped. Through the blanket, he heard these voices, but he couldn't understand what they were saying. Then somebody grabbed him and lifted him out of the cage and dropped him down on something hard and cold. Big hands stopped him from moving, and then somebody took off the blanket around him.

At last, his arms and legs were free, but wherever he was seemed to still be as dark as inside that blanket. In the darkness, he could make out two shadowy shapes standing near him. He tried to get to his feet, but the big hands pushed him down again. "You sit still, boy."

Not wanting them to hurt him again, he obeyed, putting his body against a damp wall behind him with his legs out in front. Then somebody twisted his body and grabbed both of his hands, pulling them behind him. What he guessed was a skinny rope was wrapped around his wrists. His arms were pulled some more, touching something cold and hard. Within a few seconds, they tied his arms to something, and he couldn't move them. Then they grabbed his feet and wrapped the same skinny rope around his legs.

"So how ya like that, snotty brat. You ain't gonna cause me no more trouble now, are ya?"

Sammy was left all alone in a cold, dark silent space.

Chapter Twenty-Seven

*Sunday morning, the search.*

Detectives Hamilton and Atkinson waited for the crime scene team to show up at the Blood of Jesus Pentecostal Church. After explaining to the crew what had transpired on the scene, the detectives left them to their work. Atkinson drove them to Market Street on the lower south side to join the SWAT team in their search for the two men suspected of kidnapping Sammy Nagy. Since it was early Sunday morning, this part of Youngstown was nearly deserted except for the accumulating presence of police vehicles gathering on the scene.

Atkinson pulled her police cruiser into a parking lot next to an abandoned building where the SWAT van and several other police vehicles were located. The two detectives exited their cruiser and approached Russell Tedesco, captain of the SWAT team.

Detective Hamilton asked, "Any luck yet, Russ?"

"Naw, we've covered a couple of blocks. Came up with a couple of drug busts, but no luck finding the kid or the perps who took him. But we haven't covered the entire area yet. My men are being as discreet as possible, so we don't wake anybody and spook the kidnappers into running or hurting the kid."

"Anything we can do to help?"

"Yeah, sure. We can always use some extra hands.

My team is concentrating on the east side of the street. You two can start on the west side."

"Glad to help," replied Hamilton, as he and Atkinson took off toward an abandoned building on the opposite side of the street.

The two detectives didn't draw their guns, but they treaded cautiously and silently as they approached the boarded-up building. They ventured around to the back of the structure, eyes roaming and searching behind every large, abandoned object on the way. When they reached the rear of the building, Atkinson tried the back door. It was locked. A high window next to the door was broken, leaving a gaping hole. Atkinson saw a discarded, ratty office chair nearby. She pulled it over to the window. With Hamilton's help to balance her, she climbed on the chair to reach the window.

Removing her gun from its holster, she used it to knock out the remaining glass on the edges of the window to allow her an unencumbered entry into the building. Struggling through the narrow opening, she carefully dropped down onto the cement floor inside, went over to the back door, and unlocked it to allow Hamilton's entry into the building. The two of them searched the abandoned structure from top to bottom, finding no child or any other humans—plenty of rodents, trash, and drug paraphernalia, but no kid.

They left that structure, Atkinson locking the door and also making a note to get somebody from maintenance there to board up the broken window and went on to the next building.

For the next few hours, they unsuccessfully joined the search in that area for Sammy Nagy. Several arrests were made for unlawful entry and drug possession, but no Sammy.

When they met back with Captain Tedesco, Hamilton questioned, "What now? Where do we go from here?"

Captain Tedesco shook his head. "Well, as far as we know from the information I received from headquarters, the two men we're looking for have no means of transportation. So wherever they are, they have to be on foot, meaning they can't be too far from downtown. We're gonna spread out and look at some of the other areas where we might find them. You guys wanna still help in the hunt?"

"Yeah, sure," answered Hamilton. "We've been on this case from the beginning. We have a stake in finding these two scumbags and especially the kid. Where do you suggest we go?"

Tedesco looked around at his crew. "I'm gonna send my guys to the lower north side, near the church. Maybe the perps stayed in that area. How about you two taking on the lower part of Mahoning Avenue. There's a lot of places to hide a kid around there."

"Sounds like a plan," said Hamilton. We'll start near the Mahoning Avenue Bridge."

The two detectives got in their vehicle and made their way to their new search destination.

Chapter Twenty-Eight

*Sunday morning, the search continues.*

Patricia Karis, mother of Alyssa Nagy, was dozing on her living room sofa when the cellphone on the end table beside her rang. The loud, unexpected sound immediately brought her to a sitting position and wide awake. She had given up trying to sleep in her king-size bed in her chic bedroom. Just like her body, her mind had tossed and turned all night. Her daughter was dead. Yes, they had been estranged for so long. But dead? No, that was impossible to accept. But accept she must.

Then, of course, her thoughts always went to her poor grandson. Where was he? How was he? So many times over the years she had tried to beg Alyssa to let her back into their lives. But that door was slammed in her face every time. Never picking up her phone when she saw her mother's number. Hanging up the phone immediately if Pat called from someone else's phone. Never answering any of her letters. Never opening the door the times she tried to physically visit at their house. Yet Pat still blamed herself for not doing something, *anything,* to force a relationship with her daughter and ultimately, the grandson she had never even seen. And now it was too late to ever connect with Alyssa, and her grandson could be in grave danger.

She answered the ringing phone. "This is Pat Karis."

*"Mrs. Karis, this is Chief Rutherford. Uh, I have*

*some information on your grandson."*

"Oh, oh, has he been found? Is he okay? When can I see him? I—"

*"Hold on, hold on, Mrs. Karis. Let me explain."*

Her heart dropped to her feet. No, he couldn't be dead. No! "What is it, chief? What happened?"

*"It appears your grandson was found by a street woman near the main library north of downtown. He—"*

"Oh thank God, thank God. When can I see him?"

*"Let me finish, Mrs. Karis. The boy was found late Friday night and was kept safe until early this morning. However, it appears that in the middle of the night, two men actually came into where he was staying with two street ladies, and they kidnapped him. We have a manhunt searching to—"*

"Oh God, no! That poor little guy! What can I do? Do you know who took him? Can my family help find him?"

*"Slow down, ma'am. Calm down. We have every available officer hunting for the boy and his captors. At this point, there is nothing you can do. I did, however, want to inform you of what has happened so far. I have confidence that we will find the boy and the men suspected of taking him. We have a good description of them and know their general habitat and lifestyle. I will keep you posted of any further developments, but that's all I can tell you at this time."*

"Captain Rutherford, please, I'm coming down to the police station. I want to be there when they find my grandson. I too have confidence in your police force, but I have to be there for the boy."

*"That's fine, Mrs. Karis. I think that would be wise. Whenever the boy is found, they will bring him straight-*

*away here. And having his grandmother nearby may help ease his trauma and confusion."*

Pat Karis wasn't so sure if she would be able to put the boy at ease. After all, she was a perfect stranger to him. But she planned to change that. With the murder of his parents, he had no one. No one to care for him. Nowhere to live. She had to show the boy that she was there for him as long as he needed her. She would convince him that she loved him even though they had never actually met.

As soon as the conversation with the chief ended, Pat called her daughter, Madelyn, and Sam Nagy's brother, Adam. Both of them had also been tossing and turning all night. Madelyn told her mother she would pick her up to go with her to the police station. Adam Nagy said he would also drive there within the hour.

At the station, the family members were comfortably seated in a small room with a few easy chairs and a table. From a local restaurant, Pat Karis ordered breakfast delivered for the family members and all the police staff on duty. The two families spent the waiting hours drinking coffee and pop, reminiscing and sharing events from their memories of their prior relationships with Alyssa and Sam. Both tears and laughter were expressed while they impatiently awaited news of little Sammy.

\*\*\*\*

After they completed their statements at police headquarters, Preacher Anton, Aggie Bee, and Thin Lizzy took Detective Rose Kemp's suggestion and went to the break room for coffee and donuts. Thin Lizzy didn't remember ever having a donut so delicious. And the coffee? So steamy hot and perfectly brewed. The only coffee she had had for so long was found discarded in a trash can, cold, curdled, and grainy. But she actually felt guilty enjoying every morsel of the donut and every mouthful of the coffee when poor Sammy's fate was yet unknown. No telling what Darkman would do to him.

Aggie Bee sat next to Thin Lizzy, also enjoying her treat but also concerned for Sammy's safety and welfare. As the women finished eating and wiping their hands on the napkins provided, a large, imposing man wearing navy blue trousers and a white shirt with a silver badge that read, Youngstown Ohio Chief of Police, entered the room. Thin Lizzy looked up with fear in her eyes. She was getting used to all of the officers and detectives since she had met so many of them this morning. But this man was the chief, the boss. She looked down at the coffee remaining in her Styrofoam cup, hoping to avoid eye contact with him.

Preacher Anton got out of his chair and went over to greet the chief. "Chief Rutherford, good morning."

The chief stopped, then clasped Preacher Anton's outreached hand. "Uh, good morning. Do I know you?"

"Yes, yes. I'm Preacher Anton Morris from the Blood of Jesus Pentecostal Church. I've met you a few times over the years at various events in the city."

"Oh, yes, I remember now."

Preacher Anton continued, "I also tried to get in touch with you yesterday, but you were out of the office. Yesterday afternoon was when the little boy was in my church, and I was trying to find out any information on him, anything the police might know."

"Well, yesterday was a very busy day, incidentally, because of that boy. I'm sorry I missed your call. I understand he spent part of last night in your church."

197

"Yes. As a matter of fact, these two ladies," Preacher Anton pointed in the direction of Aggie Bee and Thin Lizzy, "were the ones who brought the boy to me."

"Oh?" The chief looked toward the women. Thin Lizzy immediately looked away from his gaze.

Chief Rutherford walked over to the ladies and sat in the seat next to Thin Lizzy. Her heart was beating a mile a minute. She was so nervous. What was he going to say to her?

The chief looked at Thin Lizzy. "Ma'am, are you the woman who saved that young boy's life?"

With a voice so faint the chief had difficulty hearing, Thin Lizzy stuttered, "I-I g-g-guess s-so."

"What is your name, ma'am?"

"E-elizab-beth Th-thorpe."

"Well, Ms. Thorpe, on behalf of the city of Youngstown and the family of Sammy Nagy, I'd like to thank you. It was a bra—"

Suddenly, in a very loud, very clear voice, Thin Lizzy fretted, "But he ain't safe now. Darkman's got him."

Her outburst startled the chief, but he took her hand. "I know, but we will find the boy, and those men will pay for what they've done. We have the entire police force looking for them."

She looked down at her coffee again. "I-I hope so."

The chief got out of his chair. "Would you ladies come with me, please? There are some people in the other room who would like to meet you."

Both Aggie Bee and Thin Lizzy gave the chief a strange look. Who would want to meet them, two women dressed in soiled clothes and who lived on the street? But he was the chief of police. They had no choice. They got out of their seats, removing their trash from the table, and throwing it in the waste basket as they followed him out the door. Preacher Anton trailed behind them.

The chief led them to a larger room down the hall. Inside, sat the family of Sammy Nagy, who were gathered together, eating breakfast from take-out containers, and in a deep discussion. When the chief entered the room, the talking stopped and everyone in the room looked toward him and the three individuals behind him.

After Preacher Anton closed the door, the chief said, "I'd like to introduce you to two special women whom I'm very sure you will want to meet."

He turned to the women who had come with him into the room. "This is Agnes Washington and Elizabeth Thorpe. These brave ladies kept little Sammy Nagy safe since—" He didn't get to finish his statement.

"Oh, my God!" exclaimed Pat Karis. She rushed out of her chair. "You saved my grandson!"

While others stood and made similar shouts of surprise and gratitude, Pat Karis didn't hesitate. She went over to Thin Lizzy and Aggie Bee and enveloped both of them in her arms. "Thank you, thank you, from the bottom of my heart."

In a soft, raspy voice, Thin Lizzy lamented, "But he ain't safe now. Darkman got him. He a very bad man."

Pat Karis pulled away. "Oh, I know. I know. But at least we know more than we did Friday night. Before this morning, we didn't know if he was alive or dead, where he was, if he was safe or not. Then we were told that he had been rescued by you, Elizabeth Thorpe." She looked affectionately at Thin Lizzy. "I know that the entire city is searching for him now. Those men will be found and so will my grandson. But if it hadn't been for you…" She couldn't hold back the tears.

Thin Lizzy felt uncomfortable, and she surely wasn't used to all this attention and praise. Yet she knew what Darkman was capable of doing, and she feared for Sammy's safety.

The chief led Aggie Bee and Thin Lizzy over to two vacant chairs. "Ladies, please sit down. If you will agree, I think the boy's family might like to ask you some questions." The women sat on the designated seats. Preacher Anton also found a vacant one.

The chief spoke again. "I'm going to check on the progress of the search and will give you updates as soon as they become available." Then he addressed the preacher. "Preacher Anton, will you see that Agnes and Elizabeth get back safely to wherever they wish to go?"

Preacher Anton nodded his head. He then decided to take charge of the situation in the room. "Perhaps we should all introduce ourselves before we get down to any questioning. I'm Anton Morris, the preacher at the Blood of Jesus Pentecostal Church where little Sammy was brought in by Elizabeth Thorpe yesterday morning." He turned toward Thin Lizzy and Aggie Bee. "You've met these ladies. I'm sure they would like to know who you are also."

Pat Karis gazed around the room at the relatives, and began, "I'm Patricia Karis, the mother of Alyssa Nagy, Sammy's mother." She took a moment to dab at her eyes with a tissue she had removed from her pocket. "Sadly, she was shot and killed the night of the fire." Then she glanced at her daughter sitting next to her.

"I'm Madelyn Winthrop, Alyssa's older sister and

200

Sammy's aunt." Turning toward the gentlemen sitting next to her, she said, "This is my husband, Corey."

The man on the other side of the room introduced himself. "I'm Adam Nagy. Sammy's dad was my younger brother." He shook his head. "He was also shot and killed in the fire." Hesitating, he continued, "I'm also Sammy's uncle, and," glancing next to him, he said, "this is my wife, Naomi."

Thin Lizzy couldn't believe what she was hearing. So what little Sammy thought happened to his mother and father truly did happen. Both of them, dead. And now he was in the hands of that monster, Darkman. He must be so terrified. Oh, if only she could have kept him safe for just a little while longer, until his family found him.

There were a few moments of silence before Pat Karis then questioned, "I-I'm not accusing or anything, but could someone tell us what they know about Sammy and how he ended up being kidnapped?"

Preacher Anton said, "Lizzy, would you like to tell these family members how you found Sammy, or would you prefer me to explain it to them?" He remembered how skittish she had been and her reluctance in speaking to new people.

With wide eyes filled with angst, she mumbled, "You."

Preacher Anton cleared his throat and reiterated the long chain of events that Sammy, Thin Lizzy, and Aggie Bee had previously relayed to him—the gunmen entering Sammy's house, his hiding place, the gunshots Sammy heard, the fire, his escape, his long, long walk in bare feet, his rescue by Thin Lizzy from the speeding car, his night spent in the public library, and eventually

Sammy's arrival at the church and the subsequent events that took place there the day and night before, including his abduction. The emotional faces of the family members must have changed a dozen times during the twenty-minute recitation.

As for Thin Lizzy and Aggie Bee, they sat calmly listening to the preacher's words. When he completed his summation of the events, he asked them, "Do you ladies have anything to add?"

Both Aggie Bee and Thin Lizzy simply shook their heads.

For several moments, Sammy's relatives were speechless. This was an extraordinary and unbelievable account of what that poor boy had gone through. Even the men were wiping away moisture from their eyes with their fingers.

Then Pat Karis broke the silence. "Oh, that poor boy. Oh, how he must be suffering. And now to be in the hands of another set of cruel men."

Again, there was silence while everyone composed themselves, bringing their emotions under control while Aggie Bee and Thin Lizzy patiently watched them.

Preacher Anton finally interrupted the silence. "Does anyone have any questions for either the ladies or me? We'll try to answer them if we can."

After dabbing at her eyes, Pat Karis spoke, "Yes, if I may, I'd like to ask, uh, Elizabeth, a question."

Preacher Anton interjected, "Uh, I don't think Ms. Elizabeth would mind if you called her Lizzy and Ms. Agnes wouldn't mind if you called her Aggie." He turned to these two ladies. "Is that right?"

Both Aggie Bee and Thin Lizzy nodded their heads in agreement.

Mrs. Karis addressed Thin Lizzy, "Uh, Lizzy, I know this is difficult for you, but would you be able to tell us a little more about Sammy?" She shook her head and more tears appeared. "I'm so ashamed to admit, and someday I will explain to you, but not one of us here, not one of these family members, knows anything about my grandson. To make a long story short, his parents wouldn't let us know him. They wouldn't let us into his life." She gulped for breath as the tears grew more abundant. "So whatever you can tell us, anything at all, about Sammy, we would be most appreciative."

Thin Lizzy really didn't know the circumstances involving Sammy and these relatives, but she could see they were extremely concerned about him. She definitely was shocked to find out that they knew nothing about the boy. When her daughter Ashley was small and Thin Lizzy's parents were still alive, they doted over the girl with love, affection, and gifts the way grandparents should. And Lizzy and her husband Dennis welcomed their attention on Ashley. Dennis' parents also were devoted grandparents. Because of this, it was difficult to understand how Sammy's parents wouldn't allow these people present here, so concerned about him, to be part of his life.

She decided she had to be brave and answer any questions they might have—for their sake as well as her dear little friend, Sammy. She looked directly at his grandmother. "I-I tell ya about him."

Everyone grew silent and came to attention.

Faltering, Thin Lizzy sighed, "Sammy, he a really, really good boy. He didn't cry much at all when I found him. And his feet was hurtin' real bad. Dey was bloody with li'l stones stickin' to 'em 'cause he had ta walk in his bare feet ta get away from da fire. I tried ta clean 'em and make 'em feel better. He didn't even cry when I was fixin' 'em. And his hand was all burned from when he opened da door at his house ta get outside. I wrapped some rags 'round it too. And when we was in da church cleanin' da pews, he even helped us clean. He didn't have to, but he akst if he could help, and Aggie Bee said 'sure you can help,' so he did."

She paused for a few seconds. "And he liked da choc'late cake I got us from da hotel. We had it for breakfast yesterday. It was good."

Everyone was listening attentively with slight smiles on their faces. Then Madelyn asked, "What does he look like?"

Thin Lizzy stood. "Well, he 'bout dis tall." She patted the side of her hand against her waist. "And he got all dese really, really big curls on top his head."

"What color is his hair?" asked Adam Nagy.

Thin Lizzy points to Adam. "Uh, it kinda like yours but only more yellow. It a real purty yellow."

Naomi asked, "How about his eyes? What color are they?"

Thin Lizzy thought for a second, and then responded, "They a real purty blue color."

Pat Karis asked, "What did he say about the fire?"

"He say he was real scared, and he couldn't breathe. That's why he got outta his hidin' place and den got outta da house. Den, he said when he heard da sirens, he got even more scareder. Dat's why he started walkin' away."

Then Pat Karis asked, "What did he say about his parents?"

"He didn't talk much 'bout 'em, but I knowed he was worried 'bout 'em 'cause he heard dose shots and not nobody come ta take him outta his hidin' place."

Corey Winthrop asked, "What was he wearing when you found him?"

"He had on some red jammies wit some kinda hero on da front. He tole me da hero was somethin' like Titaniman or Titaman, I don't know. I can't remember. But dey was all dirty with smoke and stuff. And he smelled like a fire. Uh, at da church Aggie Bee helped us find some other clothes for him, so he went in da bathroom and cleaned up a li'l bit and put on da different clothes."

Pat Karis looked toward Aggie Bee. "That was nice of you. Thank you."

Aggie Bee smiled and nodded her head.

The family also directed a few questions to Aggie Bee, who willingly answered them. Then a couple more were asked of Thin Lizzy, who did her best to respond to them. Both Aggie Bee and Preacher Anton were proud of Thin Lizzy, her poise, her control. Perhaps this was good for her to have the opportunity to break out of her shell a little.

Before Preacher Anton, Aggie Bee, and Thin Lizzy left the gathering to go back to the church, Pat Karis made sure she got the preacher's phone number. "I need to have some way to get in touch with these ladies. I'm not finished with them yet."

In the hallway, Aggie Bee asked Preacher Anton, "What did that lady mean by that?"

He shook his head. "I really don't know, Aggie. But I'm sure we'll eventually find out."

Chapter Twenty-Nine

*Wednesday evening, 2 days before the fire.*

Melanie got back to the hospital around seven-thirty. Ryan had his eyes closed when she walked back into his room, but he immediately opened them when he heard the sound of the curtain being moved. "You're back?"

"Yeah, I stopped and grabbed a sandwich on my way. I hope you don't mind me eating in front of you."

"No, no, they brought me dinner about an hour ago. It actually was better than the lunch, but I wasn't very hungry. I don't have much of an appetite."

Melanie opened the bag with her food, the aroma permeating the room. Ryan looked over toward her. "Smells good."

"You want a couple of fries?" she asked as she popped one in her mouth.

"No, I don't feel much like eating."

She gave him a rueful look. "I'm sorry."

Curious again, he asked, "Mel, why do you keep saying you're sorry? None of this is your fault."

She stopped chewing. "I just feel bad for you."

"I actually feel lucky to be alive. I know I'll be okay after a few weeks. So everything is going to be all right eventually."

Melanie had a hard time swallowing her current bite of the hamburger. She wasn't so sure that everything was going to be all right. Not at all. She knew how concerned her Uncle Rocky was about Ryan saying to her as little as he did about his businesses. Hell, Ryan hadn't ever mentioned his name. So as far as Melanie was concerned, Ryan could've been talking about anybody, not necessarily her uncle. But she knew Ryan was talking about her uncle. She knew because she kept prodding him about it, just as it had been her and her uncle's plan from the beginning.

But never in her wildest dreams had she thought her Uncle Rocky would retaliate the way he did. She knew he was tough, even somewhat unscrupulous at times, but to actually endanger Ryan's life? That she never had expected.

Now she had a serious dilemma. Inadvertently, she had grown to love Ryan. Did she love him enough to tell him the truth about her uncle? About how she and Ryan met—this thing she first thought was a game that then turned into a tragedy? If she did, what would Ryan do? Hell, what would her Uncle Rocky do? It could mean she would lose Ryan forever. As for her uncle, the consequences could even be greater. If he could try to kill Ryan, what would he do to her, his own niece?

Besides, she couldn't tell Ryan now when he was in such physical pain. She couldn't add that type of emotional stress to him when he was in that condition.

So she swallowed her bite of hamburger, took a sip of her cola, and pretended that Ryan had just been in a simple accident. Nobody's fault. Just an accident. At least for now.

Chapter Thirty

*Sunday morning, the search.*
Detective Atkinson drove herself and Hamilton to the lower part of Mahoning Avenue just next to the bridge to search for Sammy Nagy and his kidnappers. A few working businesses were still located in this area, but those were closed because it was Sunday. Besides those businesses, several abandoned, boarded up buildings stood barren and empty near the street. A few vacant and neglected houses were set back at the end of rutted and pitted long driveways.

Atkinson pulled into one of the crumbling parking lots next to a dilapidated building. "I'll park here. It'll be easier to go on foot from here to the other buildings."

They both exited the vehicle, Hamilton, stretching his legs as he stood. These maximum working hours and lack of sleep were taking their toll on his aging body. They both removed their revolvers but pointed them down toward the ground as they walked toward the first abandoned property. They checked each one along the street, searching especially for any means of easy entry, such as broken windows, loose boards, or missing or unlocked doors. They entered each structure to which they had an access, thoroughly searching every room on every floor, using their flashlights when needed.

After they determined that they had exhausted their search of the abandoned buildings on both sides of the street, Hamilton suggested, "Let's check out those vacant houses on the other side. Maybe you'd better drive us there. Those are some long, pot-holed driveways, and my legs are gettin' a bit shaky."

"Yeah, yeah, old man. Guess after this case is over, you're gonna really be ready for your retirement and a long, relaxing trip to the beach."

"That's no joke, kiddo. I thought my last few months were gonna be easy-peasy. Oh, was I ever wrong."

Atkinson chuckled as they trudged up the faded, cracked blacktop driveway to the first house, a two-story structure with peeling paint. Every window on the ground floor was boarded up. The detectives walked around the house through the tall weeds and brambles, searching for a point of entry. An exterior door on the west side was surrounded by wild trees and high grass. Atkinson stopped suddenly, raising her gun. "Look, Will. These weeds have been trampled down very recently."

Will Hamilton also raised his gun. "I see that Stace. Hmm."

A few crumbling cement stairs led down to the door. Atkinson slowly and silently crept down the stairs. After squeezing her hands into a pair of latex gloves she removed from her pocket, she tried the door. Whispering, she turned to Hamilton. "It's locked. Maybe the owner was here recently."

Talking in a low tone, Hamilton uttered, "Could be, but let's check the other doors."

Suddenly, Atkinson stiffened. "Wait!" She stood like a statue. "Do you hear that?"

Hamilton came to attention, then he shook his head. "No, what do you hear?"

She put her ear up against the wooden door. "I-I'm not sure. Could be a cat or some other kind of animal. Maybe squeaky old pipes." Then a little more excited, she blurted, "Could be something else, like maybe a kid crying." She immediately jiggled the door again, but it was locked tightly. She turned to Hamilton. "We gotta get in here somehow to see what that noise is. Maybe it's an animal, but we gotta make sure."

Hamilton backed up to let Atkinson lead the way to finding another entry. They went around the back of the house where a set of deteriorating stairs led to a decrepit and decaying back porch. "Wait down here. These steps look treacherous. Lemme see if this back door is open," She carefully ascended the rickety stairs, avoiding several sharp holes in the wood. The porch was also in a very run-down condition, so she was especially careful how she stepped.

The upper window on the back door was boarded up, but someone had pulled the bottom plank away and threw it on the porch. She first tried the doorknob, but it was locked. Then she reached through the open space created by the missing board and was able to unlock the door. Without speaking, she signaled with her arm and a nod of her head for Hamilton to join her. He crept up the stairs and onto the porch, being extra careful to avoid any damaged areas.

When Hamilton arrived at the doorway, Atkinson slowly opened the unlocked door with gun ready. They entered a musty kitchen minus any appliances. Broken pipes jutted out of the worn, cheap linoleum floor, and loose wiring dangled from the ceiling where once a lighting fixture had been. Cupboard doors were missing or dangling from their hinges. In the middle of the room, they stopped to listen for the noise she thought she had heard while outside. Atkinson bobbed her head at Hamilton and pointed to a door on the opposite side of the room. He, hearing nothing, lifted his hands and shrugged his shoulders.

But she, apparently with better hearing, bobbed her head again to soundlessly indicate that she heard something. She slowly twisted the knob on the door, opening it to a set of stairs in total darkness. She mouthed silently, "Be careful." Then, as quietly as possible, she crept precariously down the staircase with him following in the same manner, grasping tightly on the railing.

At the bottom of the stairs, she stopped a couple of yards from them to allow room for Hamilton to stand. She listened intently for any noise. Hearing nothing, she took out her flashlight and turned it on. Hamilton did the same. First, she shone the light around the area where they had landed. Various types of debris lay scattered throughout—dank, mildewed boxes, here and there, broken cement blocks against a wall. Closer to an open doorway on their left, a rusty and mangled grocery cart rested on its side in a puddle of rancid water. A clean, beige blanket sprawled next to the cart lay sopping up the fetid water underneath it. The cleanliness of that blanket caused her to give Hamilton a knowing look.

As they moved forward, she saw a couple of mice and rats scamper to other hiding places. Roaches and other insects joined them in their escape.

When she determined that no other movement or sound resonated from the area in which they were currently standing, she silently moved toward the open doorway with Hamilton still following close behind.

Walking through the opening, the light shone on

more debris and scampering bugs and rodents. This was a larger room, damp and humid with stagnant water accumulating in areas along the wall. They kept walking, shining their lights behind every soaked box, every abandoned piece of furniture, and every pile of dank rags until they arrived at the back wall of the house. There, in a cleared area attached to a dangling pipe was a frightened little boy whose bright blue eyes stared back at them.

**Chapter** Thirty-One

*Sunday morning, the search continues.*

Melanie Carlini took a sip of her second cup of coffee while she put a slice of ten grain toast into the toaster. She asked her brother Nick, "Do you want me to put a piece of toast in for you, too?"

Nick made a scowl. "Naw, that crap tastes like a piece of cardboard. I'll pass. Do we have any donuts left from yesterday?"

"Don't know. You can check the cupboard. They'll probably taste stale by now. Put them in the nuke for a few seconds."

She wore black jeans, a silky, white blouse and black flats on her feet. She planned to get to the hospital early today to see Ryan because there was a possibility he would be going to rehab tomorrow. She wanted to find out the details so she could take off work and accompany him to help get him settled into the new facility.

The small television located on the other side of the kitchen was tuned to a local news station. Melanie had been so busy lately that she hadn't had time to catch up on anything happening recently in the area. As she removed her toast from the toaster, preparing to spread on a spoonful of honey, she heard the news commentator say, *"We have an update on the Friday night fire that destroyed a home on upper Fifth Avenue in Youngstown.*

*The bodies recovered from the scene have been positively identified as Samuel and Alyssa Nagy, a prominent Youngstown attorney and his wife. An Amber Alert has been issued and the police are still looking for their missing son Samuel Junior. Sammy is five years old with curly blond hair and blue eyes. If you have any information on his whereabouts, please call this hotline number, 330-555-4400. We hope to have more information later in the broadcast."*

An enhanced photo of a blond boy was shone on the screen.

When Melanie heard the names of the victims in the fire, she was paralyzed. The spoon filled with honey dropped from her hand and clattered to the floor.

Nick, searching in the cupboard for the donuts, moved quickly out of the way. "Shit, Mel! You got that crap all over my new shoes. What's wrong with you?"

She couldn't move, holding the toast stiffly in her one hand, squeezing it until it crackled and flattened.

After wiping off his shoes with the nearby dish towel and standing back up, Nick noticed that Melanie hadn't moved. "Mel?" She didn't respond. "Mel, what's the matter? Are you all right?"

Finally, shaken out of her trance, Melanie dropped the crumpled toast on the counter, rushed to the hall closet, grabbed her purse, and ran out the side door to her car in the garage.

Melanie had to get to the hospital. She had to tell Ryan what had been on the news. She was overwhelmed with thoughts and emotions foreign to her. Could her uncle have done this? No. He could be ruthless, but to actually burn someone's house down? No. And two bodies in the house? What about the boy? Where was he?

If it was her uncle, would he kidnap the boy? No. Look how he treated her. He loved her and would do anything for her. He couldn't harm a child. He wasn't that kind of a man. Was he?

On her way to the hospital, she decided to call her uncle and ask him. She knew he'd be up. He was always up early. He was probably getting ready to go to Mass. Sometimes he'd pick her up, and she would go with Aunt Stella and him. But not today.

She pressed his number on the dashboard. It rang twice, then he picked up. *"Melanie, sweetheart, how are you this morning? What can I do for you? Are you going to Mass with us today?"*

"Uncle Rocky, have you heard the morning news?"

There was a slight pause on the line. *"Uhh, actually, no. I had some paperwork to look over before church."* Another slight pause. *"Why are you asking, hon?"*

"Uncle Rocky, the Nagy's are dead, and their little boy is missing. Please tell me you had nothing to do with this. Please!"

Another pause. *"Of course, I didn't, sweetheart. I'm sure it was an accident. These things happen, you know. What a shame. Sam was a good man. So sorry to hear this."*

Melanie didn't like the tone of her uncle's voice. He sounded deceptive. And casual. Too calm and nonchalant. Was he actually capable of such inhuman and cruel policies? Was he even the man she thought he was?

When she said nothing for several seconds, her uncle prompted, *"Mel? Are you still there?"*

She had to respond. "Uh, yeah, I just dropped my sunglasses. Sorry. Well, I have to go now." Another hesitation and she wasn't sure if she should say her usual type of goodbye, but she did. "Love you, Uncle Rocky."

After his niece hung up, Rocco Banetti sat back on his desk chair in his home office and took a few heavy breaths. He knew his niece well. He had a nagging feeling that she didn't believe him.

****

In his hospital room, Ryan was growing restless. Most of the severe pain from his injuries had lessened, and the nurses were just giving him extra-strength acetaminophen to alleviate his discomfort. One nurse informed him he would be in the hospital at least until Monday. Not much ambulance transporting was done on weekends except for emergencies. He was also getting bored.

Mel came to visit every day, but his mother had gone back home. Who knew when he'd ever see her again? Sam Nagy was in on Wednesday and said he'd get in touch with Ryan regarding his suspicions about what caused his accident after he checked into some things. They both had strong beliefs that it had to be Banetti's men. He had a brief chat with Sam on the phone Friday afternoon, but Sam said he had been busy and hadn't learned anything yet. He had mentioned trying to get up to see him on Sunday to tell him everything he knew. Perhaps he'd be in this afternoon.

Boredom caused Ryan to flick on the television to a local news station just as his breakfast arrived. He immediately turned off the television but not before he saw a drawing of a young child on the screen. *Hmm, another child must be missing. Poor kid. I hope nothing serious has happened to him. It's probably some kind of domestic dispute. Mother and father are fighting, and the kid is in the middle of their custody battles. Such a shame.*

He took the thermo-lid off his breakfast, steam escaping as he did. Scrambled eggs, wheat toast, and a sick little sausage patty. Sliced canned peaches and a hot cup of coffee rested on the side of the tray. He shouldn't complain. It was better than he usually made for himself at home. It would be a quick bowl of cereal with a cup of coffee. Sometimes he didn't have time for the coffee and would pick up a cup at the nearest fast-food joint on the way to work.

The breakfast didn't taste as bad as he expected. And he was hungry. He was also getting adept at using his left hand to do things. It took a little longer, but at least no one had to feed him. That would be way too embarrassing.

After he finished the peaches, he turned the television back on to the news. Saturday football scores were being broadcasted with shots of the players running on the field. He liked to watch the games, even the high school ones. He was a diehard Browns fan ever since his dad had taken him to one of their games when he was eight years old. Hell, that was so long ago. He hadn't seen his dad in years. Who knew if he ever would again? Who really cared? His life was good now, except for this damn accident. But the doc said he'd be fine after a few months. And he had a beautiful and loving fiancée now. What more could a guy want?

He picked up his coffee cup and was sipping the hot drink carefully when the picture of the same missing boy came back on the screen. As he stared at it, the kid looked familiar. Then the pretty, dark-haired newscaster started to talk about the segment. *"An Amber Alert was issued for little Sammy Nagy and a search party yesterday had turned up no news on the boy's whereabouts. His parents perished in Friday night's fire on the north side of Youngstown, but Sammy is unaccounted for. If anyone has any information about him, please call the police hotline listed at the bottom of your screen."*

Ryan dropped the cup of coffee, splashing it on the dirty breakfast dishes and all over himself. *No! What did she say? Sam and Alyssa dead? There must be some mistake. I just talked to him on Friday. Oh, my God*!

He was still staring at the screen wondering what to do, who to call, when the curtain pulled back and Melanie entered the room. Her face looked like she had applied makeup that was ten shades too light for her skin. The moment she saw Ryan and the picture of Sammy on the television, she knew he was aware of what had happened.

He stared at her. "Oh, my God, Mel, Sam's dead! He's dead! I can't believe it." He bowed his head and kept shaking it back and forth as if he were trying to clear the tragedy from his brain.

Melanie took hold of his good hand and gently bent to kiss his cheek. "I just saw it on the news this morning and came right over to the hospital. This is terrible, Ryan. Oh, my God. That poor little boy."

She didn't know how to tell Ryan what she thought might have actually happened to Sam Nagy and his wife, but she had to get Ryan's thoughts. She pulled a chair closer to the bed and sat down, again clasping his hand. "Did you watch the entire clip? Did you see where they said the fire was suspicious?"

Puzzled, he stared at her. "What do you mean?"

"They said they don't think the fire was started

accidently. They think somebody set the fire intentionally."

All the color drained from Ryan's face. He had been sitting up in the bed, but his body collapsed backward as he closed his eyes and breathed heavily. "No, this can't be happening."

Melanie waited a few minutes until Ryan seemed able to deal with the heartbreaking news of his boss's recent demise. Then she asked, "Ryan, what's going on? Why are all these terrible things happening?"

He covered his eyes with his good hand. "I don't know, Mel... I don't know."

Melanie's emotions were split right down the middle. If she told Ryan her suspicions, she'd have to admit how their relationship was based on lies and deceptions. How their meeting in that bar had been just a game to her. She thought it had also been just a game to her Uncle Rocco too. But her recent distrust of her uncle's sincerity had completely changed her thinking. It was definitely not a frivolous thing to him—nor to her anymore either. It was a matter of extreme importance—a matter of life and death. How could she not have known this?

All these years, she had been completely blindsided, thinking he was her devoted uncle who would look out for her and her family not out of duty but out of love and affection. So many times he had told her how he had cherished and adored her mother, his sister Angela. Was that a lie also?

She knew she had to talk to Ryan. To tell him this secret. Whatever would happen after that, she'd have to accept the consequences. She couldn't live with this type of lie for the rest of her life, whether with or without

Ryan.

The two hadn't spoken for several minutes. Both were deep in their own appalling thoughts, Ryan coming to terms with the fire and Sam's death and Melanie finally conceding to what her uncle was capable of doing. Quietly, she dropped Ryan's hand, pushed back her chair, and walked over to the large window on the opposite side of the room. Looking out at the view before her, but not seeing it, she folded her arms in front of her. She didn't turn around as she said, "I have to tell you something."

Ryan, realizing she was no longer sitting next to him, looked in her direction. Without turning around and in an unfamiliar tone to her voice, she said, "Do you remember when we met, Ryan?"

Confused and wondering why the hell she was bringing this up at this time, he agreed, "Of course, I do. Why would you ask me that?"

"I have a confession to make."

"What are you talking about? A confession?"

"Yes, a confession?"

"Well, what is it?" He knew he sounded annoyed. What could she be telling him that was more important than the death of his boss and the disappearance of a small child?

Gaining her courage and composure, she blurted, "It was a set-up."

Even more confused, he asked, "What was a set-up? You're talking in riddles, Mel."

She turned around to face him but didn't move from the window. "Our meeting that night. It wasn't a chance meeting like it seemed. It was planned and arranged. I knew you were going to be at that bar. I singled you out.

That drink I spilled on you? It wasn't an accident. I did it on purpose."

He was appalled. "What? You knew I was gonna be there?"

She came a little closer to the bed, but still keeping distance between them, her body still straight and stiff. "Let me finish." She looked down at the floor and took a deep breath. "My uncle wanted me to get to know you. He knew you would be in the bar. I wore that sexy outfit so you'd notice me. And you did. I was to get acquainted with you so you'd reveal personal and business information about my uncle to me. Then he'd know that he couldn't trust you or the law firm you worked for."

Ryan's head was reeling. What was she talking about? Was this for real? He couldn't speak. First, the news about Sam, and then Melanie, standing before him and telling him their relationship was all a planned lie. A fake. How could that be?

Melanie didn't give him a chance to say anything. She walked closer to him. "But the thing is, Ry... The thing is, I fell for you. I fell head over heels in love with you. And I thought that setting you up was all a game. I thought my uncle just wanted to see how far you could be pushed. So I agreed. I thought it would be fun. A challenge. But then it turned serious for me. I fell in love with you, Ry. I really did."

His whole world was falling apart. He looked at Melanie as if he didn't even recognize her. Was this his fiancée, the woman he wanted to marry? This all had to be a nightmare, and he would wake up in his cheesy apartment ready to go to work. He even closed his eyes and shook his head to try to erase all these images invading his mind. But when he opened them again,

Melanie stood next to him, tears running down her face, with a look he didn't recognize.

Without even asking her who her uncle was, he fell back on the bed and muttered, "Rocco Banetti."

Melanie approached the chair and sat down on it. She reached for Ryan's hand, but he jerked it away and turned his face to the other side. He didn't want to look at her. He couldn't accept any of this. His accident. Sam's death. The realization that his fiancée had lied and deceived him during their entire relationship. She was a two-faced bitch!

Melanie tried to reason with him. "I really love you, Ry. I really thought it was just a game. I didn't mean to fall in love, and I certainly didn't know what my uncle had in mind for you or your boss. Just the thought of all that has happened because of him makes me sick to my stomach and crazy out of my mind. I'm so, so sorry. He's always been so good to me and my family. I didn't know he was the monster that he is. Please believe me, Ryan. I didn't know. I never, ever would have agreed to any of this had I known what he had in mind. You know me. I'm not that kind of a person."

He jerked his head around and stared at her with contempt visible on his face. "Know you?" His eyes were full of anger—and disgust. "I don't know you at all." He raised his hand. "Go! Get the hell out of my life!"

She stood up and reached for him. "Ryan!"

He batted her arms away. "Go! Get out!"

She looked down at him one last time. Then she turned and pushed the curtain aside. Before scurrying out the door, she turned back to look at him. "Ryan, I love you. I truly do, and I'm so, so sorry!"

Chapter Thirty-Two

*Late Sunday morning, the search continues.*
At police headquarters, the police hotline rang constantly as a result of the many missing person flyers posted throughout the city, the Amber Alerts, and the TV and radio updates broadcasted since the news of Sammy's disappearance. Several leads came in regarding sightings of a boy or suspicious looking characters in the area. The volunteers manning the phones gave those leads to the officers assigned to the hotline to determine if they were authentic or bogus. Those that seemed credible were followed up with some type of action, thus far without any success.

One boy was seen walking alone into a pharmacy on the north side. It turned out he was eight years old and had ridden his bike to the store to buy some aspirin for his sick mother. Two men dressed in shabby clothes and looking suspicious were seen walking down Federal Street. Apparently, these men, who had ID's, were on their way to work at one of the construction sites going on downtown. Another boy was seen sitting on the porch steps outside a house on Norwood Avenue. It seemed this young fellow was upset with his brother because he wouldn't take him to play baseball with the bigger kids who lived down the block.

At 11:56 that morning, a call came into the hotline that caused the entire room to become fully alert. A gruff voice revealed, *"You know dat boy his face is on dat poster? Well, I knowed where he be."*

All calls were being recorded, but this one was immediately put on speaker, just in case it was legitimate. "Sir, can you tell me where he is, so I can send help to pick him up?"

*"No, I ain't gonna do dat just now. Suppose I want da reward."*

"There hasn't been any reward offered yet, but I can talk to the authorities to see if there might be one coming forward. Can you tell me where the boy is?" While the volunteer spoke with the caller, the tech department frantically tried to determine the location of the call.

*"No, I ain't gonna do dat. I ain't gonna tell ya 'less I gets some money."*

"Well, can you tell me how he is? Is he safe? Is he hurt?"

*"Oh sure, he okay. He ain't hurt. He just fine."*

The volunteer heard a slight snicker in the caller's voice before asking, "Can you give me your name and your location so we can deliver any money for a reward."

*"No, I ain't gonna do dat either. I ain't no dummy, ya know. I'll call back in a li'l while to see 'bout da money."* And he hung up.

By this time the room was filled with police and other personnel. Chief Rutherford quickly asked the tech worker, "Did you get the location of the caller?"

"No, the conversation was too short."

"How about the telephone number?"

"It was a burner phone. It won't do us any good."

"Damn!" The chief was frustrated. Then he quickly enquired to anyone, "Have those two women from the church left the station yet?"

One of the officers answered, "I just saw them leave with the preacher in a white van."

"Quick! Call the preacher. Tell him to get those women back here ASAP."

"Yes, chief." The sergeant left to get the number of the preacher."

**\*\*\*\***

Preacher Anton's cellphone rang as he was pulling out of police headquarters, heading for the Blood of Jesus Pentecostal Church. From his dashboard he answered, "Preacher Anton Morris here. How can I help you?"

*"Sir, this is Officer Tedrow of the Youngstown Police Department. The chief has requested you bring those women back immediately."*

"Is there a problem, officer?"

*"I don't know, sir. We received a call on the hotline, and he just told me to have the women returned to headquarters."*

"Uh, okay, officer, I'll turn around." He entered the nearest business parking lot, turned around, and headed back to headquarters.

With her forehead wrinkled, Thin Lizzy, having also heard the phone conversation between the police officer and the preacher, frowned at Aggie Bee. Aggie Bee, not knowing anything more than Thin Lizzy knew, simply opened her eyes wide and shook her head. But she also was concerned. Why would the chief want them back at the police station? Well, she couldn't worry for too long because they were pulling back into the parking lot.

As they entered the main entrance, the officer at the reception desk directed them back to the room where the call center was being conducted. As soon as they entered the room, they were greeted by Chief Rutherford. "Ladies, we just got a suspicious phone call from a man who says he knows where the boy is located. He hung up because he expects to receive a reward. He told the volunteer he would be calling back. We've recorded the call. Could you women listen to the call to see if you can identify the caller?"

Aggie Bee glanced at Thin Lizzy. "Yes, sir, we can do dat."

The tech had the recording ready. He played the entire conversation for the women. After it ended, Aggie Bee exclaimed, "Dat's him. Dat's Darkman, all right. I'd a knowd his voice anywheres. Ain't no doubt. Ain't dat right, Thin Lizzy?"

Thin Lizzy quickly nodded her head. "Yes, sir, dat's Darkman. I'm sure."

The chief grabbed both of their hands. "Thank you so much." He paused. "Can I ask you to stick around the station for a while longer? He's expected to call back soon. Maybe you can help us out some more."

The ladies looked at each other again. What else did they have to do? They had nowhere to go but to roam the streets. Aggie Bee responded, "Sure, sir, we can do dat."

"Great! Thank you." The chief looked around and saw Officer Tedrow. "Can you send someone to get lunch for the ladies and Pastor Anton while we wait for this Darkman to call back?"

"Certainly, sir." Then he asked the women what they would like to eat.

Again, Aggie Bee looked at Thin Lizzy, who frowned and slowly shook he head. Since Aggie Bee knew Thin Lizzy wasn't much of a talker, she answered, "Sir, we don't much care whatchu get us 'cause we eat just 'bout anythin' at all." She chuckled and Thin Lizzy had a slight smile on her face. These ladies were overjoyed. They had never eaten so well in so many years.

Preacher Anton, who had been standing nearby, addressed the chief, "Sir, if you don't mind, I need to get back to the church. I had one of the deacons take over for me this morning, but I have services the rest of the afternoon."

The chief instantly agreed, "Oh, by all means, go back to your church. I'm so sorry we kept you here so long."

"Oh, no. That was no problem. I had it covered, but it seems like I'm not needed anymore. Do you want me to send someone to pick up the ladies when you're through with them?"

"No, that won't be necessary. We'll see that they get back to their ho—, uh, the church."

The women found seats near a small table away from the phone banks while the hustle and bustle continued in the large room. About a half hour later, Officer Tedrow returned with a feast of fried chicken, mash potatoes, hush puppies, and cold drinks. The women were ecstatic. They couldn't remember the last time they had been treated to such a banquet. Of course, they devoured the food, never knowing if they'd ever get a meal like that again.

Then, like everyone else in the room, they waited for the return call from Darkman.

Chapter Thirty-Three

*Early Sunday afternoon, the rescue.*
Sammy couldn't see much around him because it was so dark, but he kept hearing squeaking noises and sounds of dripping water nearby. He was also certain that mice and bugs crawled across his body. He really didn't mind the bugs so much. He liked them. Sometimes Jace and he would dig holes in Jace's backyard, trying to see how many different bugs they could find. One time he caught a grasshopper and put it in a dish to have for a pet, but his mommy wouldn't let him keep it. She told him that grasshoppers and bugs aren't supposed to be pets. They need to live outside.

So the bugs were okay, but he didn't like the mice. He shivered when he felt them go across his legs. That's all he could do with his feet and hands tied. Even just shivering, made the ropes on his wrists and ankles get tighter. Every time he tried to move, they sliced into his skin a little bit more. He was also so very tired. Defeated, he dropped his head down against his chest and continued to cry softly.

Through his tears, he thought he saw a flicker of light out of the corner of his eye. Immediately, he stopped crying and looked in the direction of the flash. Soon the light came closer and closer to him. Had Darkman and Mojo returned? Please no!

The light got very bright and shone directly in his

face so he couldn't see anything. Then he heard a lady's voice shout, "Here he is! Call 9-1-1 and tell them we found him. We found the boy!"

The light was then removed and no longer shone directly on his face. The woman holding the flashlight approached him and bent down. "Hi there, are you Sammy?"

Sammy nodded his head and weakly affirmed, "Y-yes."

"Well, we're gonna get you out of here and take you to your family."

Sammy looked like he was going to cry harder. "I don't think I have a family anymore."

The woman removed a small pocketknife from her jeans and carefully cut away the rope binding Sammy's hands and then his feet. "My name is Detective Stacey and that big man over there is Detective Willy. We're from the police, and we've been looking for you since we found out you weren't in your house that caught fire."

"For real?"

"And we're gonna first take you to the hospital to make sure you're okay before—"

"I'm okay. I'm okay. I'm really, really glad you found me. I thought you were Darkman coming back. Thank you, thank you."

"Well, you're very welcome, and even though you say you're okay, we're gonna get you to the hospital just to get you checked over. Right now, I see you need some bandages for those wrists and ankles of yours. Do they hurt much? What's that on your hand? Bandages?"

Sammy smiled, "No, they don't hurt very much." He looked at his wrapped, right hand. "Yeah, those are bandages Thin Lizzy put on my hand 'cause I burned it on the door."

"Was that at your house?"

"Yes, ma'am."

"Well, we'll make sure the doctors at the hospital take care of that burn and anything else that hurts you, okay?"

With a tiny smile on his face, Sammy answered the detective, "Okay."

While Atkinson had been taking care of Sammy. Detective Hamilton had called 9-1-1 and gone outside to await their arrival and direct the paramedics and other officials back to the abandoned house. Ten minutes after the detectives had found Sammy, with sirens blaring, the emergency and police vehicles pulled into the rutted driveway of the house where Sammy was held captive. A rush of activity took place. The stretcher was taken from the ambulance down the basement of the house. Sammy was gently loaded onto it, and covered with warm blankets, which felt terrific on his clammy body. The paramedics swiftly but carefully then guided the stretcher out the side basement door, which had been broken open, then up the crumbling cement steps to the ambulance parked outside.

Atkinson had followed the stretcher out of the basement and over to the ambulance. Sammy saw her as they raised him into the ambulance. "Will you please come with me in the ambulance?"

Atkinson was somewhat surprised at his request, but responded, "Sure, Sammy, I can come with you." She asked the paramedics to wait a second while she told her partner, who was now in the basement with other officers examining the crime scene. She got on her phone to call him. "Hey, Will, the boy wants me to ride with him to the hospital. Can you take the car and meet us there?"

*"Sure thing. I'll see you when I'm done here."*

Then Atkinson climbed into the ambulance to be with Sammy.

On the way to the hospital, the paramedics checked all of Sammy's vitals and kept him warm. As for his cuts, burns, and bruises, they knew that the doctor on call would want to see the extent of his injuries and perhaps take photographs of them. After determining that his wounds were superficial and the hospital was just five minutes away, there was no danger in waiting until the doctor saw him and decided his necessary treatment.

During the short ride, Atkinson stayed directly by Sammy's side and answered any questions he had as best she could. Sammy seemed to calm down with her responses and seemed less stressed as the ambulance got closer to the hospital.

When they arrived at the emergency entrance, a crowd of reporters had already gathered there, trying to get answers to their questions. While Atkinson followed the stretcher inside the hospital, she quickly informed them, "The chief will make a statement later. I have no comment at this time."

Sammy was wheeled back to a small cubicle in the emergency area. After he was settled onto a warm, white bed, a tall woman dressed in green scrubs entered his cubicle. She came closer to him. "Hello, I'm Doctor Dresden. Can you tell me your name?"

With eyes wide open he spoke, "Sammy Nagy."

"That's a very nice name. Can you tell me how old you are?"

"I'm five years old."

The doctor began examining him while still asking

questions. "Where do you live, Sammy?"

He hesitated, and tears formed at the corners of his eyes. "I-I lived at 2255 Fifth Avenue, Youngstown, Ohio, but my house was on fire, and I don't know where my mommy and daddy are. Thin Lizzy took care of me, but I don't know where she is either. Do you know where she is?"

Atkinson couldn't help but notice the look of concern on the doctor's face as she went about her examination. She removed the rags wrapped around his hand. Then she took off his shoes and socks. She looked closely at each area of concern. Then the doctor pointed out, "Sammy, I'm going to have the nurse take some pictures of your injuries. Then she will clean up all those burns, cuts, and bruises on your body. After that, we'll see if we can get some answers to your questions. How's that?" She patted him on his leg.

Sammy, though frightened and anxious, was still an inquisitive, bright five-year-old, asked, "Why do they need to take pictures of my boo-boos?"

"They just want to make sure they know how you were hurt by all that happened to you. Will that be okay?"

"Yeah, I guess so."

The doctor told him she would see him later, and the nurse came in and took photos of all Sammy's injuries, especially his feet and hand, which seemed to be the most serious ones. Then the nurse cleaned him up and treated and applied antibiotic cream and bandages to all areas needing attention. She helped him into a fresh, crisp hospital gown and new, disposable underwear.

"This is a funny looking dress," he remarked to the nurse. "Is this a diaper?" he asked when pulling up the disposable underwear.

The nurse chuckled, "No, it's not a diaper. Your underpants are very soiled. The doctor thought you might be more comfortable in something nice and clean. These are just underwear we throw away after they are used."

"Oh, okay."

Sammy was very tired after the many ordeals he had dealt with over the past few days. When he was cleaned up, the doctor came in to see him. "Sammy, we're going to let you rest for a while before we allow anyone in to see you."

With his eyes closing, he was so tired he barely heard a word she said. He mumbled, "Okay," and finally was in a deep sleep.

****

Two important things happened at the Youngstown Police Headquarters that afternoon. First, Thin Lizzy and Aggie Bee patiently waited in the call center for the return call from the suspected kidnapper of Sammy Nagy. The chief wanted them to verify the voice of the caller to determine if it was either Darnell Manson, alias Darkman, or Jose Morales, alias Mojo. He would occasionally check in on the activities in the center for any updates or to see that Thin Lizzy and Aggie Bee were comfortable as they waited. The two ladies talked to each other and occasionally dozed as they hung out. With each phone call answered, they would stop their conversations in anticipation of hearing Darkman's raspy voice. Finally, one of the volunteer operators quickly raised her hand, signifying that this was the call on which they were waiting. She immediately put it on speaker. *"You got my money for me yet, woman?"*

233

All of the operators had been told to inform this caller that the families were offering a $15,000 reward if and when the boy was returned unharmed. This operator informed the caller of this arrangement. She attempted to keep the kidnapper on the phone for as long as possible to get a trace on the location, but Darkman wasn't quite as stupid as some thought.

When the operator informed him of this arrangement, he warned, *"Oh no, sister. Dat ain't how it gonna happen. Here da way it gonna be. I gets my money, and den I tells you where da kid is. You git dat?'*

That's how this might have gone down if it hadn't been for the second thing that transpired at the headquarters that Sunday afternoon. About fifteen minutes before the call from the kidnapper came into the phone bank, the 9-1-1 operator had received a call from Detective Will Hamilton revealing that Sammy Nagy had been found in an abandoned home on lower Mahoning Avenue, and the boy was currently on route to Saint Elizabeth Hospital for examination and treatment, though he appeared to have no serious injuries.

Of course, Darkman, a.k.a. the kidnapper, was not in the same location as Sammy Nagy because he had to make this phone call to the hotline. Darkman had no phone of his own, but Whistler, one of his acquaintances, had allowed him the use of his phone to make the call the first time. He charged him one dollar for that privilege. However, Whistler told him he'd charge two dollars for this second phone call, which Darkman didn't have at the time and had to beg on the corner of East `Federal and Walnut Street until he accumulated it, which led to the postponement of the second call.

Therefore, the volunteer operator, along with keeping Darkman on the phone for as long as possible, was to feign no knowledge of the rescue of Sammy Nagy and go along with whatever the kidnapper requested.

Darkman gave his demands. *"I wanchu ta put my money in a big brown envelope and put it in da bottom of da trash barrel near da ticket office at da bus station. Don't have no cops around either or ya don't get da kid back. I'll kill him. Understand? I want da money dere in a half hour. No later. Den I'll call ya back so's you can get da kid."* Of course, he had no intention of ever calling back again after he got the money, which he would never see.

The call wasn't long enough to pinpoint a location, but both Aggie Bee and Thin Lizzy positively identified the speaker as Darkman. Since he had scheduled a drop-off for his "reward," the police no longer were concerned about his current location. They knew where he would be in a half hour. A team of officers was immediately sent to the bus station disguised in plain clothes, some dressed as the homeless, some in jeans. One female officer was dressed in skintight short shorts, five-inch-high heels, low cut cropped top, and makeup as thick as plaster. An officer dressed in khakis and a polo shirt was sent in advance to plant the package filled with newspaper, slip it into the bottom of the trash can near the ticket booth, and keep an eye on it.

An hour later, a man identified as Darkman was seen entering the bus station by other plain clothed officers on duty outside. Inside the station, Darkman thought he was being clever by first meandering around the room, then approaching several trash bins and pretending to scavenge in them, taking out various items that he really didn't care about. When he finally got to the bin containing the pack of newspaper, he reached down into the barrel digging deep. He latched onto the planted package, and as he pulled it out with a huge grin on his face, he felt something stick into his back.

When he turned around, this beautiful woman with skin like creamy caramel and a bosom exploding from her shirt smiled at him through thick, ruby red colored lips. "You are under arrest, Darnell Manson. You have a right to remain silent. Anything you say can be used against you in a court of law…"

Chapter Thirty-Four

*Sunday afternoon, after the rescue.*

Pat Karis and the other family members of Sammy Nagy were still sitting comfortably in the small room at police headquarters when Chief Rutherford burst into the room. "He's been located. He's safe and they're transporting him to Saint Elizabeth Hospital to check out his physical condition. You may want to go directly to the hospital to greet him."

After cheers of joy and relief, they hurried out of the station and quickly drove to the hospital. When the group arrived, journalists and cameras were awaiting them, but the family members ignored them completely and surged into the emergency area. Pat Karis rushed up to the nurse reception station. "We're the family of Sammy Nagy, the little boy who was recently brought here."

"One moment, please," the nurse said as she moved from her desk and went back into the adjacent hallway.

"What's the matter?" asked Adam Nagy. "Can't we see him?"

"I don't know," replied Karis. "I think the nurse is checking on it."

Those waiting for the nurse to return were anxious and restless. Some paced back and forth rather than standing. Soon the nurse returned. "The boy is currently sleeping, and the doctor doesn't want him to be disturbed. As you are aware, he's had a rough few days."

Mrs. Karis asked, "Can we perhaps just take a peek at him, please?"

The nurse gave her a sympathetic look. "Let me check with the doctor." She went back down the hallway. When she returned, she instructed, "The doctor said two of you at a time can go back, but please be very quiet and don't disturb him."

Madelyn looked around at the group. "Mom, you go first by yourself. Then Adam, you and your wife can go next. Corey and I will go last."

Pat Karis clutched her daughter's hand. "Thanks, Maddie." Then she followed another nurse who had come to direct her back to Sammy's cubicle.

The jittery feeling in Pat's stomach increased as she trotted down the hall getting closer to Sammy's cubicle. She couldn't believe she would finally see her grandson. And at last, he was safe. For over five years, she had fretted and prayed that someday she would be able to see him, to hug him, to show how much she loved him. She never even considered that these would be the horrible circumstances of that first meeting. The boy's entire life had been turned upside-down. The deaths of his father and mother, her daughter. The horrifying fire destroying his home. The ordeal he had to go through to get safely to this hospital. But finally, he was safe, and she was about to see him for the very first time.

The nurse stopped at a cubicle on the right side of the long corridor. She gently pulled the muted green curtain aside enough so Pat could look into the room. Oh, how her heart ached with every emotion possible when her eyes rested on the small child sleeping peacefully on that bed. His curly blond locks spread out on the pillow. She could see the rise and fall of his small chest against the lightweight blanket covering his tiny body. She saw his bruised arms resting on the blanket. Tears welled up in her eyes. If love could cause a heart to burst, hers would have exploded in a million pieces. He was so perfect, this little boy, so very exquisite.

She stood there just staring at him for at least five minutes. When the nurse touched her arm, Pat finally stopped staring at the child. Shaking her head, she blew a silent kiss to him before turning around and returning to the reception area.

After everyone had their chance to peek in on Sammy, they returned to the reception area to await what would happen next. The nurse had told them that Sammy had no life-threatening injuries, but he had been extremely exhausted upon his arrival at the hospital. The doctor suggested letting him sleep until he awakened on his own before trying to determine what his future fate might be.

It was late afternoon when the two detectives, who had previously talked to them in the hospital chapel early Saturday morning, approached the group as they waited.

Pat stood. "Is he awake? Can we see him?"

Detective Hamilton responded, "He is awake. They want to keep him overnight just to keep an eye on him and to be sure he has no internal injuries. They also need to work out what will happen to him when he leaves the hospital. That's why we need to talk to you, the family, again. Children Services is not formally open today, Sunday, you know. So their representative, Mrs. Lanisha Scott, would like to meet with the family tomorrow morning at nine o'clock in her office."

Pat broke in, "Wait... Let me write down this information." She reached for her purse and took out a small tablet and pen. "Lanisha Scott, you say?" She wrote it down. "What's the address?"

Hamilton said, "222 West Federal Street. It's on the fourth floor."

Karis wrote down the address on the page. "I'll be there." She turned to Madelyn.

Madelyn immediately responded, glancing at her husband, "Corey and I will be there too."

Hamilton looked toward Adam Nagy. "How about you, Mr. Nagy?"

Adam answered, "Yes, of course. My wife and I will also be there."

"Good," Hamilton commented and paused. "Now, Sammy will be in his own room shortly, room 4006, if you want to make your way upstairs about now so you can see him."

"Yes, we do," Pat Karis replied.

They all began marching toward the elevators.

****

Sammy woke up disoriented. Where was he? Oh, yeah, he was in the hospital. He had been in so many strange and frightening places these last few days that it was no wonder he was confused. One good thing—he felt rested. And he didn't feel so afraid anymore. Not like after the fire or when Darkman took him from the church. Kind of like how he felt when he was in the library with Thin Lizzy. He knew she would help him. It wasn't her fault that Darkman and Mojo were such bad guys. He was learning quickly that there were lots of bad guys in the world.

Just as a nurse came into his cubicle, he realized he had to go to the bathroom. She came over to his bed, "So you're awake, Sammy. How do you feel?"

"I have to go to the bathroom."

"Okay, I'll show you the way. Then we're going to move you to a room."

"This isn't my room?"

"No this is in the emergency ward of the hospital. People just stay here for only a short time. The doctor wants you to stay overnight to make sure you're okay."

"I'm okay. I-I thought maybe Thin Lizzy was gonna come and get me."

The nurse looked at him kindly. "That'll all be figured out tomorrow. Right now, let's get you to the bathroom and up to your room."

She unwrapped a pair of yellow cloth slippers and put them on his feet. Then she helped him off the bed and supported him while they walked across the hall to the bathroom off the corridor. "Do you need me to help you?"

"No. I can do it myself."

"Okay, you come out when you're done. I'll be waiting."

Sammy went into the bathroom and did what he needed to do. When he opened the door and looked down the hallway, he saw the nurse coming toward him. "Your room is ready, and transport is on the way to take you up. Let's get you situated back in your bed."

Five minutes later, a tall, burly man entered Sammy's cubicle, wheeling another bed. He looked at Sammy and then at a paper he had in his hand. "Are you Samuel R. Nagy Junior?"

Sammy was a little intimidated. The man sort of looked like Darkman. He knew it wasn't, but... He answered in a small voice, "Yes, sir."

"Mr. Nagy, my name is Tyrone, and how would you

like to go for a ride up the elevator on this classy bed I brought especially for you?"

Sammy was feeling a little more at ease. This man didn't sound at all like Darkman sounded. "Okay." And he started to climb out of the bed.

"No, don't get down. I'm gonna lift you over."

"Oh, okay." He lay back on the bed in the cubicle.

With strong, muscular arms, the man lifted Sammy onto the transport bed as if he were a feather, covered him with a clean, warm blanket, and put up the safety side rails. "Here we go!"

Sammy was maneuvered swiftly out of the room, down several very cool and long hallways to an elevator. When the elevator door slid open, Tyrone adeptly steered the bed into its small space. He hummed a song while the elevator went up. Sammy saw the numbers of the floor highlighted as the elevator rose. It stopped on number four. Tyrone was still humming when they exited the elevator.

His bed was pushed down another long, carpeted hallway and around a couple of corners. Some of the doors to the rooms on each side were closed; some were open. He heard muted conversations coming from a few of the rooms. He also heard someone crying from another, which concerned him a little.

Tyrone stopped at a room that showed the number 4006 on a plaque next to the door. He halted the bed, nudged the door open wider, and then placed Sammy's moving bed next to another wider, clean bed in the room. Sammy noticed it wasn't the only bed he saw. Another one was on the other side next to a large window. Someone was in that bed, but Sammy couldn't see the person because whoever it was, faced the window and was bundled in several blankets.

As Tyrone placed Sammy on the bed in the room, another nurse came into the room. "I guess you're Sammy Nagy, right?"

"Yes, ma'am."

"It's nice to meet you, Sammy. I'm Emma, and I'm going to be your nurse for a few hours." She began taking care of Sammy, piling on another warm blanket, taking his temperature, his heart rate, and his blood pressure."

"Why do you have to do all that stuff? I'm okay now. I'm not sick. And that other nurse did it all before."

Nurse Emma smiled. "Oh, this is just procedure. We have to do it to all the patients. I'm glad you're feeling better but be prepared: we'll be doing this many times while you're here."

"Oh, okay." He didn't quite understand, but many things occurred to him as of late that he didn't understand. He was learning to accept some of them.

When the nurse finished with all the routine procedures, she asked, "Are you hungry? I've been told you haven't eaten all day."

With everything that had been going on, Sammy hadn't realized, but he was very hungry. "Yeah, I am kinda hungry."

"I'll have some food sent up to you." As she was about to leave, she noticed movement from the other bed. "Oh, Sammy, the young man on the other side of the room is Eli. He's eleven years old."

Eli had turned around and curiously looked at Sammy and raised his hand. "Hi."

Sammy responded, "Hi, I'm Sammy."

The nurse smiled as she left the room to order something to eat for the boy.

Sammy looked around the room. A television was attached to the wall in front of him, but it wasn't turned on. A light green curtain on a bar was bunched up between Eli and Sammy's beds. Another curtain was also on his other side, also all bunched up at the end. He was wondering how long it would take before he'd get some food. His stomach was growling, and it felt like something was moving inside it. He looked toward the large window to determine if he could see anything, but his bed was too far from it.

When he turned his head back the other way, a man dressed all in blue entered his room and came over to his bed. "Hello, Sammy, I'm Dr. Silverman."

Sammy looked around. "What happened to the other doctor?"

"Are you talking about Dr. Dresden?"

"Yes, sir."

"Well, Dr. Dresden just works in the emergency area. I'm going to take care of you up here, just like I take care of your roommate, Eli, over there." He looked toward Eli. "Right Eli?"

Eli nodded his head.

Then Dr. Silverman turned back to Sammy. "I think Nurse Emma told you that we're keeping you overnight just as a precaution."

"Where am I gonna go tomorrow? Back with Thin Lizzy?"

Kindly and softly, the doctor responded, "I don't know the answer to that yet, Sammy. I believe that will be determined tomorrow." He paused. "What I wanted to talk to you about now is that there are several people who want to see you as soon as possible."

Sammy squinted his eyes. "Who? Is Thin Lizzy

here?"

"I don't know about Thin Lizzy, but your grandmother, your aunts, and your uncles are here."

Confusion took over Sammy's entire face. "I-I don't have any grandmother or any aunts and uncles."

"Yes, you do, Sammy. That's what I'm here to tell you. Your grandmother's name is Mrs. Patricia Karis. She is the mother of your mother Alyssa."

Not only was Sammy's stomach flip-flopping now, but his brain was in turmoil. He knew nothing about a grandmother. His mommy and daddy told him that all his grandparents were dead, so how could he have a grandmother? His parents wouldn't tell him a lie, would they? Sammy didn't know what to say to the doctor. He just stared at him with his mouth half open.

He finally shook his head and uttered, "No, I don't have a grandmother."

Dr. Silverman tried to convince him about his newly found relatives. "Yes, you do, and she wants to meet you very much, as well as your Aunt Madelyn, who is your mother's sister, and your Uncle Adam, who's your father's brother."

No! His mother didn't have a sister and his father didn't have a brother. They would've told him about them. Why is this doctor saying these things? If they were true, why didn't his mom and dad tell him about these people? The more he thought about it, the more confused he became.

The doctor's eyes were filled with compassion. The poor child's mind was so befuddled. He wasn't sure if with all that had happened to him, perhaps he wasn't ready to meet these newly found kinfolk. He asked, "Would you agree to see these people?"

His entire world had fallen apart and everything new was jumbled and chaotic, making no sense to him at all. He felt almost as terrified now as when he had hid in the bathroom closet during the fire. "I-I don't know. I-I don't know."

The doctor gave him a little more time to toss it around in his head. He waited.

Finally, Sammy mumbled, "Can I eat first?"

The doctor smiled. "Sure. You can eat first. Then we'll let them in your room just one or two at a time. Okay?"

"Okay."

The doctor started to leave. Before he went out the door, Sammy pleaded, "Can Thin Lizzy come with all of them?"

Chapter Thirty-Five

*Sunday afternoon, the hospital.*

Nothing could explain how Ryan Nesbitt truly felt. In addition to some exceptionally horrible catastrophes that had recently affected him, his fiancée, the woman he thought he loved and with whom he expected to spend the rest of his life, was a cheat, a liar, a bitch!

After Melanie had left that morning, he lay in the bed with his mind going back and forth over the total mess his life had become. How could he recover from all this? Sure, his broken bones would mend. The cuts and bruises on his skin would heal. But how could he fix a broken heart and a shattered mind?

With his one free hand, he seized the edge of his blanket, soiled from the earlier coffee spill, pulled it toward him, and covered his face. He lay there weeping softly for what seemed like an eternity. He wanted to die. What was the use of living anymore?

"Ryan?"

Someone had entered his room.

"Ryan? Are you all right?"

Someone gently pulled the blanket away from his face. His mother stood looking down at him, her expression showing serious concern.

"Mom. it's you. You came back?"

"I saw the news on TV about the fire and your boss. Oh, Ryan, I'm so sorry. I had to come back to be with you. This is horrible. You must be out of your mind with grief. And with your accident and everything…"

Ryan couldn't handle it anymore. He began to wail like he did when he was a child. He couldn't help it. The sight of his mother coming to be by his side, to comfort him in his dire time of need was overwhelming.

His mother reached down and hugged him as best she could despite all his constraints. She whispered in his ear, trying to find words to comfort him.

Ryan's tears began to slacken. "Mom, how could all this stuff happen? How? Sam and Alyssa are dead. I can't wrap my brain around that."

His mother sat at the side of his bed, lifted his hand to her lips and gently kissed it, but she let him express his feelings.

"And, Mom, worst of all…" he began to tear up again. "The fire at Sam's house?" He took a deep breath. "It wasn't an accident. It was deliberately set. And my accident wasn't an accident either."

Maureen suddenly dropped his hand. "What are you saying?"

"I'm saying they killed Sam and Alyssa, and they tried to kill me too."

"What! Ryan, who tried to kill you? I thought somebody just forced you off the road."

"They did, but it was no accident."

His mother's mouth shot open, and she continued to blink her eyes as if she were trying to erase what Ryan had just told her. "Are you serious? Who Ryan? Who did this to you and Sam?"

Ryan looked directly at his mother. He decided he was through keeping secrets. No more. He had never mentioned Rocco Banetti's name to anyone except Sam,

Carl, and Alyssa. He had kept his word. And look what happened. Look what it got him. It was time to reveal what a scheming, degenerate bastard Rocco Banetti really was.

"It was Rocco Banetti."

Stunned, Maureen dropped down onto the chair. "Ryan, I know this man owns quite a few businesses and has made a name for himself in this part of the state. What makes you think Rocco Banetti had something to do with your accident and your boss's death?"

He stared directly into her eyes. "Mom, he's a client I work on at the law firm. Actually, he is the *main* client I work on. Part of my contract when I was hired was that I was never to tell anyone *anything* about him, not even the fact that he was a client."

"Why would all this secrecy business be a part of your contract? Why would you think he is responsible for all this?"

"Because he is an unscrupulous, deceitful, lying bastard. That's why!"

When she continued to stare at him, he said, "I'm definitely sure of this, Mom. That man is in cahoots with cartels as far away as Mexico. He operates a sex slave ring with very young girls from several foreign countries, including Russia and China. And those are just some of the stuff he fronts. He's into so much illegal and degenerate shit, the man is worse than the devil himself."

"All right then, Ryan. If this Banetti person is so awful, you have to do something to stop this, or he'll kill you next time for sure. You have to tell the police before he comes after you again."

He shook his head. "I'll go to prison. When I went to work for the law firm, I knew what my job would be.

Of course, at the time, I really didn't know just how wide the scope of his corruption was, but when I learned, I continued to work there anyhow. I didn't quit. So my being complicit with the knowledge of his crimes, I'm also guilty of a crime too."

His mother was anything but convinced. "Think about the damage he has done to so many lives. If you don't do something now, he'll continue to hurt many more people with drugs and his sex crimes. And who's to say he won't come after you again? That's almost a given. Next time, you won't just end up in the hospital. You'll end up in the morgue. You have to do something, *now*!"

He groaned, "I don't know, I don't know. I'm scared, Mom. I'm really scared."

She leaned over and kissed him on his cheek. "I know, son. I know." She sat back down and was silent for a few seconds. Then she quietly admitted, "Ryan, I know you think of me as some religious zealot." She chuckled. "Maybe I am." Pause. "I know as a kid, you hated always going to church with me, and you rebelled against religion as you grew up." Another pause. "But I also know that you are basically a good man. You wouldn't intentionally inflict pain and anguish on another person. And if you thought you could help other people, you would do it."

She turned her head toward the ceiling and rubbed her chin. "I remember when you were, oh, maybe about ten years old. Remember that old lady who lived down the street who had all her utilities shut off because she couldn't pay her bills? Without me or anyone else prompting you, you opened up a lemonade stand on the corner of the street to raise money to help her out.

Remember?"

Ryan nodded his head.

His mother continued, "Of course, you didn't make enough money to put a dent in her bills, but you were able to bring attention to her problem, so she got help somewhere else." Another pause. "You cared, Ryan. You cared. And this is your chance to help so many people. To save your own life as well as others. Think of those poor girls involved in that horrible man's corruption. Or those whose lives are devastated by the drugs he puts out on the market. Ryan, there is more than just your own self to think about."

Sadly, he responded, "But I don't want to go to prison, Mom."

She clasped his hand again. "I know you don't, son. We'll get a good lawyer for you. And I'm sure if you provide evidence about this monster's inhumane corruption and testify against him, the law will go easier on you. Ryan, it's the right thing to do. You know it as well as I do."

Ryan's head was spinning. He knew his mother was absolutely right. Sure, he was aware of Banetti's unlawful activities, but to him, it was only on paper. He didn't see the victims of the crimes committed by the man. He didn't see the bodies that the man left behind. And he had to admit—selfishly, he blocked the consequences of it all out of his mind. Yes, his mother was right. It was time for him to own up to his own transgressions and take what punishment he deserved.

For a moment, he thought of Melanie. Isn't that exactly what she had done? She didn't have to tell him when she did about Banetti being her uncle. Surely, she knew Ryan would be very upset with that admission and

251

might break the engagement. But she told him anyhow. Granted, he would probably have eventually found it out. But she took the initiative and confessed to him, which was probably very difficult for her to do. Maybe she did it because she really did love him…

But for now, he had to make his own decision about the direction his life would go. "You're right, Mom. I have to take responsibility for what I've done and to stop that man from killing and corrupting anyone else. Will you call the police station and tell them to send somebody over here to talk to me. Tell them I have information on who killed Sam and Alyssa Nagy."

****

Wasting no time, Maureen Nesbit pulled out her cellphone and looked up the non-emergency number of the police department. "Hello, my name is Maureen Nesbit. I'm calling for my son, Ryan Nesbit. He's a patient in Saint Elizabeth Hospital because of injuries he received in a car accident."

The dispatcher asked, *"Was there an officer at the scene of the accident?"*

"Oh, this isn't actually about the accident. What he wanted was for an officer to come talk to him. He has information about that fire that killed Mr. and Mrs. Sam Nagy. He knows who is responsible for their deaths."

She turned to Ryan, who was intently looking at her. "She told me to hold for a few seconds." They waited.

Soon a different voice came on the line. *"Hello, ma'am, this is Detective Willard Hamilton with the Youngstown Police Department. I understand you have information about the fire at the Nagy household?"*

"I don't have that information. It's my son, Ryan Nesbit. His boss was Sam Nagy, and he has some things he'd like to tell you."

*"My partner and I will be there in five minutes."*

\*\*\*\*

Detectives Atkinson and Hamilton were about to leave the hospital after Sammy was settled in his room and they had discussed the situation with the doctors. They left a police officer on duty to watch the boy. When Hamilton received the call from dispatch about a man in that very hospital who wanted to speak to the police regarding the Nagy fire, their plans changed. He looked at Atkinson. "The woman said her son has information about the fire."

"Her son?"

"Apparently, he was in some kind of car accident, and he told his mom he has some information to give us."

"Well, ain't that somethin'!" remarked Atkinson. "Guess our luck is really changing for the better. About time. What room is he in?"

They took the elevator up to the floor where Ryan Nesbitt was located. When they walked into the room, they saw a woman standing by the window while a young man lay stiff as a log on the bed. His head was bandaged, casts covered one leg and one arm; bruises spotted his entire body. His eyes, red and swollen, indicated a recent bout of tears.

"Geez, man," Atkinson said, "you really were in some accident."

Ryan said nothing, only looked at the detectives with both dread and conviction.

Hamilton said, "Your mother told us you have some information on the Nagy fire?"

Ryan blinked his eyes a few times and asked his mother, "Mom, will you raise my bed up a little."

The detectives moved out of her way so the un-named woman could take care of the man's request. Atkinson took out her note pad and pen, readying for this man's unofficial statement.

Ryan took a deep breath. "My name is Ryan Nesbitt. I 'm an attorney working at the Padgett & Nagy law firm in downtown Youngstown. My duties at the firm almost exclusively involve working on the business and personal accounts of Mr. Rocco E. Banetti, who I believe is responsible for the deaths of Sam and Alyssa Nagy."

Both detective's eyes bulged as Ryan began to make this statement. Atkinson's pen stopped in mid-air. Hamilton cautioned, "Are you sure you want to make this statement without an attorney present?"

After glancing at his mother, with a sober face, Ryan replied, "Yes, I'm sure."

Hamilton and Atkinson tilted their heads toward one another. Hamilton agreed, "Well, then, go ahead, Mr. Nesbitt."

Ryan briefly told them about the work he did for the law firm, focusing on the unscrupulous activities of Rocco Banetti. Then he mentioned how he thought Banetti's men had been following him for several weeks leading up to his car accident. He told them the circumstances and his suspicion about the nature of that accident. He stated that when he heard that the fire at the Nagy house was suspicious, he had to conclude that his accident and the deaths of Sam and Alyssa had to be the work of Rocco Banetti. Finally, he told them unbeknown to him, Banetti's niece was his fiancée. He didn't go into any details about their relationship but did mention that Melanie had recently confessed to him that their original hook-up in a bar had been orchestrated by Banetti. He also mentioned that she too thought her uncle was responsible for his accident and the deaths of the Nagys.

After Ryan completed what he had to say, Hamilton asked, "Are you willing to make this an official statement, Mr. Nesbitt?"

"Oh, yes. Yes, I am."

Hamilton advised, "You know this means you will be taken into custody as soon as you have recuperated sufficiently, and we'll be putting an officer outside your room until that time. Also, while in the hospital, the only visitors you will be permitted will be your attorney and your mother. So, are you sure about your decision?"

"Yes, detective, I'm sure." He sarcastically chuckled, "Hell, after what I've told you about Banetti, I welcome the protection of a police officer outside my door."

"Then I'm going to read you your rights and I advise you to get an attorney as soon as possible."

Chapter Thirty-Six

*Sunday afternoon, after the rescue.*

On most Sunday mornings, Rocco Banetti attended Mass at the Holy Family Parish in Poland, Ohio. This bright September Sunday had been no exception. He always dressed in a smartly tailored linen suit, crisp white shirt, and a luxurious Italian tie, while his wife Stella usually chose a flowing designer dress, four-inch heels on her narrow, delicate feet, and styled her raven black hair coiffed to perfection.

When Rocco and Stella returned to their lovely home from church after Mass that afternoon, their personal chef had prepared the perfect meal of honey-glazed spiced roast goose and herby comfit potatoes for them and their guests, the head of a prestigious research hospital in Pittsburgh, Dr. Alexander Galanis and his wife Darla. They had just sat down in the huge dining room to enjoy their early dinner when the door chime echoed from the front of the house.

As the server was passing out their appetizers of gruyere and crab palmiers, the housekeeper quietly entered the dining room, walked over to Rocco and in broken English whispered in his ear so no one else could hear, "Sir, two detectives come to see you. They say very important and must talk now."

Rocco was only slightly concerned. He was sure the police were looking into the Nagy fire. Benny Ricci and his men would have done an excellent job and not left any incriminating evidence. He breathed a heavy sigh and proclaimed, "Please excuse me for a few moments, Alex and Darla. I have some urgent business to attend. Enjoy the crab, and I'll be back shortly."

His two guests nodded their heads as they munched on their appetizers.

Banetti followed Olga to the foyer where an older man and a much younger woman waited for him. "What's this all about, detectives? You've interrupted my dinner this afternoon."

Hamilton and Atkinson stood at the entranceway. Their first impressions of Rocco Banetti were spot-on. Cocky, arrogant, just an overbearing, high-and-mighty ass. But they were professional law enforcement officers and would not treat this egotistical son-of-a-bitch any different than they would have treated Mother Theresa. Hamilton stated, "Mr. Rocco Banetti, you need to come with us to police headquarters to answer a few questions."

The surprise on Banetti's face was very evident. He had expected them to ask a few simple questions about Sam Nagy and that terrible fire, and that would be it, not haul him off to police headquarters. But he responded in his typical contentious manner. "I'm sorry, detectives. I'm unable to leave my guests at this time. How about I join you there in a few hours after my guests have departed?"

Hamilton countered, "I'm afraid that won't do, Mr. Banetti. This is not a request. You need to come with us now."

Before Banetti had a chance to respond to the detective's demand, he heard loud sirens approaching the house. Screeching tires resounded from the other side of the doorway. Soon, a pounding on the door startled them. Banetti quickly opened the door to a mass of uniformed officers—FBI, DOJ, the DEA. With weapons drawn, several of them charged through the heavy, oak doorway. An officer with FBI emblazoned on his jacket stepped forward. "Rocco E. Banetti, you are under arrest."

The look on Banetti's face was indescribable. The faces of the two detectives revealed complete shock. They were totally unaware of any ongoing federal investigation involving Banetti. Hamilton quickly asked the FBI arresting officer, "What is going on? We're here to take Mr. Banetti in for questioning about a suspicious fire in our city."

"I'm sorry. Who are you?"

"Detective Willard Hamilton of the Youngstown

Police Department. This is my partner, Detective Stacey Atkinson." Both detectives pulled out their badges to verify their identities.

"Well, it appears we're in a quandary here. Rocco Banetti is coming with us."

Hamilton asked, "What are you charging him with?"

The FBI agent smirked. "The list is very long."

The agent next to him pulled out the lengthy warrant and began to read some of the charges, "Money laundering, tax fraud, tax evasion, securities fraud, extortion, kidnapping, sexual exploitation of children... Need I go on?"

Hamilton held up his hand, "No, no, that's enough." He looked around at all the agents in the foyer. "Are you here to search his home?"

The FBI agent replied, "Yes, we are. After we take him into custody."

"Do you mind if my partner and I observe?"

"Not at all. Just stay out of our way."

Another agent of the FBI moved forward and approached Banetti. "Turn around, sir." Roughly, he aided Banetti in obeying his command.

Without a word, Banetti turned and placed his hands behind his back as the agent clipped the handcuffs tightly around his wrists.

Chapter Thirty-Seven

*Sunday afternoon, after the rescue.*

An orderly dressed in gray scrubs came into Sammy's hospital room carrying a tray of food. He looked at a small slip of paper on the tray. "Are you Sammy Nagy?"

Sammy responded, "Yes, sir."

The orderly moved the over-bed table in front of Sammy and placed the food tray on it. "Enjoy your lunch."

Sammy looked around the room before he took the lid off his food. As he lifted it, steamy, pleasant odors permeated his nose. Softly, he commented, "It smells good."

He lifted a juicy hamburger with melted cheese and took a big bite. "Mmm, good." He sat the burger down and picked up a crispy French fry, biting a piece, then putting the entire fry in his mouth, chewing it well. "Mmm."

"That food must be pretty good with all that noise you're making over there," joked Eli from the other side of the room.

Between bites, Sammy mumbled, "Sure is. I was really, really hungry."

Eli questioned, "Why? When was the last time you had something to eat?"

Sammy paused his chewing. "Uh, I think it was

yesterday at supper at the church. Yeah." He continued chomping on his food.

"You ate in a church?"

Sammy placed the hamburger back on his plate. "Yeah, lots of bad stuff has happened to me."

In a caring voice, Eli asked, "Do you wanna talk about it?"

Sammy picked up his burger again. "No, not right now. Maybe later."

"Okay," Eli agreed and was quiet for a while. Then he mentioned, "I fell off my bike and hit my head. My mom was really mad at me 'cause I forgot to wear my helmet. She yelled at me at first. Then when I started actin' goofy, she wasn't mad anymore. She just brought me to the hospital."

Between bites Sammy asked, "Are you still acting goofy?"

"Naw. I think I'm okay now. The doctor just wanted to keep me here to make sure. I'm supposed to go home tomorrow." He paused. "How 'bout you? The doctor said you can go home tomorrow, too."

Again Sammy stopped eating and became sullen. "I don't know where I'm gonna go?"

"What do you mean? Are your mom and dad divorced or something?"

"No, not that?"

"Why don't you know where you're gonna go then?"

Sammy completely lost his appetite. He placed the lid over the half-eaten food on the tray. "'Cause my house burned down and I think my mommy and daddy are dead."

Eli was speechless for a few seconds, then said,

"Wow! That's a bummer." He looked over at Sammy and saw tears running down his roommate's cheeks. He decided he didn't want to pursue this conversation anymore, and simply said, "Uh, sorry, uh Sammy." Then he rested back on his pillow with thoughts of gratitude for his own life running through his head.

Sammy shoved the over-bed table out of his way and leaned back on his pillow. The events of the last few days were bombarding his brain full force. Yes, he finally admitted to himself that his mom and dad were probably dead, and he would never, ever see them again. What would happen to him now? Would Thin Lizzy let him stay with her? But she didn't live anywhere either. How would he even go to school?

And that doctor said he had a grandmother. No, he couldn't have. His mommy said that his grandmas and grandpas were all dead, so how could he still have a grandma? And aunts and uncles too? His head was swimming. He squeezed his eyes shut, hoping everything would come back to normal when he opened them. As he bowed his head with is eyes tightly closed, he felt someone touch his arm. "Sammy?"

He opened his eyes to see that doctor, Dr. Silverman, standing near him. "Sammy, your grandmother and Elizabeth Thorpe are here to see you. They're right outside the door. May they come in?"

Sammy was confused. "What about Thin Lizzy? Doesn't she want to see me?"

Elizabeth Thorpe, a.k.a., Thin Lizzy, who was standing on the other side of the long curtain, heard Sammy's pleading voice. She was not a forceful person, and her mind didn't always catch on to things like she wanted, but in Sammy's voice, she heard pain and torment. Over the past few days she had learned so much more about him and the sorrow to which he was dealing. Thus, though she was shy and maybe a little backward, she knew Sammy needed something familiar, something he could depend on, something stable in his life.

She pushed the curtain back. "I'm here, Sammy. I'm right here."

****

When Thin Lizzy moved the hospital curtain aside and walked into Sammy's room, his blue eyes brightened, and he beamed, "Thin Lizzy, you're here!"

The doctor moved aside, so she could reach down to hug him. "Yeah, Sammy, I been waitin' and waitin' for dem to find you. I was so mad when Darkman stole you. I feel real bad he did dat. I'm so sorry."

With happy tears in his eyes, Sammy responded, "It wasn't your fault, Thin Lizzy. You been so good to me, and I didn't know if I'd ever see you again." Then his voice quieted, and his body slackened. "You know, I think my mommy and daddy are dead."

Thin Lizzy's eyes also misted with tears. "I know, Sammy. I know." She held the boy while they both cried.

Pat Karis, who had also stepped into the room from behind the curtain, tried to contain the tears that also had accumulated in her eyes. Even though the loss of her daughter had such a devastating impact on her life, she knew this poor child had suffered too many inconceivable losses. The events of the past few days would affect him for his entire life.

Pat slowly walked over to Sammy's bed and stood beside Thin Lizzy, who had released Sammy to dry her tears with her sweatshirt sleeve. Pat moved a little closer to Sammy. Thin Lizzy stepped back to allow her to approach the boy. Pat gently touched his arm. "Sammy, I'm your grandmother."

Sammy's eyes opened wide. "You look just like Mommy, only with different hair!"

Pat smiled wistfully. "Yes, I've often been told that." She took his hand. "You know, I've wanted to meet you for a very long time."

Sammy let her hold his hand. "H-how come you didn't come to visit us? Didn't you know where I lived?"

"Yes, I knew where you lived, but... Perhaps we can talk about that some other time, okay?"

"Okay, I guess."

Pat continued in a soft, tender voice, "I've been told about the terrible things that have happened to you, and I want you to know that you don't have to worry about anything anymore. I'm going to take care of you."

"What do you mean?"

"I mean everything is going to be okay. You're going to come live with me."

"With you? What about Mommy and Daddy?" He hesitated. "Oh yeah. They're dead. I forgot."

With downcast tear-filled eyes and quivering lips, she replied, "Yes, they are. I'm so sorry."

"What about my house? Are we gonna live there?"

"No, I'm afraid the fire destroyed it completely."

"You mean all my stuff was burned up, my toys and everything?"

"Yes. Yes, they were." She paused. "But we're going to buy you new clothes and new toys just like your old ones, or if you like, we'll buy different ones."

"What about my school and my friends, Corbin and Jace?"

"Well, you'll go to a different school, but I'll make

sure you'll get to see Corbin and Jake."

"It's not Jake. It's Jace."

Pat chuckled, "Oh, I'm sorry. I meant Jace."

"That's okay. Daddy always calls him Jake too. He got confused sometimes."

That remark caused all those in the room to chuckle a little—even Eli, who had been listening in on the conversation from the other side of the room.

Chapter Thirty-Eight

*Monday morning, after the rescue.*

At nine o'clock Monday morning, Patricia Karis, her daughter and son-in-law, Madelyn and Corey Winthrop, and Sam Nagy's brother and sister-in-law, Adam and Naomi Nagy, met with Lanisha Scott, a case worker with the Mahoning County Children Services. The purpose of the meeting was to give temporary custody of Sammy Nagy to Patricia Karis until the court could appoint her sole and legal guardianship of the boy. Since Sammy had literally become an orphan, it was imperative that arrangements were made immediately to determine who would care for him. Also present, was Pat's attorney, Donald D. Dugan.

After introductions were made, Ms. Scott proceeded, "Mrs. Karis, I understand you are the grandmother of the child and wish to take full responsibility for his financial and physical care and upbringing."

"Yes, that is correct."

"Pardon me for bringing this up," Scott said, "how old are you, Mrs. Karis?"

Somewhat surprised, Karis answered, "I'm sixty-three."

Scott continued, "You do realize you will be in your mid-seventies when the boy graduates high school—if you live to that age."

Pat was getting a little miffed. "What is your point, Ms. Scott?"

"My concern is for the boy and his future. I want to be sure there is no danger of him being abandoned before he is able to reach his full potential."

Pat held her temper in check. "Two things here, Ms. Scott. Number one, I am a very wealthy woman. I have had a trust fund set up for this boy since I learned of his birth. So financially, he is set for life. Now, number two, my daughter, Madelyn, and her husband, as well as Sam Nagy's brother, Adam, and his wife, who are all here this morning, have all agreed and will put in a signed, legal document that they will care for the boy if anything should happen to me. In other words—if I die before he is capable of being on his own." She breathed a heavy sigh. "I hope that is sufficient enough to show that the boy will not be on the street again."

"I'm sorry if I upset you, ma'am, but understand, it is the duty of this office to make sure that does not happen again."

Pat's temper subsided a little. "I do understand that, Ms. Scott. However, I know you are not aware of what my relationship had been with my daughter. That fire, the deaths of my daughter and her husband, I don't think any of it would ever have occurred had my daughter allowed me to be part of her life. And, then my grandson would never have ended up all alone miles from his home."

"Mrs. Karis, are you insinuating that perhaps your daughter never would have wanted you to have custody of her child?"

Pat hesitated before answering. "I don't know."

No one spoke for several seconds. Then the

attorney, Donald Dugan, exclaimed, "Ms. Scott, since my client's daughter and son-in-law are not available to express their wishes, under the urgency of the circumstances and with Mrs. Karis' financial means and relationship to the child, don't you think it warrants immediate action on this matter? For your information, at Mrs. Karis' request, I have contacted the offices of Padgett & Nagy, LLP, inquiring if they are in possession of any legal documents, such as the wills of the boy's parents, that might negate Mrs. Karis' right to take custody of the boy or provide any other information regarding the guardianship of him in the event of their deaths. However, currently we are unable to locate the other managing partner, Carl Padgett. In the meantime, I have also begun a search with the Probate Court to see if such documents exist. I will certainly provide you with this information as soon as it becomes available to me.

Lanisha Scott glanced around the room. Then individually she asked the relatives present their opinions regarding Mrs. Karis taking guardianship of the child. Each one unanimously agreed that her care would be the best solution to this pressing issue. After further consideration and additional questions, Ms. Scott presented papers to grant temporary custody of Sammy Nagy to his grandmother.

Thus, as the family members of the child left the children services office and made their way to the hospital to see Sammy, their spirits were somewhat lifted, knowing the boy would have a home with his grandmother for as long as he needed and wanted it.

****

Sammy hadn't slept well the night before. Even for a five-year-old, he was scared. What would happen now?

It was verified that his mother and father had died, though he wasn't exactly sure of the circumstances. He knew there had been bad men. He had seen them. He also heard the sound of the gunfire while he was hiding. Then there was the actual fire. He knew something very bad had happened. And now, though unaware, at that very moment while he lay in his hospital bed, his fate was being decided for him.

Since it was Monday morning, the regular cartoons that he usually watched on weekends were not on the television. At home, he would have been in school, sitting next to Corbin and Jace at their table. The class would probably be taking turns standing beside their chairs and telling Mrs. Eckhart what they had done over the weekend. Sammy would never want to tell his friends and teacher about this past weekend. He wanted to forget it forever.

Since he wasn't in school and he was bored, with the TV remote, he finally found a cable cartoon channel of which he was unfamiliar. He put that channel on for a while and watched it, waiting for what would happen to him next.

Eventually, in the next bed, Eli, who had gone back to sleep after breakfast, awakened. Sammy asked, "Is the TV on too loud?"

"Naw," replied Eli. I'm just tired of being here. I wanna go home?"

Sammy thought the same thing, but he didn't say it because he knew he couldn't go home, and speaking about it would only make him sad again. He asked, "When is your mom coming to get you?"

"Oh, I dunno. Everything takes forever in this hospital. I got football practice today. I sure want to go.

They'll kick me off the team if I miss too many practices. But I'm not sure if my mom will let me go."

"Is this at your school?"

"No, this is just a league me and my friends are in."

"What school do you go to?"

"Austintown Middle School. I'm in the sixth grade. How 'bout you?"

Sammy didn't answer right away. "Well, I did go to Saint Joseph the Provider, but... I don't know what school I'll go to now."

Eli muttered, "Oh yeah, I forgot about all that stuff you have goin' on." A pause. "Sorry."

"That's okay."

Their conversation ended as Eli turned on his TV to a sports channel.

About ten o'clock Eli's mother arrived at the hospital to take him home. He dressed while he waited for the transport to take him down in a wheelchair. When he left, he had his mother write down his cellphone number and give it to Sammy. As he was led out of the room, he said, "When you find out what's happening to you, call me and we can maybe hang out sometime. Right, Mom?"

His mother smiled and nodded her head.

After they were gone, Sammy was all alone again. He turned off the television, closed his eyes, and lay back on the bed. His mind was jumbled with past horrors and future scary unknowns. When he heard the rustle of his curtain, he opened his eyes to see the morning nurse come in again. "I'm going to take your vitals one last time. You're going home today."

"I'm gonna go home?"

The nurse, knowing Sammy's predicament, felt

remorse. "I'm sorry. I just meant you're leaving the hospital."

"Where my gonna go?"

"The doctor and your grandmother will be in to talk to you about that."

"What about Thin Lizzy?"

"Uh, I don't know anything about a Thin Lizzy. Talk to Dr. Silverman about that."

"Oh, okay."

The nurse completed taking Sammy's vitals and logging them into the computer. As she was leaving his room, she said, "I'll be back a little later to change your bandages."

"Oh, okay."

Sammy lay in the bed, not knowing what he was supposed to do now. Should he get dressed? Where were the clothes from the church that he had on when Darkman took him? Was he supposed to just walk out the door or what?

About a half hour after the nurse had gone and just when he was about to jump down from the bed to do something of which he wasn't sure, Dr. Silverman entered his room. "Well, Sammy, are you ready to get out of this place?"

"Yes, sir." A pause. "But where my gonna go?"

"That's definitely a good question. And an important one too. You see, your grandmother should be here soon. She stopped at the store to buy you some fresh clothes."

"What about my clothes from the church?"

"I don't know anything about them. We'll probably give then back to the church."

"Oh." Another pause. "What about Thin Lizzy? Is

she coming with me?"

"Thin Lizzy?"

"Yes. She's my friend. She saved me from being killed by that black car. She took care of me."

"I think that is something you'll have to discuss with your grandmother." The doctor went to the computer to look at Sammy's medical statistics so he could release him.

The curtain moved again, and the lady who said she was his grandmother came over to the bed carrying a plastic bag. "Hello, Sammy. How are you this morning?"

"Okay, I guess."

"Did they tell you that you're going home with me today?"

"Yes, ma'am."

"I've brought you some new clothes. Would you like to put them on? I've removed all the tags for you."

Dr. Silverman interrupted, "Perhaps, Sammy would like to take a shower before the nurse changes his bandages." He looked at the boy. "Do you need any help? I can call the nurse in to help you."

"No, I can do it myself." Confused, he looked at his wrapped, right hand. "What'll I do with all this stuff on my hands and feet?"

Dr. Silverman came over closer to him. "Just peel them off and leave them on the floor in the bathroom. The nurse will dispose of them." He touched his arm. "Are you sure you don't need any help?"

"Yes, sir."

Pat Karis lowered the bed so he could step down more easily. She handed him the bag. "Here are your new clothes."

He took the bag from her. "What'll I do with the

stuff I got on?"

The doctor answered him, "Leave them on the floor also. We'll take care of them."

"Okay," he responded as he carried the bag into the bathroom with him.

What now? He was frightened. He removed the clothes from the bag and placed them on the sink counter. Then he stripped off the night shirt and the disposable underwear, placing them in a pile on the floor as he was told. He tore off all the bandages on his feet and hands and put them in another pile on the floor. Then he used the toilet before going into the shower stall.

This shower looked different than the one he had at home. It didn't even have a door on it. When he looked at the faucets, they were much too high for him to reach, and he wasn't sure how to turn them on. Maybe he should get his new grandma to help him get started.

He stepped back out of the stall, slipped on the disposable underwear—he didn't want to be naked—and went over to the bathroom door. Opening it up just enough to stick his head out, he looked around the room. The grandma lady was sitting on the edge of his bed. He needed to get her attention. "Uh, Gramma Lady, I-I need some help turning on the shower."

Pat Karis quickly looked his way and got off the bed. "Sure, Sammy, what can I do?"

"It's too high, and I can't figure out how to turn it on."

"Well, I can help you with that."

Sammy moved away from the door to allow Pat to enter.

Pat looked at the faucet mechanism. "I see what you mean." Standing to the side, she turned the water on and adjusted the temperature to medium hot. "Do you want to see if this is too hot or too cold?"

She moved away so Sammy could check the temperature.

He put his hand under the streaming water and looked up at her. "That's okay."

"Do you need anything else?"

"I-I don't think so."

"Do you want me to stay in here while you wash?"

Sammy hesitated. "Do you have to?"

She gently smiled. "No, I don't." Her smile grew a little wider. "How about if you call me in when you're done, so I can turn off the water?"

"Okay."

Pat left the bathroom.

After his grandmother had gone, Sammy removed the disposal underwear again and climbed his naked, little body into the shower.

Oh, the water felt so good on his sore muscles, the bruises, the cuts, the aches. His injured hand burned a little when the water touched the tender skin but after a while it felt good. He stood in the shower and let the hot water fall on his entire body. He didn't know how long he stood there with the hot water cascading over him. He wanted to stay there forever. But he heard a distant knock on the door. "Everything all right in there, Sammy?"

Quickly, he answered, "Yes, ma'am."

He grabbed the washcloth and rushed to wash himself before he exited the shower. After drying with the white, scratchy towel nearby, he dressed in his new clothes—underwear, blue sweatpants, red and blue T-shirt, and blue hoodie sweatshirt. He left the blue socks and white sneakers in the plastic bag and exited the bathroom. "I'm done now. Will you turn off the water for me?"

As Pat got off the bed to go into the bathroom, she remarked, "My, you look very nice,"

The nurse was also in his room. "I'm going to put some clean bandages on your feet and hand, Sammy. They need some protection for a couple more days, so they can heal."

Sammy sat back on the bed while the nurse tended to his injured feet. Pat returned to the room and sat on the chair while the nurse took care of Sammy's wounds. When the nurse had medicated and bandaged all the injuries, she also put on his new socks and shoes. "There!" she said. "You are ready to go. The transport will be here shortly." She left the room.

Sammy glanced around. Bewildered, he asked his grandmother, "Is Thin Lizzy coming with us?"

Somberly, Pat replied, "No, she's gone back home."

"But she doesn't have a home. She's just like me."

Pat gently clasp his hand. "You will have a home with me now. You're my grandson. I'm going to take care of you."

"But why can't Thin Lizzy come live with us, too? She's my friend." A sad pout took over his face as he concentrated his doleful eyes on his bandaged hand.

Pat was somewhat caught off balance. "Well, I-I don't know. Perhaps she wouldn't want to live with us."

He abruptly looked up at her, widely opening his eyes. "We can ask her, can't we? She doesn't have a home to live in."

The boy was right. The woman who saved her precious grandson's life and who kept him safe deserved some type of recognition more than a simple *thank you*.

In fact, Thin Lizzy deserved so much more.

The boy gave her an idea. A good idea. Hmm. Since she was still in charge of Karis Industries and needing to keep it thriving and profitable, Sammy would need a nanny of some sort to look after him when she wasn't around. No way was she able to retire at this point in her life. That Elizabeth Thorpe woman was definitely a caring person. Evidence of that was how she took care of Sammy as best she could after she found him. If it hadn't been for her, who knows what would've happened to her grandson. What if...

"You know what, Sammy. You're right. We *can* ask her."

## Chapter Thirty-Nine

*Monday afternoon, after the rescue.*

Ryan Nesbitt's hospital room remained heavily guarded. In fact, the entire hospital enjoyed a heavy police presence throughout the building and grounds. His mother did not return to Cleveland but had spent the night at his apartment. He was under house arrest, but the police decided to allow his mother to stay with him. She had retained Kirk Huxley, a Cleveland criminal attorney, to represent her son. Kirk had been there in the morning while Ryan gave his official statements to the two detectives and the court reporter.

Ryan's mood had improved since he gave his statement. He was aware his confession would implicate him in serious crimes, but Banetti's crimes were far reaching. No way was he safe, knowing the man killed Sam and Alyssa and tried to kill him as well. He didn't exactly feel joyous with his decision—more like relief. Like a burden had been lifted off his shoulders.

As they often did these days, his thoughts turned to Melanie. He went over and over in his mind what the deception she and her uncle had played on him. Sure, he had been really angry she had deceived him. But he was now able to look at it more from her perspective. She'd thought it was just a game. At the time, he was just a stranger to her, just some guy in a bar. And as far as she knew, her uncle was just a loving teddy bear, always looking out for her interest. Ryan clearly remembered the look of horror on her face when she learned what lengths her monster of an uncle had gone to.

Had he stopped loving her when she admitted her wrongdoings? Or was he simply so angry at the time that he wasn't thinking clearly at all. He couldn't just stop loving her because of something she did when she didn't really know him. Besides, he was no angel either. Look at where he was right now—under house arrest.

When it came to him keeping quiet about Banetti's crimes, the exploitation of minors—and so much more— how could he have the gall to chastise her for merely playing a game?

He had to make this right. He had to talk to Melanie. Maybe she would refuse to talk to him, but he had to try. "Hey, Mom?"

Ryan's mother who'd been gazing out the window, turned to him. "What is it, son?"

"Would you ask the officer outside to step in here?"

"Sure." She went to the door, carried on a whispered discussion with the guard.

The officer entered Ryan's room. "Mr. Nesbitt, how can I help?"

"I know I'm not allowed to speak to my fiancée, her being Rocco Banetti's niece," Ryan said, "but I'd like to get a message to her."

"I dunno about that, Mr. Nesbitt. The chief would have my butt if I allowed that."

Ryan thought for a few seconds. "Well, can my mother call her and just give her a message from me?"

The officer clasped his lips tightly and slightly shook his head. "What's the message?"

Ryan was embarrassed to tell the officer what he

277

needed his mother to say to Melanie, but he had no choice. "Just that I'm sorry, and I love her."

Chapter Forty

*Monday afternoon*

Before Sammy and Pat Karis left the hospital, Pat had sat on the chair next to Sammy's bed and made a phone call to the Blood of Jesus Pentecostal Church. "This is Pat Karis. May I speak to Preacher Morris, please?"

She waited a few seconds before she heard Preacher Morris' voice. *"Hello, Mrs. Karis. This is Preacher Anton Morris. What can I do for you?"*

"I was wondering if Thin Lizzy, oh, I mean Elizabeth Thorpe, happens to be in your church today."

*"Why, no, ma'am, she is not. I'm sorry."*

"Do you know where I might get in touch with her?"

A pause. *"Uh, no, I do not. After seeing the boy in the hospital yesterday, I believe a police officer brought her and Agnes Washington back to the church. But after the evening church service, I don't know where the ladies went."*

"Oh, I assumed they slept at the church last night."

*"Oh, no. We don't normally provide overnight shelter for the homeless community, only on emergency situations, such as when the young boy was in their custody. Usually, they all disperse after the service and go their separate ways. We just don't have the funds or personnel to add that type of shelter. I'm sorry."*

"So you have no idea where I can find Ms. Thorpe."

*"No I don't. The women could be anywhere."* Another pause. *"I will tell you that every weekday morning I hold church service at nine o'clock. Agnes Washington occasionally attends the service. If she comes by tomorrow morning, I'll see if she knows where you can find Elizabeth."*

Disappointed, Pat added, "Well, I guess that's all I can do for now. Thank you, Preacher Morris." She gave him her phone number and disconnected the call.

Then she looked over toward Sammy, sitting patiently on the edge of the bed. "I'm sorry, Sammy, but I don't know where to find Thin Lizzy. She isn't at the church."

He pleaded, "Maybe we can go look for her, okay?"

Pat protested, "But I don't know where to even look, son."

"She just walks around the streets all over town. That's all. We can just drive around until we find her."

Pat was very concerned for the boy. He was agitated and quite reluctant to go with her without Elizabeth's companionship. "I don't know… I don't know."

"Please? Please?"

Almost to herself she remarked, "But where would we even start looking?"

Sammy, seeming a little more positive, exclaimed, "She likes to go to the library and the un-i-versty, too. That's where she took me. She says she walks downtown, but she's careful to stay away from the bad men. We can start at those places."

Pat couldn't help herself. The boy looked so determined. She gave in. "Okay… We'll go search for her. For a little while, anyhow."

Just as Sammy hopped off the bed, the transporter

arrived to wheel him out of the hospital. When the three emerged from the elevator on the main floor, they were joined by Madelyn Winthrop, Pat's daughter.

Pat thanked the transport worker for wheeling Sammy down. She took Sammy's hand as he got off the wheelchair to guide him to her car. While they walked toward it, she said to him, "Do you remember Maddie? She's your mommy's big sister. That makes her your Aunt Maddie."

With reluctance and shyness, Sammy looked up at her and briefly uttered, "Hi… Aunt Maddie."

Madelyn patted him on the shoulder and smiled, "Hello, Sammy, my nephew. Very nice to meet you again."

Pat had also purchased a child's car seat that morning before picking up Sammy at the hospital and had installed it in her back seat. She opened the back door for him, and he immediately climbed into the car seat and fastened the safety belt himself. Pat was surprised at some of the things the boy was capable of doing on his own as well as being amazed by his politeness and temperament, especially after all he had endured these last few days. She had to give her daughter, Alyssa, credit. Even though they had irreparable differences in their relationship with each other, she seemed to have done a great job in raising her son. The thought of Alyssa made her sad, not only because of her tragic death, but now she never would have a chance to reconcile with her.

After fastening her seatbelt, she said, "Maddie, we aren't going directly back to the house. We have an errand to do."

Madelyn looked puzzled. "Where are we going?"

She glanced at Sammy in the back seat. "I thought you wanted to show Sammy his new home."

"Well, I do, but something else has come up. Sammy has given me an idea."

Still confused Madelyn remarked, "Oh?"

"We're going to find Thin Lizzy."

"Uh, who is Thin Lizzy, Mom?"

"You remember Elizabeth Thorpe? She's the lady who found Sammy in the middle of the street."

"Oh, that's Thin Lizzy? I didn't know." She hesitated. "Why do we need to find her?"

"Well, for right now, Sammy wants her with us. But besides that, I want to talk to the woman. I have a deal to make with her."

"O-okay? Can I ask what that deal might be?"

"You'll find out soon enough." With a gleam in her eye, she started her car, drove out of the parking garage, and turned toward downtown.

****

Pat Karis drove as slowly as possible through the streets of downtown Youngstown, searching for Thin Lizzy. Both Maddie and Sammy scoped out the sidewalks as Pat drove up and down the various streets. Having no luck downtown, she then drove around the area near the university. Many co-eds walked along the sidewalks, crossed the streets, and entered and exited various buildings to attend classes, but there was no sighting of Thin Lizzy.

Next Pat took random streets near the main library, up and down, crawling along when she was not blocking any traffic. But no Thin Lizzy. She even drove back to Belmont Avenue near the hospital, going up and down the streets in that area. Finally, she reluctantly conceded,

"I don't know, Sammy. We can't seem to find her. Maybe we should give up."

"Can we maybe try one more time downtown? Maybe we missed her the first time."

Pat released a sigh. "Okay, okay, one more run through town. If we don't find her this time, we'll have to stop looking for today. Okay?"

Sammy face showed his disappointment. "I-I guess so."

By this time, traffic was picking up in the area with offices, restaurants, and shops closing. It was more difficult for Pat to drive slowly. She did the best she could, weaving down street after street while Maddie and Sammy kept scanning the sidewalks and street corners. She was on West Front Street, driving past the courthouse, when suddenly, Sammy yelled, "There she is! There she is! And Aggie Bee too." He started to unhook his car seat safety belt.

Maddie yelled, "No! No, Sammy! Mom will pull over. Just wait a couple of seconds."

"But she might get away. We have to stop her."

Just at that moment, a car pulled away from a parking spot on the street. Pat swiftly maneuvered her vehicle into the space. All three exited the car. Maddie tightly clutched Sammy's hand before he could beeline across the street on his own.

Thin Lizzy and Aggie Bee were about to turn the corner and walk up Market Street toward Federal when Sammy yelled as loud as his lungs would allow. "Thin Lizzy! Thin Lizzy! Stop! It's me, Sammy."

Hearing her name, Thin Lizzy stopped and turned to see who was calling her. She saw Sammy between those two women that were at the police station and hospital,

Sammy's grandmother and her daughter. Why was he calling her name?

Aggie Bee turned around also. "What dey want? Are we in trouble? Do ya think we should run?"

Thin Lizzy said, "No, Sammy is callin' me. I don't think we in trouble."

Dodging the traffic, the trio finally made it across West Front Street. Pat and Maddie let loose of Sammy's hands so he could run to Thin Lizzy. To her complete surprise, he latched around her waist and hugged her fiercely. "I was so scared we wouldn't find you," he wailed, burying his face against her front. "So scared."

Stunned, Thin Lizzy looked down at Sammy, then at the two ladies approaching them. She didn't know what to say.

When Pat and Maddie reached the other two women, Pat, slightly out of breath, spoke, "Elizabeth, I know this is a very strange thing to ask, but could you come back with us to my house? I'd like to talk to you about something. I'll bring you back downtown afterward, if you like."

Thin Lizzy was even more confused. Why would this lady want to take her to her house? "Am I in trouble?"

"Oh, no, on the contrary. I have a proposition to offer you."

"What's a proposition?"

"Well, it's something I'd like to talk to you about that will benefit you, me, and Sammy."

"I ain't in trouble then?"

"No, you are definitely not in trouble."

Aggie Bee touched Thin Lizzy on the shoulder. "Go with da lady, Lizzy. She ain't gonna hurt chu."

After a moment of thought and hesitation, Pat added, "Uh, Agnes, could you come with us also? I'd like to talk to you, too.

Aggie Bee's eyes popped open. "Me? You wanna talk ta me, too?"

Pat agreed. "Yes, both of you."

Thus the parade of four women and a small boy ventured back across Front Street to Pat's luxury SUV. Sammy's car seat was in the middle of the second row of seats. Thin Lizzy sat on his left and Aggie Bee sat on his right. They fastened their seatbelts, and Pat drove them all to her spacious home on five acres just outside of Poland, an upscale suburb of Youngstown. Sammy's face broke with a wide smile as he glanced back and forth between Thin Lizzy and Aggie Bee.

As Pat pulled into a long, circular driveway and up to the house, Aggie Bee whistled, "Whew! Ain't dat house a beaut!"

Pat got out of the car, as did all the passengers. She led them up the wide front stairs to an expansive front door. The door was opened by a woman dressed in a tailored pant suit. Pat made introductions. "Elizabeth, Agnes, this is my personal assistant, Dinah Burkholder. Dinah, would you get us some tea and cookies? Bring them out to the sunroom. We're going to have a conference."

Without asking any questions concerning the two new female guests dressed in trashy, suspicious attire, Dinah responded, "Yes, Mrs. Karis. I'll take care of that right away."

Pat led the group back to the spacious sunroom at the back of the gorgeous house. Thin Lizzy and Aggie Bee couldn't help but admire the décor and design of this beautiful home as they followed Pat. Neither of them had ever seen anything like it before. Sammy, also having lived in a spacious and opulent home, paid no attention to his surroundings. He was, however, anxious to see what his new grandmother had in store. Plus, the idea of cookies sounded pretty good.

When they entered the sunroom, Pat suggested, "Please, ladies, take a seat." She sat in a white wicker chair against the bank of windows facing the expansive swimming pool in the back yard. Maddie sat on a matching chair off to the side of the room. Thin Lizzy and Aggie Bee with Sammy between them sat on the wicker couch, also matching the chairs, with bright floral upholstery. Once everyone was settled, Pat began, "As I mentioned before, I'd like to offer the two of you ladies a proposition. In other words, a job."

Both Aggie Bee and Thin Lizzy's mouths dropped open. Aggie Bee asked, "Did ya say a job, ma'am?"

"That's what I said." She paused and then outstretched her arm and moved it in a wide arch. "As you can see by my beautiful home, I'm not in the same predicament as you two ladies are. But I need your help—both of you. First, you, Elizabeth. I have a business to run to keep a lot of people happy and employed. And now, thankfully, and to my greatest joy, my grandson has finally come into my life." She smiled at Sammy. "It seems that since I need to keep working to keep the business going, I need someone to help me give Sammy a good home."

She again looked at her grandson. "I have noticed that Sammy has grown very fond of you, Elizabeth. He knows you cared as well as you could for him when he was in desperate need of help. And it was actually his idea for me to ask you if you would come to live with us and help me take care of him. What do you say?"

This time Thin Lizzy's mouth opened even wider, but she was speechless. Her eyes darted every which way around the space. Finally, they focused on Sammy, beside her. "You want me ta live which you in dis big house?"

With tears in his big wide eyes, he simply nodded.

Tears began to flood from Thin Lizzy's eyes also. "But I'm just a dirty, old homeless person. I ain't no good for nothin'."

"No, no, Thin Lizzy, you're wrong," Sammy objected. "I-I love you. You took care of me so nobody could hurt me. I-I don't care if you have dirty clothes. My new grandma lady can wash them for you." He turned to Pat. "Can't you… Grandma?"

Pat, also in tears, replied, "We'll buy her some new clothes, Sammy."

Sammy clutched Thin Lizzy's hand. "So will you stay and help take care of me, please, please?"

Thin Lizzy quickly glanced at Pat. Then she looked down at Sammy. Immediately, she bent down and pulled him onto her lap to give him a deep hug. "Yeah, I-I guess I'll stay."

After everyone somewhat regained their composure, Pat had more to propose. "As for you, Agnes, I've been told that you are a very good cook. My last cook recently retired and moved to Florida. I've had an agency sending over several different candidates for the permanent position, but none of them have worked out. I'd like to offer that position to you."

Aggie Bee's head twittered around the room. "Ya want me ta be yer cook, ma'am?"

"Yes, I do. You've been highly recommended."

"But I'm a street person, just like Thin Lizzy. I ain't no fine lady like you,"

Pat shook her head. "Believe me, Agnes. You are just as fine a lady as any of us." She turned to her daughter. "Isn't that right, Madelyn?"

With emphasis, Maddie responded, "Absolutely!"

Aggie Bee kept shaking her head. "I can't believe it. Ma'am, you is askin' both a us ta live in dis fine and fancy house which you?"

"Yes, I am. You will both have your own bedroom on the third floor, and you will share the bathroom on that level. I'll show you the facilities after we have our tea and cookies."

Maddie got out of her seat. "Speaking of tea, Dinah is bringing it in now. Let me help serve. Ah! Chocolate chip and sugar cookies. And a glass of chocolate milk for Sammy."

## Epilogue

*Six months, after the fire*

Rocco Ettore Banetti was tried in a federal court, found guilty, and convicted of multiple white-collar offenses as well as multiple counts of murder, including those of Samuel and Alyssa Nagy. He was ultimately sentenced to life imprisonment without the possibility of parole and was then incarcerated in the United States Penitentiary Hazelton in Bruceton Mills, West Virginia to lead out his life until his natural death. Whether or not he would make it that far remained to be seen.

Several individuals in his entourage, Benny Ricci, his head of security, among them, were also sentenced to life imprisonment without parole, with some also being sent to Hazelton. Banetti had pleaded not guilty to all charges against him, but the evidence presented to the jury was so overwhelming that all twelve jurors found him guilty with only being sequestered for five hours. Also, to avoid the death penalty, the two hitmen who had shot the Nagys testified against Banetti, adding more credence to his guilty verdict. As the saying goes, Banetti will never see the light of day again. The fires of Hell will be his next location.

The irony of it all for Banetti was that *no one* at the law firm of Padgett & Nagy LLP had ever leaked or revealed intentionally or unintentionally one iota of Banetti's legal or illegal personal or business information. The Department of Justice was the culprit responsible for uncovering many of Banetti's white collar crimes, which then led to the discovery of his more serious infractions, such as the murders of Sam and Alyssa. Banetti will have a long time to mull that over in his mind while in his prison cell that he shared with other members of the country's infamous scoundrels.

As for Carl Padgett, the senior partner of the law firm, he did not wait around long enough to see the outcome of the investigation into the deaths of Sam and Alyssa Nagy. The Saturday morning after the fire, he rounded up all of the cash he could get his hands on and booked a flight for his wife and him to Spain, which had no extradition policies with the United States. As far as anyone knows, they are sitting comfortably in their villa on a beach along the Mediterranean Sea. Or maybe not.

It took Ryan Nesbitt four months to heal completely from his injuries received in the car accident, later proven to be caused by Banetti's men. In addition to Ryan's own account of the accident, an eyewitness had seen the black SUV threatening Ryan's compact car and had taken down the plate number. When the witness came forward with that information, it led to a vehicle registered to REB Enterprises.

Because Ryan had fully cooperated with the police and the DOJ, he was sentenced to only two years of community service and put on probation for five years. His community service required him to work as a public defender in Youngstown for those individuals charged with crimes who were unable to afford their own attorney, receiving only a nominal salary for his work. He considered himself lucky to get off with such a light sentence.

Melanie Carlini actually testified against her uncle at his trial, explaining the set-up for her getting to know Ryan so Banetti might catch him in some act of betrayal. Rocco Banetti refused to even look at his niece during the trial. Even though he had been so good to her, especially since her mother's death, Melanie finally realized that her uncle was evil to the core. Her father and her brother both supported her and were by her side during the time leading up to Banetti's conviction.

The police had eventually permitted Melanie to make one visit with Ryan while he was in the hospital under house arrest, but with police supervision. Both Ryan and Melanie spent the first ten minutes hugging, kissing, and apologizing to one another. All was forgiven regarding both of their misdeeds and misunderstandings.

After being transferred to the rehab facility, Melanie was permitted to visit Ryan, and they proceeded to make plans for their pending nuptial to take place the following September. Since Melanie no longer had a rich uncle available to pay for her wedding, the event would be a much smaller affair. Ryan's mother Maureen helped the couple make plans and would provide a large amount of financial support for it also. Ryan had saved a good amount of money from his salary at the law firm, so the couple was able to put a down payment on a cute three-bedroom bungalow in Austintown, a modest middle-class neighborhood of Youngstown.

Darnell Manson, a.k.a. Darkman, was charged and convicted of the first-degree kidnapping of Samuel Nagy Junior. He was sentenced to twenty-five years in prison and fined $20,000. How that would be paid was anybody's guess. Jose Morales, a.k.a. Mojo, was also tried and convicted on kidnapping. Since he was not the mastermind of the crime, he was sentenced to fifteen years with a fine of $15,000. For safety reasons, many of the street people in Youngstown were glad those two rogues were finally off the streets.

Detective Willard Hamilton retired from the Youngstown Police Department in December after the fire on Fifth Avenue. The deaths of Sam and Alyssa Nagy, and the ensuing murder case resulting from their deaths, had taken its toll on Hamilton's aging body. In November, he had turned sixty-seven. He was more than ready. Of course, his former partner, Detective Stacey Atkinson, reluctantly took on her new partner, a rookie detective just out of training. It would take her a while to get used to the transition. Hamilton continued to tell her he was available for advice whenever she needed him, but no more all-nighters for him.

The tragedy of the fire brought about significant and gratifying changes in the lives of Lizzy Thorpe, a.k.a. Thin Lizzy, and Aggie Washington, a.k.a. Aggie Bee. Prior to living on the streets of Youngstown, both of these women had led basically normal lives. Aggie, then a single woman in her mid-thirties, had been a cook at a popular barbeque restaurant on Youngstown's north side. However, when the owner of the restaurant had a sudden massive heart attack and passed away, the establishment had to close, leaving Aggie without a job. Unable to find another, she eventually ended up living on the street—until she met Patricia Karis.

Before her life terribly changed, Lizzy Thorpe, a cashier at a local grocery store, her husband Dennis, a plumber, and their eight-year-old daughter Ashley lived a happy life in a modest two-story home on Youngstown's west side. But several years ago when

Lizzy was thirty-three, Dennis and Ashley were brutally murdered. A local drug cartel and his heinous henchmen had burst into their home, in error, searching for stolen drugs. Her husband was shot and died instantly. Her daughter, coming down the stairs, was trampled and kicked by the robbers as she descended. Ashley Thorpe lived for a week before succumbing to her injuries.

As a result of being bashed in the head with the butt end of a pistol, Lizzy suffered a fractured skull, leaving her with injuries that seriously affected her mental capacity. After the incident, she struggled to support herself, but she no longer was capable of holding on to her job or maintaining the financial obligations of her home. Thus, she too wound up destitute and living on the streets.

Now these two proud women, Elizabeth Anne Thorpe and Agnes Beryl Washington, led respectable lives. Aggie proved to be an excellent cook. Delicious meals were always ready whenever Pat needed them. And her food expenditures actually decreased with Aggie's frugal supervision.

As for Lizzy, she couldn't believe that she was given food, shelter, and wages just for spending time with her little friend, Sammy. He was such a joy to be with, and he helped to fill that hole in her heart left by her daughter's death. With Madelyn Winthrop's assistance, Lizzy learned to drive again. She transported Sammy back and forth to his new school, The Montessori School of Mahoning Valley. She would take care of him after school, tending to his needs—preparing him snacks, washing his clothes, shopping for his clothes, helping him with his schoolwork, or playing games with him when he was bored or lonely. In time, with loving care and attention to her basic needs, along with extensive therapy, Lizzy's mental capabilities greatly improved.

It goes without saying, Lizzy and Aggie were very happy in their new jobs and their new lives. Aggie convinced Lizzy to join the choir at the Blood of Jesus Pentecostal Church, creating a satisfying social life for the women. Because of the role the church and Pastor Anton Morris had played in keeping her grandson safe, Pat Karis began to support the church on a regular basis with her donations. She would be forever grateful to them. This financial support, in turn, helped Pastor Morris supply more help to the area's homeless community.

On the subject of who would have permanent guardianship of Sammy Nagy Junior, a court date was held in February. The last wills of Samuel and Alyssa Nagy had been found with no mention of custodial choices for Sammy in the event of his parents' deaths. There was also no mention in either a positive or a negative way about Patricia Karis. In addition, no one attending the court appearance contested Patricia Karis's appeal for guardianship. Therefore, the judge granted permanent sole custody of Sammy to his grandmother.

Regarding Lizzy's two trash bags she and Sammy had hidden in some high weeds at the church near the art museum, they hadn't even lasted a day in that location. The custodian of the church took that day to do some special yard work and noticed the bags in their spot. When he opened one to look inside, the smell was so putrid that without hesitation, he immediately tossed both of them into the nearby dumpster.

What about the boy? What about Sammy? Was he happy? Did he miss his old life?

Yes and no, to both of those questions. He was young enough that he could move on with his life, hopefully without too much damage to his psyche. Pat Karis and Sammy's aunts and uncles tried to make the transition for him as gentle as possible. Sammy met his cousins on both sides of the family, Adam and Naomi's preteen daughters and three-year-old son, and Corey and Madelyn's daughter. Even though three of his cousins were all older than Sammy, he was just so glad to have them in his life. As for Adam's little boy, Owen, Sammy felt like a big brother to him. Finally, he had an extended family.

Sammy also got together with his friends, Jace and Corbin from Saint Joseph, his old school. But he was making new friends at his new school, and his friendship with Jace and Cody would probably fade in time. He and Eli, his roommate at the hospital, also became close friends despite their difference in age.

Yes, Sammy was adjusting to his new life. Yes, he was young and still adaptable. However, the things he had seen and the trauma he had endured would be etched in his mind forever. But as he snuggled in his bed each night with his newfound grandmother in the next room and his two special friends, Aggie Bee and Thin Lizzy, sleeping in the rooms above him, he felt safe and protected. For now.

## A word about the author...

Besides What Happened to the Boy, June is the author of six other published novels: Let Freedom Ring, Before We Fade Away (nominated for the Paranormal Romance Reviewer's Choice Award in 2018), A Conflict of Time, Whatever It Takes, There Was an Old Woman, and At Rope's End. She is also currently under contract for her non-fiction memoir that deals with her daughter's battle with cancer while the two of them operated a forever home for neglected and abused animals. June, now an eighty-four-year-old woman, lives in Ohio and spends her retirement writing, hanging out with what family she has left, and staying alive.